WINTER'S POWER

THE POISONED KINGDOMS
BOOK TWO

AMELIA MACLEOD

AUTHOR'S NOTE

Dearest Readers:

For your convenience, you can find a glossary of terms in the back of this book.

Note: Skip the remainder of this note if you prefer not to read content warnings.

CONTENT NOTES

Winter's Power contains themes of grooming and abuse. Though these are not detailed on the page, they nonetheless contribute to trauma. The book also contains violence in the form of fantastical fights and battles, attempted murder, and death. In one scene, a character worries that another may be suicidal.

There is discussion of human enthrallment, which amounts to a form of slavery. None of the sympathetically portrayed characters utilize or sanction this power. This book also contains explicit sex scenes.

Sincerely,

Amelia

WINTER'S FATE RECAP

PREVIOUSLY, IN THE POISONED KINGDOMS...

!! SPOILER WARNING !!

The passage below provides a **FULL RECAP** of the events in Book 1, *Winter's Fate*. It's intended as a reminder of what happened.

If you haven't read *Winter's Fate*, you should stop now and pick it up before continuing!

The passage below *will* spoil the ending of the book.

You have been warned!

—✳—

Princess Laena of Etra abdicated her throne five years ago, officially for love of a stablehand named Ben, but secretly because she possessed dangerous ice magic. Now living as a commoner, she discovers a poisonous crystal in her garden that spawns a shadow monster. When her sister Queen Katrina refuses to take the threat seriously, Laena reluctantly agrees to serve as emissary to Aglye in exchange for Katrina's investigation.

Captain Callum Farrow of Aglye's Royal Guard—recently demoted by King Hawk for failing to prevent the previous king's murder—steals the diplomatic mission to prove his worth. Despite his reputation as a ruthless magic hunter, Callum protects Laena from assassins and kidnappers, and the two fall for each other during their perilous journey.

Their ship is destroyed by an unnatural storm created by heart-tither Milla, who serves mysterious masters. After being shipwrecked and captured, Laena uses her ice magic to save them both, revealing her secret to Callum. Though magic is forbidden in Aglye, he chooses to trust her.

At the monastery of Inasvale, they learn from Prince Thaddeus (now a poisonkeeper) that the barrier between the Vales and the Miragelands is weakening, and that the mages seek to return. King Hawk arrives and shocks Callum by revealing he also possesses magic: fire that complements Laena's ice.

The devastating truth emerges: Queen Katrina has been working with the mages all along, using heart-tithe magic powered by the pain of those she loves. She planted the crystal, orchestrated the attacks, and plans to kill both Laena and Hawk to ensure the mages' return in exchange for keeping her throne.

In a climactic battle, Laena and Hawk combine their powers to fight Katrina, but the queen escapes after murdering her lover, Regent Declan, to fuel her magic. Realizing that the Vales chose them as magical heirs to protect the realm, and that her abdication allowed evil to take Etra's throne, Laena makes the ultimate sacrifice: she agrees to marry King Hawk to legitimize her claim and unite their powers against the coming magical threat. Despite her love for Callum, as she chooses duty over desire to save her world from the returning mages and her corrupted sister.

And now, the story continues...

For Dad, who might be horrified, but whose love of soap operas is probably to blame.

I miss you.

CHAPTER 1

KATRINA

*K*atrina kept expecting the magic to fail.

The last remnants of Declan's heart-tithe clung to her blood, his death—his murder—drawing so much more power than she had anticipated, and for so much longer. The magic had carried her to Inasvale with no trouble, an expensive spell, and yet she could still feel it keening within her, anxious to spend itself.

She crept through the streets of the poisonkeepers' city, breathing in the sea-thick scent of the air, the morning mist beading fresh dew on her cheeks, her lips, her knuckles. Should any of the townspeople flick their curtains aside to look out into the pre-dawn streets, she imagined she would resemble a spirit, drifting through their town with dark purpose.

The thought appealed. She found herself leaning into the idea as she straightened her spine, infusing grace and lightness into every step.

If she'd thought she could spare the magic, she'd have floated.

Soon, she would have all the power she craved. And more.

For now, her heart-tithe magic was enough to lift the locks

on the monastery gates and the pitiful locks on the interior halls. It was enough to lead her to the staircase she sought, to drop a pair of poisonkeeper guards into a deep slumber, their robes pooling around their bodies as they crumpled, unconscious before they hit the floor. All with a flick of her fingers.

Declan's sacrifice enduring, just a little longer.

Her mentor. Her lover. Perhaps the magic could taste the poison in that love. Perhaps it savored the bitterness.

He'd defied her, in the end. That made it easy.

She left the guards in the hall, descending the narrow staircase until it dumped her into an equally narrow passageway. Just as the old tomes in Etra's library had described. The books were as dusty as this hall, their pages difficult to read for the mottles of dirt and mold. Concentration had always been a slippery thing, when it came to books and study. She'd rather be scrambling along Etra's rocky coast, investigating hidden caves and poking at tide pools. She'd rather be scaling the castle walls.

But rocks and caves and sheer walls would not give her the power she craved.

And so she'd persevered. She knew, even before the passage opened into the forest, that she would find what was promised: mossy trees, with canopies thick enough to blot the early-morning sky. A stone path, kept free of weeds and overgrowth.

And the magepool.

All these months of heart-tithing, of attempting to call the mages and their power back to the Vales, of trying to figure out how to weaken the barrier further. And then finally, *finally*, one of the crumbling books had revealed the path with a line in passing, as though it was of no consequence at all, when to her it was everything: a still, black pool set in a cradle of stone, and a drop of royal blood. Her blood.

According to the book, there was something more to the poisonkeepers' traditions than pure religious fanaticism. She hadn't thought to imagine that they were truly protecting something of value.

Though 'protecting' was a rather strong word, when she'd sliced through their pathetic defenses with such ease.

Katrina moved up the shallow steps to stand before the magepool, her throat dry despite the mist in the air. The pool stared up at her, a lidless pupil. It might be an inch deep, or a mile; it might be an endless abyss.

She tugged her sleeve up, bustling it around her elbow, and withdrew her dagger from the belt at her waist. Heart-tithers were always cutting each others' palms or knuckles. It seemed to her that there were less annoying places on the body to nurse a stinging wound for a week.

Holding her arm out over the gaping pool, Katrina parted the flesh on the back of her wrist with the tip of the dagger. An inch would do; there was no need for theatrics with only trees for an audience. Still, she didn't wince at the bite of stinging pain. She would not give even the trees a chance to judge her weakness.

Blood welled into the cut, a shock of red, and then it was falling, trickling down her arm until it bumped the heel of her hand and, with nowhere to go, dropped directly into the pool.

It landed without so much as a ripple. She had the sense, though she could not have said why, that there *were* ripples— invisible to her eyes but plunging deep into the pool, reaching downward instead of circling along the surface.

Katrina held her breath.

And nothing happened.

She waited a beat, and another. The pool stared back at her, like a blank slate.

And then, anger. It came like an inferno, as it always did these days. It came with the urge to burn every last leaf in this awful grove to ash.

The book had *lied* to her. It had dangled the knowledge like a sliver of hope, only to snatch it away. How could she make up for her own ignorance, her own stupidity, if the books she struggled her way through turned out to be full of lies?

Katrina squeezed the cut, scattering drops of blood into the pool with a scream of rage. When she got back to Riles, she would set it on fire. She would set the entire library on fire. She would set all libraries on fire.

"It screeches like a wounded weasel."

Katrina stopped flailing, her arm now marbled with rivulets of blood. The voice was light, its tenor dripping with disdain.

She looked down.

Two men gazed up at her from the pool, their expressions unimpressed. One appeared to be young, maybe twenty—her age—and she had the impression that he was the one who had spoken. His lips twisted in contempt for her outburst, but his face was otherwise a handsome one: a sweep of blond hair, a casual tilt to his posture, and cheekbones that might've been chiseled by a renowned sculptor.

The second man was older, his graying hair hanging loose to his shoulders. Yet the two men resembled one another; they shared the same bold nose, the same underlying handsomeness.

Father and son, perhaps. She knew, without a doubt, that she was gazing into the Miragelands. That these were mages.

The books were not overly forthcoming about the nature of the Miragelands. One thing she'd gleaned, though, was that the pool on their side was part of the mage king's palace. Or so it had been, a few centuries ago. Which meant that, in all likelihood, she was looking at the mage king himself. And his heir.

Katrina dropped her hand. "I've come to thin the barrier."

The younger man scoffed, but the older one merely held her gaze. Her waning power surged in her blood, a fresh wave of magic beating along her veins as if reignited by his stare. She flexed her fingers, and curls of black smoke leaked from the tips, following the movement of her hands. That was... new.

"We need *royal* blood of the Vales," the older mage said. "That is how we were locked away. That is how we will return."

It took an effort to return her gaze to the pool. "You have *my* royal blood."

She knew what he was going to say even before his lips parted. It was the same thing everyone had been saying for years.

"Yours was enough to summon us. To unlock the barrier, the pool requires your sister's."

Always. From before Laena's abdication to well after it. *Wasn't there a way to bring her back?* people asked. *Wasn't there a way to convince her, to make the stablehand a king or a consort, a prince of some kind?* From councilors to maids and cooks, they begged for Laena's return. As if Katrina had not been sitting right there, ready and willing to take her sister's place, to learn whatever was required.

Only Declan had supported her. Even as naive and uncultured as she was, she knew that he'd done so for reasons of his own. But he *had* supported her. He'd stood beside her, and he'd defended her.

Until, just like everyone else, he'd chosen to betray her.

Katrina lifted her chin. "*I* am Queen of Etra."

The mage returned her stare. "You are a play queen while your sister lives."

Don't worry. Declan's words echoed in her mind, as if triggered by the mage's dismissal, and as real as if he'd been standing beside her. *The council won't think of you as silly if I am beside you.*

He'd been right. They had accepted her, in time, as a necessary evil.

And so to prove herself, she'd had to become one.

"You are the mage king," she said, infusing her tone with a confidence she did not feel.

The mage met her stare, his eyes like pools of unblinking

ink. Though that might have just been the look of them through the pool. Finally, he inclined his head, just the barest sliver, as if deciding to trust her with this one taste of information. "Valdric," he said. "And my son. Koreth."

The prince, or so he must be. Koreth just stared at her, that sneer pasted on his lips. Like he couldn't quite believe they were lowering themselves to have a conversation with her. When he turned his head to look at his father, she saw a stripe of leather cord twisted around his neck, the glint of a pendant. She could not make out what it was. "She knows too little of us to be of any use."

Katrina decided to ignore Koreth's existence, focusing instead on his father. "I know that the mages have suffered in the Miragelands for centuries. I would grant you access to the Vales again."

The prince straightened, anger flashing in his eyes. "Our people are strong. You cannot begin to fathom how we have—"

King Valdric held up a hand, and Koreth went silent. "You will need our guidance in this."

I will show you what to do. When to smile.

Throat dry, she nodded.

"You must either get your sister's blood to add to the pool," King Valdric said, "or else kill her so you will be the true queen."

Heat burned in her chest. And with it, she realized with horror, the threat of tears. She swallowed hard, forcing the tears down. "*She* was the one who gave up her title. I stepped in because she abandoned us. Abandoned Etra."

How did no one else see it?

The mage king merely shrugged. "The Vales do not accept it."

The Vales must accept it at least a little bit, else she would not be talking to him. Perhaps the pool would respond to any human blood spilled, anyone who wished to speak to the mages. Just as a heart-tithe could be worked by anyone.

Katrina rolled her shoulders, forcing her back upright. These people would not make her bend. This *task* would not make her bend. At least her tears had dissipated. Had they spilled down her cheeks, or even done more than sting her eyes, she would not have recovered from it. Not with these two. And certainly not with herself.

Collect Laena's blood, or kill her. Fine. She could do that. "Easy enough," she said.

"The pool will also require blood from the King of Aglye."

"I don't see an issue."

"And then," King Valdric said, his tone darkening, "there is Evren Avery."

Katrina frowned. She didn't know the name. "Who is that?"

Koreth flinched, almost imperceptibly. But Valdric merely held her gaze, his hatred digging deep lines into his brow and sharpening the glint in his eyes, though Katrina couldn't see how he could know anyone in the Vales well enough to hate them. "You call him the Ruthless King."

CHAPTER 2

LAENA

*L*aena's shoes were too tight.

Her feet ought to be the very least of her concerns.

But maybe that was precisely why, as she followed King Hawk's sister through the Vunmore palace halls toward the throne room—toward her *wedding*—she found herself fixating on her feet, on the pinch of pain that radiated with every step. The big toe on her left side—*pinch*—the heel on her right—*burn*—the shoes constraining her in a way that made her want to rip them off and throw them down the hall.

Instead, she focused on the pain. Anticipated it. Because if she allowed herself to think of anything else, her ribcage would crack open and a much worse pain would spill out, for all to see.

"Laena?"

She blinked, forcing herself to focus on Emilia. The princess had stopped in front of the pair of oversized doors that Laena knew would open into the throne room. String music came to her in muffled strains, the doors hiding the shuffling and rustling and whispers of anticipation that would certainly be rippling through the crowd. A pair of guards stood at attention to either side, waiting for her word to throw them open and reveal the crowd, and the flowers, and her soon-to-be husband.

It would have been nice to see Edmun's kindly face right about now, or even Godfrey's. But she didn't recognize these men.

Emilia's hair was pinned into an elaborate network of braids, a few strands of golden-blond brushing over her shoulders. Her bridesmaid's dress was bright Aglyean blue, with purple embellishments along the neckline and sleeves. She looked fresh and lovely, her excitement plain in the blush of her cheeks, the way she bounced on her feet. They'd spent a good deal of time together in the two weeks since Laena's engagement, and Laena had come to like her a great deal.

The princess was smiling, nodding her encouragement, as if Laena's hesitation was born from the type of nerves that a kind look could help to quell. "Are you ready?"

Laena didn't trust her voice to sound past the lump in her throat, so she only nodded.

Instead of heading through the doors, though, Emilia stepped forward and clasped Laena's hands. "I get nervous, too," she whispered. "In front of so many people. But I'll be right there next to you on the dais. Plus, I bet as soon as you get in there, you'll have eyes for no one but Hawk."

Laena's heart thumped painfully against her ribs. She squeezed the princess's hand, grateful for her kindness. "Thank you." Her voice was unsteady, but she didn't mind. "For everything."

Emilia pecked a kiss onto her cheek, then turned back toward the throne room. At her signal, the guards turned simultaneously and unlatched the doors, their movements synchronized to the second. Or so it seemed.

How often do you practice that? a frantic, stalling part of Laena's brain wanted to ask. *Are you special ceremonial guards? Is that why Edmun isn't here?*

The doors swung open, washing her face in a breath of wind, and Emilia floated out into the aisle, beaming like she was the one getting married.

And then, as if time had skipped a beat, Emilia drifted into place on the dais, and it was Laena's turn to face the sea of strangers. Guests had come from across the land, and she hadn't met fully a third of them yet—though even if she had, their faces would still be blurring together in this moment, the audience heavily splashed with Aglyean blue. All she could smell were the lilacs.

The one person she wanted to see was nowhere in sight.

No one had seen or heard from Callum since he'd grabbed that bottle of whiskey and disappeared after her rejection, her insistence that marrying Hawk was the right thing to do. He'd taken off with a small contingent of soldiers, apparently telling the king that they needed training. And that was that.

Not that she'd expected him to return for the wedding. Not truly. If he hadn't come before now, it hardly seemed likely he'd appear simply to stand beside his king. She wasn't even sure if she hoped for that or dreaded it.

She couldn't blame him. She *wouldn't* blame him. It was just as well that he wasn't here.

If she kept repeating that, she might convince herself it was not a lie.

The strings were louder now, though she would have expected the sound to disappear into those cavernous ceilings. The music rose over the rushing in her ears, blending with it until she could hardly distinguish the two.

"Smile, Your Highness," one of the guards whispered, and then Laena's treacherous feet were moving her forward into the room—*pinch, burn, pinch, burn*—and down the aisle to where King Hawk waited.

The golden king, the fire king, and her ally. Her husband,

soon. Handsome, young, and intelligent. He was everything she should be happy to want.

Laena focused on Hawk, tried to mirror his smile as she made her way toward him. Too slowly, perhaps, but who could fault a bride for taking care not to slip? With the lump still lodged in her throat and the mass of knots tying holes in her stomach, she didn't know how she would manage to speak at all.

One problem at a time. A step, a smile. When she got there, the words would come.

A flicker of movement on the upper balcony caught her eye, and her steps slowed even more as she followed the shape of a person drifting along the row of stained-glass windows. At first, it seemed it was merely a regular guest, or even a guard, silhouetted against the bright light.

At first, she thought it might be Callum, hiding, watching the proceedings from a distance.

But then the light shifted. The figure sharpened.

It might have been made of smoked glass, sculpted into the form of a person, if its edges had been at all solid—which they were not. It stood as if wreathed in steam, resting wispy hands on the stone rail, watching her now-stalled progress down the aisle.

Laena's magic gave a jolt of recognition, sending a sour bite of bile into her throat. It felt like a pull to the ribcage, drawing her so strongly she nearly took a step toward the balcony—which would have sent her detouring among the seats. That would certainly get people talking.

If they were not already. Laena wrenched her gaze away from the ghost—for that was certainly what it resembled—to focus again on King Hawk. He was still smiling, still kind, still handsome, though the slightest hint of a crinkle had formed between his eyebrows. Beside him, Emilia shifted her weight from one leg to the other, giving Laena an encouraging nod.

When she risked a glance up to the balcony, the smoky figure was gone.

She could feel the weight of the guests' curiosity, their assessment. The way that, collectively, they seemed to be leaning forward, wondering what would happen next. Whether she would falter.

Laena took a deep breath. She could still salvage this. Smile pasted on her lips, she recalled her attention to the dais.

A second ghost flinched into sight behind Hawk, and Laena's magic uncoiled without warning, nausea twisting the knots at her stomach as it wrenched her forward. She missed a step, her toe catching on the hem of her dress—*pinch*—and someone was reaching for her, but she swerved away, fear making her stagger again.

Her power had always felt fresh, calm. Gentle. Now, it was oil and poison. It was blood on snow, pulling her down. The floor careened toward her in a blur of blue carpet and gray stone, her legs disobeying her slipping command to keep her upright.

Strong arms caught her before she hit the floor, wrapping her in the smell, the feeling, the *home* of woodsmoke and leather. And then she was looking into Callum Farrow's stormy blue eyes. He'd caught her beneath the knees, his other hand circling protectively around her back. She was aware, distantly, that people were murmuring in concern. But all she could feel was the safety of his arms around her, the solidity of his body as he cradled her to his chest.

"Did I summon you here?" she whispered.

"Not by magic, my lady," Callum said. His dark hair was tousled, and he wore his uniform jacket, the top two buttons of his shirt undone and revealing a triangle of his muscled chest. Dressed for travel. Not for a wedding.

His gaze dropped to her hands, where ink-black lines were

spreading across her palms, her wrists, the inside of her forearm. Following her veins, then branching out like cracks.

Fear sparked in her gut, but then the world was tilting, her magic burning hot, the poison threatening to pour out of her throat.

The last thing she felt was weightlessness as Callum lifted her up and away, and the vibration of his voice ringing through her body as he called for help.

CHAPTER 3

CALLUM

*C*allum carried Laena out into the hall, fear clawing at his gut like a wild thing.

The guards had the sense to shut the doors behind them, barring their retreat from view and keeping the guests at bay until further notice. Callum didn't give a shit what happened to the gawking nobility. He just needed Laena to be well.

The only comfort he could take, the only thing keeping him from flying into a full-on panic, was in the gentle rise and fall of her chest as he cradled her, the warmth of her too-shallow breaths on his neck.

One moment she'd been on her feet, her fingers curved gracefully around the purple bouquet, her hair partially restrained in twisting braids—he could still feel the phantom softness of the loose curls around his fingers, the press of her lips against his—

One moment, she'd been on her feet and looking beautiful in an unearthly kind of way, like light scattered through a prism. And heading down the aisle, albeit slowly, to marry the mages-damned King of Aglye.

One moment, she'd been well. At least, as well as could be expected under the circumstances.

And in the next, she'd wavered.

Callum was lucky he'd been there in time to catch her. His instincts had wanted him to brood in some shadowy alcove like a phantom, but in the end, he hadn't been able to abide the idea of keeping so much distance between them.

He didn't know where to take her now. He only knew he had to get her out. Away.

"Here." Thaddeus hurried up beside him, taking two steps for every one of Callum's long strides, as he pointed toward the line of wooden doors that dotted the corridor. For a moment, Callum thought they were heading for the guards' room where he and Laena had parted two weeks ago, and he didn't know if he would be able to endure that.

No. For her, he'd endure it.

Thankfully, Thaddeus skipped the guards' room, instead opening the next door down to reveal a sitting room with a fire in the hearth and a sofa in the corner, a few half-drunk glasses of whiskey abandoned on side tables. Callum supposed he'd known of the room's existence, but he couldn't remember ever entering it. There were just too many damned rooms in this palace.

"Hawk prepared for the ceremony here," Thaddeus explained.

That explained the drinks, at least. Callum carried Laena to the sofa, laying her head gently on one of the sky-blue cushions. Her lips were parted, her eyebrows pinched as if something pained her. But she breathed, if a beat too quickly, too shallowly. She still breathed.

He touched the back of his hand to her forehead. She didn't feel overly warm, though her skin was damp with perspiration. *Just nerves*, a panicked part of his brain insisted. *Wedding day nerves.*

But nerves didn't send poisonous lines crawling up a woman's arms, darkening her veins to an alarming shade of purple. He traced a finger along the inside of her wrist, ignoring Thaddeus's hiss of warning. If the affliction was contagious, then Callum would die beside her. He didn't care.

The door opened, and he didn't have to look up to know it was Hawk. He was fairly certain that the king's boots would click like that no matter where he walked. A carpet. A meadow.

With reluctance, Callum dropped his hand away from the king's betrothed.

"It would have been best to wait for the physician," Hawk said.

There was always something Hawk thought Callum should have done differently. But if he expected Callum to linger another mages-damned moment before getting Laena to safety —not to mention out from under the heat of the nobles' stares— then he was a fool. The people here might like her, might find her supposed love story with the king to be romantic, but Laena would not want them gawking at her when she was vulnerable. Mages, but she would *not*.

Callum ignored Hawk, turning instead to Thaddeus. "It's her magic. You have to help her."

Thaddeus crouched beside him, bending to inspect the dark lines Callum had noted on Laena's wrists.

"My magic doesn't do *that*," Hawk said.

The panic was beating at Callum's throat, and it wanted nothing more than to heat and shift into anger. Just so it would have an outlet. He let his fingers curl into fists at his side, squeezed. Let go. And still, the anger seeped into his tone. "I was asking Thaddeus."

Hawk hovered over Thaddeus's shoulder, gaze sharp as he watched his brother inspect the black lines that traced up Laena's veins.

A lover would be at her side. A lover would take her hand in his.

Her betrothed kept his distance.

"I've never had that problem with my powers," the king pushed. "I take the byflower, and I'm fine."

It wasn't Hawk's fault that Laena had chosen him over Callum. That he represented duty and safety and power, in all the ways that Callum could not. Callum knew it, knew that it wasn't fair.

In this moment, he hated the king anyway. "I was asking. *Thaddeus.*"

But the poisonkeeper was already shaking his head, gaze still trained on Laena's wrists. "I don't know. I'm not an expert on magic, Callum. Especially Vales magic. It's... new, to me. I've studied Hawk's version of it as best I can. Laena's appears to be different."

Clearly. Callum turned to Hawk. "Maybe you did something to her. When you blended your powers fighting Katrina."

"That was weeks ago." Hawk tucked his hands into his pockets, as if they were discussing some triviality. The menu for his wedding festivities, or the color he preferred for his jacket. "Weeks during which you disappeared. So you would have no reason to know that she's had no issues in the interim."

Behind the passive-aggressive accusations there was a question in there. One Callum didn't care to answer. Where had he been? Sparring. Drinking. Hiding. Sparring more. Drinking more. None of that mattered. Hawk should be climbing the walls with anxiety. He should be screaming for a physician. Instead, the king was regarding Laena like an investment that might slip away.

They had to find a way to help her. There must be someone in the Vales who knew more about magic.

"Silerith." The word left his mouth before he realized it was on his tongue. It tasted like hope. Callum stood, turning away from Laena to look Hawk in the eye. The king had always been good at meeting his gaze, had never shrunk away from Callum's looming height. "They're lenient on magic. Someone there could help."

"They're lenient on *heart-tithers*," Thaddeus said. "It's not the same."

He knew it. Demons, but he knew it.

"But they might know of Vales magic," Callum insisted. "If it showed up in their king's line, as it has in Aglye and Etra, then he might not have feared it or hidden it. They might have embraced it."

Which would mean they might know much more than anyone else at this point. The more Callum spoke, the more certain he became.

Thaddeus straightened, gripping his hair as he paced toward the fire. "It's much too risky. You know the dangers that come with Silerith. Hawk can't even reach the Ruthless King when he wants to, and people disappear over the borders never to be seen again…"

While he rambled, Callum held Hawk's gaze. Because Hawk knew what Thaddeus did not: that their father had often sent raiders over the border who returned unscathed. Including Callum, on more occasions than he could count. Including Hawk, in his young soldiering days.

Hawk knew that while Silerith was indeed dangerous, Aglye's soldiers knew how to slide inside its borders for the sake of protecting their own. For the sake of chasing down heart-tithers who'd supposedly fled from Aglye—yet often seemed too entrenched on their lands to be anything but longtime residents of Silerith.

Ever since Magnus's death and Hawk's ascension to the throne, the orders to cross the border and chase down heart-tithers had ceased.

"It's her only chance," Callum said.

If he had to get on his knees and beg, he would do it. For her, he would do it.

"Tell him, Hawk," Thaddeus said. "Tell him it cannot be done."

But for once, it was Hawk and Callum who had the understanding. The secret knowledge of a shadowy side to the crown. Hawk knew the hidden roads, had ridden on several missions himself before it became clear that he didn't have the capacity for violence. Even in the face of his own destruction.

A hesitation that had led his father to retire Hawk from the missions, keeping him safely within Aglye's borders while Callum continued his raids with a chosen group of soldiers. Because Callum was the one, Magnus had said, who was willing to get his hands dirty.

And now, his son was looking at Callum with that same brown-eyed clarity. Forming a plan. "Actually," Hawk said slowly, "there is something else I need in Silerith."

Thaddeus stopped pacing. "What?"

Callum had heard those words so many times, though never from Hawk's lips. So many times that he wondered if some part of him must have anticipated that Hawk would say them now, even though it was his father who had spoken them again and again over the years.

There is something else I need in Silerith.

A secret. A raid. A heart-tither, dragged kicking and screaming from their home. Sometimes with an injured family restrained in the darkness, hollow-eyed lovers and children bearing scars—so *many* scars—the acrid burn of the heart-tithe not quite covering the smell of blood.

But there were times, too, when it was only a couple. A family living together in peace, no ropes or chains, the scent of the heart-tithe faint. No scars on the children. No blood.

And Callum had hauled them away just the same.

Before Laena, he'd been able to tell himself that despite

appearances, those heart-tithers were evil. That working magic was evil. That anything meant to access the powers of the mages could only ever be evil, and that pain willingly offered by a friend or a lover for the sake of a spell could not make it right.

When he thought of magic now, it was not the stink of a heart-tithe that came to his mind. It was the sharp scent of fresh snow. It was the kiss of snowflakes falling on hot skin.

"What," Thaddeus said, staring at Hawk with open dismay, "could you possibly need in Silerith?"

Thaddeus had been allowed the freedom of ignorance. Callum envied that.

Hawk nodded, as if it was decided, and Callum could practically see the pieces clicking together in his mind, the plan the king would foist on them whether they liked it or not. But it was Callum's plan this time, Callum's wish. Laena's salvation, perhaps her only chance.

If Hawk had a plan to see that done, then Callum would follow it. No matter what else the king might ask of him.

"Yes," Hawk said. "Farrow will take her to Silerith. And then—"

Callum's heart stuttered. "*I* will take her?"

Hawk paused, mouth still open, the rest of his sentence stalled on his tongue. He was not often interrupted. At least, not by people other than Callum. He really had been gone too long if the king was forgetting that. "You know it best, do you not?"

It made the most sense, so much sense that it was foolish of Callum not to have predicted it. What had he been imagining? That Hawk would escort Laena to the Ruthless King personally, in a royal caravan? No, entering Silerith was a thing best done in secrecy. *Only* done in secrecy.

'The crown needs a man who's willing to get his hands dirty.'

Yes, Callum knew Silerith best. Sometimes he wished he did not.

"It's decided, then," Hawk said again, when Callum didn't

respond. "You'll take her to Silerith. You'll see if you can find someone to help with her magic."

And while they were there, Callum would take on another mission for his king. He would root out a secret, or a den of heart-tithers who'd been plaguing Aglye's trade—or not. He would burn, or he would steal, or he would kill.

Surely Hawk would not ask anything of him that might put his future queen at risk. But Callum knew better than to assume it. Before he could reply, Laena's voice broke into the silence, clear and strong.

"Decided, is it? And do I get a say in any of this?"

CHAPTER 4

CALLUM

*C*allum could no more have prevented himself from turning toward her than he could have stopped the onward march of time, the rising of the sun.

She stood beside the sofa, hands clenched at her sides, jaw set. Beautiful, ethereal. Pale as the grave, those inky lines still carving paths along her wrists and palms. When she met his gaze, a spark of heat lodged itself beneath his ribcage and pulled.

"Certainly, my lady," he said. "It is always entirely your choice, is it not?"

She narrowed her eyes. Mages, but she looked beautiful when she disapproved of him. He wanted to get down on his knees and beg her to reconsider, damn the consequences.

And at this point, there *would* be consequences.

"Some would say those choices are not as straightforward as most would believe," she said.

"And others would say the path forward is most clear." The bitterness in his tone surprised him, but he couldn't help it. He wanted to shout the truth. He wanted to kiss her until they were both panting, to taste every inch of her. He wanted... he didn't know what he wanted to do.

He only knew he wanted *her*.

Eyes flashing, she started forward. "You—"

"You should sit down, Princess," Thaddeus said, and Callum startled, suddenly remembering that he and Laena were not the only two people in the room.

Hawk should have moved toward her first, should have offered an arm to steady her. Callum would have enjoyed watching her bat it away.

But only now did the king step between Laena and Callum, though the thread of tension still thrummed between them like a tether. Hawk took her hands, and Callum turned toward the door, avoiding Thaddeus's gaze.

How he would endure a lifetime of watching Hawk touch her, he did not know.

It would pass. He had to believe it would pass.

"I didn't realize you two disliked one another so much," Hawk said, and it was a good thing Callum was turned away from them, because he could not stop himself from rolling his eyes. That was what he read from their argument? Unbelievable.

"I must have misread that," Hawk said. "I know he can be irascible, but Callum will keep you safe, Laena. You have my word on that."

Irascible. *Hawk* was the one who was irascible. Whatever that meant.

A knock sounded on the door, and Princess Emilia stuck her head inside, eyes glistening with worried tears. How she'd found them, Callum couldn't guess. She'd probably bribed the guards to tell her. "Is Laena all right? Physician Demeran says I'm to take her to her rooms, and she'll meet us there."

Callum half expected Laena to protest that she didn't need a physician. But she merely extracted herself from Hawk's hands, then slipped out of her shoes, pinching her gown between two fingers and lifting it to keep herself from tripping.

Without so much as a glance in his direction, she drifted out of the room, dress swirling around her legs as if to whisk her away to another world. For reasons he couldn't begin to guess, she left the shoes discarded on the floor.

The door slammed shut behind her like a slap in the face.

He wanted to go after her. To apologize, to explain. Most of all, to make sure she truly was well, that she could make it to her rooms with only Emilia's assistance.

And if she was well—to argue. To argue, and to let that argument turn to a different kind of heat, to press her against that wall again.

"Your first mission is of course to help her, if you can."

Callum forced himself to look away from the door, instead focusing on Hawk. Who was already talking, of course. Oblivious to everything that actually mattered and already formulating plans, assuming that Callum would be ready to hear them. Ready to jump to his command. Thaddeus hovered behind his brother, shifting his feet, and Callum wondered how much of *his* life had been overtaken by Hawk's magic, Hawk's needs, Hawk's demands.

All this time, Callum had thought that Thaddeus was the one driving his own destiny. Instead, he'd left his life behind for his brother's sake.

Callum wanted to sigh. Maybe Thaddeus would understand Laena's choices better than he could.

Outside, the sun was setting. The rays sparked glints of light off the golden crown that perched on Hawk's brow. The king was nodding to himself, his movements increasing the effect and giving the impression that the light, like everything else, responded to his every whim.

"If you can," Hawk continued, "you should get her to the Ruthless King himself."

Sure. Just get her to the most secretive person in the Vales. Callum didn't even know precisely where the Ruthless King was, only that he kept his capital in the craggy northern mountains. It was a long range, covering hundreds of miles of territory. Without help, they could wander forever trying to reach him.

"I doubt he goes by the Ruthless King," Callum said dryly.

Hawk waved the comment away. If he knew the Sil king's true name, he didn't say it. "If he shows any signs of heart-tithing, Callum, I need you to eliminate him."

Thaddeus startled, whipping his head around as if he feared a Sil spy would leap from the corner and strike Hawk down for daring to threaten their king. But they were alone, the room secure. No spies in sight.

Hawk simply stood there, golden light spilling out of his head like a fucking halo, his expectations clear: that Callum would do as he was ordered. Casually suggesting the assassination of a foreign king.

Apparently convinced that they were safe from prying eyes and ears, Thaddeus turned back, gaping at Hawk like the idea of murdering another country's leader, one with whom they shared a tentative peace, was one that had never crossed his mind.

For Callum, the suggestion was less of a surprise. Still, he had to tamp down a flare of anger at the coldness of it. Not on behalf of the Ruthless King—who might, in this moment, have accurately described Hawk the same way, and who no doubt had armies of guards to protect him—but on behalf of Laena.

"You said I would be taking Laena there for help," Callum said, choosing his words with care. The last thing he wanted was for Hawk to snatch the assignment away. If anyone was going to Silerith with Laena, it had to be Callum. He knew it best, could protect her best.

And he wanted to be near her. Demons, but it was true. He couldn't deny it.

"You are," Hawk said. "Perhaps the Ruthless King simply shares our Vales magic." Thaddeus opened his mouth to speak, but Hawk held up a hand, silencing him. "If so, excellent. All the better that we should learn from each other. But Etra has already turned on us. So if you find the Sil king working heart-tithes, you must kill him."

Callum let the words settle into the room. At least the king had said it outright, instead of hiding behind veiled words he could later claim had been misunderstood.

"Hawk," Callum said, then stopped. The king would, if pressed, dig in his heels just to prove his power. But Callum had to voice his concerns. He had to. "What if he's the only one who can help Laena?"

Hawk laced his fingers together, twisting lightly. It wasn't an affectation he demonstrated very often, and almost never in public. Nerves, wearing thin. "Heart-tithing is not like Vales magic. If that is his magic, then he would not have the knowledge to help her."

"You don't know that."

"He could destroy us," Hawk said simply. "That's reason enough to make the difficult choices."

Difficult choices. Like ordering a killing that someone else would carry out. Like murdering the only source of assistance, the most likely source of magical knowledge in all of the Vales. If Thaddeus and his magepool access and his vast library at Inasvale couldn't help, if Hawk had never seen magic do this before—the poisonous lines that crawled along her veins, the fainting—then who else could hope to help?

Callum could hardly seek assistance among the dens of magic users he'd raided over the years. He was hated, far and wide. Besides, there were not many left. Not many left at all.

"Do you agree?" Hawk raised an eyebrow, expectant. "*Captain* Farrow?"

The king dangled the title in front of him like a prize. A bribe, more like, to make him a captain once again, his disgraces forgotten—assuming he would stop protesting and go along with Hawk's plan. To carry on, as he always had, with the Aglyean crown's dirty work.

Right now, Callum just wanted to punch the king in the face.

The night he'd spend in the dungeon would be worth it. Though it was not impossible that Hawk would elect to leave him there for good.

But if Callum didn't take Laena to Silerith, who would? Hawk was needed in Aglye, and Callum would never leave her in the hands of a brute like Landon Moore. Never mind that Moore was in trouble with Hawk for insulting her, repeatedly, though Callum had not missed the fact that Moore hadn't yet been dismissed.

Hawk might send Edmun or any of the other soldiers. And Callum trusted them with his life. He simply didn't trust them— or anyone but himself—with *hers*.

"Yes," Callum said. "I agree."

"Good." Hawk thrust his hand into the pocket of his jacket and withdrew a gray pouch, which he handed to Callum. All business. As if Callum had not just agreed to act as his personal executioner. "This crystal powder will allow you to contact me during your journey. Simply toss a pinch into the fire. It will connect to mine."

Callum peered into the bag, confused. "You walk around with this in your pocket?"

"It's well to be prepared."

"What if you're not in a room with a fire?"

"Don't be difficult, Farrow. There's enough in there for you to try again."

Callum pinched a few crystals out of the bag, rolling them between his thumb and forefinger. They glittered in the candlelight. Part of him wanted to throw the damn bag across the room. He wasn't truly repulsed by magic, not anymore; but the thought of carrying this with him still made him uneasy.

"I can't tell if you're joking," Callum said finally.

Hawk frowned, affronted. "Of course I'm not joking."

Naturally not. Perish the thought.

Hawk would need to find a way to make his magic public eventually. And Laena's, too. A few short weeks ago, Callum would not have trusted himself to respond with understanding. Though even now, it was difficult to imagine that he would have arrested the king because of his powers.

Perhaps they should just tell the truth. Perhaps the people would find it comforting.

Or perhaps the idea of tossing a crystalline powder into a fire to speak across vast distances would spark riots.

Thaddeus cleared his throat. "I developed the powder, and others. It turns out that exposing certain materials to Hawk's unfettered magic unlocks hidden properties. In this case, brinestone. It appears to react by creating a connection between the magic and its source, allowing direct communication with Hawk."

Callum stared at him. "How do you even test something like that?"

Thaddeus removed his spectacles and rubbed the lenses on the sleeve of his robe. "*Very* carefully."

Callum had more questions—such as how Thaddeus had managed any of this from under the bony thumb of Inasvale's poison master—but Hawk was already reaching for the door, waving his other hand in dismissal. "I'll inform the guests of Laena's illness and reassure them that all will be well. I suggest you get some sleep."

It was almost a physical relief when the door shut behind Hawk. He'd go out there and give some flowery speech, no doubt longer than it needed to be, and then the doors would open and the guests would spill out, chattering and murmuring and gossiping about what had happened. Planning lavish gifts or home remedies. Scheming about how to curry favor.

He wasn't being fair to them, not really. But the politics of court rankled, gentle though they were.

Laena's shoes still lay discarded on the floor, and Callum bent to retrieve them before he quite realized what he was doing. They were violet, made of some silky material, and when he rose, he found his gaze returning to door through which she'd disappeared ahead of Hawk, straight-backed and barefoot, as if she were merely heading out for a picnic.

"The fate of the Vales rests on this marriage."

Callum startled. He'd forgotten, once again, that Thaddeus was still standing there. He turned to find the younger man watching him, his hands still for once. Not fidgeting. Just regarding Callum with a sad smile, a mixture of pity and understanding.

Callum stepped forward. "Does it? Do you truly believe that?"

Thaddeus glanced toward the door, as though Laena's phantom still lingered there. As though he could see her, too. "I don't know if it's fated, as such," he finally said. "I don't know that their magic needs the alliance they keep insisting it does. But if she left him now? It'd be a disaster."

The people forgave her for her own scandal, even loved her for it. As if they should have any say in the matter. They sighed at the tale of second love Hawk had so effortlessly spun throughout the realm, no doubt commissioning a bard, or ten, to compose ballads that would rival those of Laena and her stablehand.

But were the truth to emerge about her connection with

Callum... that story would be more difficult to corral. Infidelity at the least, treachery at the worst. And that was assuming Hawk did not decide to jail them both. In the face of the thinning barrier, and Katrina's efforts to restore the mages to the Vales, it might well tear the country apart.

It was done. He would never stop hating it, but it was done.

CHAPTER 5

LAENA

*L*aena tried not to appear as shaky as she felt, but she was grateful for Emilia's arm as the princess led her away from the sitting room. The corridor leading away from the throne room felt intimidatingly large. It seemed impossible that her knees would allow her to reach the end of it, not to mention the interior halls of the palace—and the staircase to her own chamber—without betraying her.

She couldn't help glancing into every alcove, fearing a ghost would reappear at any moment.

And she couldn't help wondering if her weakness was due to this mysterious illness, or if it was an aftereffect of the argument with Callum in the sitting room.

Or if it was simply because he was here. After weeks of feeling his absence in every room, he'd filled this one immediately, his presence impossible to ignore. She could still feel the strength of his chest against her body, the thump of his heartbeat in her ear as he'd lifted her into his arms.

Where had he been for the last two weeks? And who, a small voice added, had been with him?

It was none of her concern. She had no right even to

wonder, when she herself was betrothed to Hawk, had spent the last two weeks wandering Vunmore's gardens, and learning her way around the city she planned to rule at his side. If Callum had found comfort elsewhere, she could hardly blame him for it. Even if the thought made her stomach ache.

A latch clicked down the hall, and Laena startled, head swimming as she glanced over her shoulder. She wasn't ready to face the wedding guests yet. She wasn't ready to face anyone.

Emilia squeezed her arm. "Don't worry," she said, reading Laena's thoughts. "I know a shortcut. If you're up for an adventure?"

Laena raised her eyebrows. She'd spent plenty of time with Emilia over the past few weeks, at garden parties and balls and family dinners. The princess was bright and enthusiastic, and Laena had enjoyed their conversations, though they had not had the opportunity to talk in private.

Though Laena did know that the princess lived a rather sheltered existence within the palace, and that she was not allowed to step foot outside of it without Hawk's permission.

It seemed Emilia had some secrets of their own. And she was willing to share them with Laena.

"How could I refuse?" Laena replied.

The princess grinned. She tugged Laena toward the staircase at the end of the corridor which, to all appearances, led up to one of the palace's five towers. Though the Aglyeans referred to Hawk's home as a palace, it was as much a castle—a fortress, built centuries ago by the conquering mages. And retaken when the humans ousted them from the Vales.

Laena didn't see what shortcut could possibly lead from the top of the tower to her rooms on the second floor of the castle, which were accessible through another staircase. But Emilia didn't head up the stairs. Instead, she turned her back to them and knelt, her bridesmaid's dress pooling around her as she slid her fingertips along the cracks of one of the larger stones in the floor. And then shifted it aside with a loud scrape, revealing a narrow stone staircase that twisted down into the ground.

Narrow and crumbling, Laena thought as she peered into the darkness. She couldn't even see to the bottom. How on earth had Emilia found this place?

"I've never shown it to anyone before," Emilia said tentatively. "It leads directly to the private-floor staircase. Though, there are other exits."

"Your secret is safe with me," Laena said as they descended into the darkness. She touched a hand to the wall to steady herself. "But how is it that Hawk doesn't know of a secret passage in his own castle?"

Emilia withdrew a match from her bust—always good to be prepared, Laena supposed—and struck it against the wall. She then bent, retrieved a torch from the corner, and applied the match to it, illuminating the passage in a small circle of orange firelight.

She'd clearly been down here frequently.

"It's not a secret passage." Emilia reached up to shift the stone aside, hiding their descent, then nodded for Laena to continue down the stairs. "At least, I don't think it's intended to be. See the paint on the wall there? Yes, the rusty streaks—don't touch it, it's very delicate—those are pre-mage-era paintings."

"Pre-mage era," Laena repeated. She knew there had been humans in Vunmore before the mages, of course. She hadn't known there was anything left of them.

Emilia's face shone with excitement. "When the mages took over, they activated Vaelthorne. The volcano. Made it impossible for the humans to fight. They were overwhelmed, the city was covered in ash, and the earthquakes broke down a lot of the buildings. Although I guess magic had something to do with all that, too."

Emilia shuddered, and Laena flushed, tucking her hands close against her body though the darkness hid the poisonous lines that still traced up her veins. What would the princess think if she knew Laena could work magic?

She would regret showing Laena her secret. That was a certainty.

"The mages liked Vunmore's location," Emilia went on, oblivious to Laena's distress. "So they built their fortress atop the human foundations. Vunmore's full of places like this. There's a bakery in the north city where the floorboards reveal..."

She trailed off, darting a glance at Laena. "Sorry," she said. "Hawk says I bore people with my history talk."

"It's fascinating," Laena said. "I wish you'd continue."

Laena couldn't see Emilia's face, but the spring in the princess's step said she was delighted to continue. It made Laena sad to think that Hawk had been discouraging her to talk about something she loved so much. "Well, after Jyn and Sera showed me the frescoes in their basement—they run the bakery, and they sent me a note to tell me about it—I started wondering if the palace had similar secrets. So I started poking around. And, well, here we are!"

"Adventurous," Laena said. She didn't ask how Emilia had become such good friends with bakers, or anyone else, when her brother sheltered her so closely in the palace. Etra's tradition was for its royals to spend time among the people and learn about their trades, and for the queen to travel the continent before taking her throne. To see something of the world.

In Aglye, the princess was kept as if in a snow globe. Though Laena couldn't say how much of that was Aglyean culture and how much was Hawk's concern for his sister's safety after their father's murder.

Either way, she had a feeling these walls weren't very successful at containing their princess.

In truth, Emilia reminded her of Kat. Or how Kat had been, once upon a time. Certainly, Laena didn't expect that Emilia would take up heart-tithing and attempt to restore the banished mages to the Vales.

But they did share that love for physical adventure. Kat had always been hiding in the wine cellars, exploring the caves that pockmarked Etra's coast, and playing pranks on the tutors. Once, she'd convinced Laena that they ought to learn to scale the palace walls from the outside, in case of an attack. Why they would need to climb the walls rather than descend them, except that the descending would have been less fun, Laena didn't know.

Luckily, they'd chosen a side of the palace with only three stories. Still, the climb had been harrowing, leaving Laena's arms shaking by the time she pulled herself up to safety just as the sun began to sink toward the horizon.

And that view. That view had been worth the risk.

She and Kat had met there regularly after that. Though, to Laena's relief, they'd climbed out of their own chamber windows to do so, instead of scaling the palace walls.

Yes, Emilia reminded Laena painfully of the Kat she'd once known. The princess didn't seem to mind at all that her dress was now smudged with dirt and ragged along the hem. Laena wasn't sure she'd even noticed. Of course, she herself was still swathed in her wedding gown. And she, too, was finding it difficult to care. Though perhaps not for the same reasons.

She wasn't married. She still had time.

It made her want to weep with relief.

The passage curved gently ahead, the hall opening enough for Laena to step up and walk beside Emilia.

"I haven't begun to explore the gardens yet," the princess was saying. "There's a fountain where—"

Footsteps sounded down the passage ahead of them, and Emilia froze. "No one knows about this place," she said. "I've never encountered a soul down here."

But apparently, that was not the case.

They had no weapons. No way to defend themselves in case of attack.

"Whoever it is, I hope they're not touching the frescoes," Emilia whispered.

The person who rounded the corner ahead of them was a dark-haired young woman, her hair pulled back into an artful bun. She wore trousers and a gray tunic with a tuft of lace at the waist, a quiver of arrows slung over her chest and shoulder. Laena didn't know much about weapons, but she could make out the glint of silver in the feathers, and she doubted they were typical war-ready arrows.

These were show arrows. The woman was a performer.

And though it took a minute for the pieces to snap into place —given the hair and the outfit—Laena knew her.

"Gretchen!" Laena couldn't help it; she darted forward and threw her arms around the woman. Gretchen was one of the performers-slash-bandits who'd helped rescue Laena when she'd been captured by heart-tithers. Laena hadn't seen her since Inasvale. She'd thought the whole group had stayed behind there.

Gretchen startled at the embrace, then patted Laena's back awkwardly. "I don't really know you," she said.

Laena stepped back, but she couldn't keep from grinning at the sight of a familiar face. Everyone in Vunmore had been kind to her; more than kind. But Gretchen's brand of honesty wasn't common. And she knew a hint of what Laena had been through on the journey here. She'd been through some of it, too.

"The king brought us here to perform at the wedding," Gretchen said. "A surprise for you. Except I hear there's been a... complication."

There was a question there that Laena wasn't sure she was ready to face. Gretchen had been with Laena on the road, yes— which meant she'd been with Callum, too. She'd been there when they'd pretended to be married, when they'd shared a pallet. If she said anything about their closeness to Hawk...

Laena had to believe she wouldn't. Gretchen was right; they didn't know each other. But Gretchen didn't seem the type to contribute to court gossip. If anything, she seemed likely to scorn it.

If that was wishful thinking, well, it was all Laena had in her arsenal at the moment.

Laena turned to introduce Emilia to Gretchen. But the princess had gone still, her face flushed. She was staring at Gretchen with wide eyes, her lips parted.

"Princess Emilia," Laena said, "this is Gretchen... actually, Gretchen, I don't know your family name?"

"Obviously you wouldn't," Gretchen replied.

Laena waited a beat. When Gretchen didn't offer it, she went on, suppressing a smile. "Gretchen was part of the group that helped me and... she helped us on our journey here."

Emilia nodded. Swallowed. "I, um. Yes. It's nice to meet you. What a kind... a kind gesture. Of Hawk to make. For Laena, I mean."

Curious. The princess was... flustered?

It *was* a kind gesture for Hawk to invite the bandits to perform at the wedding. Another king might've thrown the bandits in jail despite their help in rescuing Laena. Instead, Hawk had given them work. Not just any work; he'd brought them to perform at their wedding because he knew that was their dream—and because it meant something to her. He was a kind man. She would do well to remember that.

"So the king brought you to Vunmore," Laena said when Gretchen didn't respond. "But what are you doing here? In the... tunnel."

She half expected Emilia to correct her with a proper term, like 'ancient walkway' or 'pre-mage-era ruins.' But the princess was staring at her hands, her bottom lip wedged between her teeth.

Gretchen dug the toe of her boot into the wall crease, dislodging a layer of crusted dirt. "I saw a messed up stone on the floor. Decided to check it out. It led me down here."

She spoke so matter-of-factly, the opposite of Emilia's gushing excitement. And yet, Laena sensed the same intensity, the same deep curiosity about this place. Judging by the way Emilia was darting glances at Gretchen with moon-wide eyes, she felt it, too.

"There was an incident at the wedding," Laena said. "I felt unwell. Princess Emilia is escorting me to my rooms."

Gretchen nodded, then gestured in the direction they'd been walking. "I'll go with you."

Emilia cleared her throat. "Not far now."

They resumed their walk, a bit more quickly now. Emilia stumbled more than once, which Laena would understand given the uneven ground—it was half stone, half dirt, with no warning as to when one might give way to the other—except that Emilia had shown no trouble with the passage until they'd encountered Gretchen.

If Gretchen noticed Emilia's attention, she didn't let on. "Where's that cranky captain who was with you before?" she asked.

Laena wasn't sure Gretchen had much room to call someone else cranky when her gripes had been among the loudest during the trip. Even now, she seemed to have no problem saying what she thought, even in front of Emilia. Bandits, captains, princesses. It was all the same to Gretchen.

It was refreshing and painful, all at once. It reminded her of Callum.

"He's here," Laena said. "Though he was gone. For a while."

At the mention of him, Emilia found her voice. "That's

Callum," she said. "He comes, he goes. He comes back, he brings a gift, he's off again."

"What kinds of gifts?" Gretchen asked.

Emilia startled, as if surprised that Gretchen had spoken to her directly. "A shell from the shore. A lava rock from the mountains. A jar of salt from the southern quarries."

Gretchen snorted. "Not very good gifts, are they?"

Emilia's entire body stiffened. "What do you mean?"

"Only rocks and shells? Doesn't exactly like to open his purse."

"He would. Only, he knows that I love to learn about Aglye and that I can't travel. He knows that what I want most, in the very depths of my soul, is to learn more about its geology and its history. So he brings that."

Laena pressed her lips together, remembering what Emilia had said about Hawk dismissing her excitement for history. Her brother thought it boring. Or at least, he feared she would bore others, which was in some ways even worse. Stifling.

The thought of Callum bringing treasures back for Emilia, validating her love of history and the land... it ignited a spark in Laena's chest that was impossible to dowse.

It sounded like him. Mages, but it did.

Gretchen looked at Emilia, as if seeing her for the first time. "Right," she said. "That makes sense. Sorry."

Laena's jaw nearly dropped in surprise, but she caught it before she could give away her shock. Gretchen, apologizing? Laena had heard the woman insult every single one of her companions, from their cooking skills to the way they smelled, and not once had one of them wrung an apology from her lips.

"Can't see why you'd want him around much, anyway." Gretchen said the words almost tentatively. Like they were an offering. "He's... big."

"And grouchy," Emilia agreed, apparently placated. "But he

does also bring back the best spiced candy from the northern villages. Sometimes."

They walked in silence for a few minutes, focusing on placing their feet without stumbling. Laena caught occasional splashes of color on the walls—the rusty reds Emilia had mentioned, as well as patches of blue and green.

Pre-mage-era paintings. Remarkable.

"Are you feeling a little better, Laena?" Emilia asked. "It's not much farther. I promise."

She was feeling better, surprisingly. The shakiness appeared to have passed, and she found herself trusting her knees to hold her weight. When she risked a glance at her hands, she had to withhold a gasp of surprise. The black lines were fading, hardly visible now. In a few minutes, they would be gone entirely.

"I'm feeling stronger now," she said. "Perhaps it's just been too much. With the travel."

Travel that had included a shipwreck, a kidnapping, and multiple battles. Not to mention her sister's betrayal.

Given all that had occurred over the last few weeks, Laena could almost convince herself that her strength had failed her due to fatigue. But fatigue didn't summon ghosts that resonated with her magic. It didn't blacken a person's veins.

"Thank goodness," Emilia said. "I hope Hawk managed to calm people down. They'll be so worried about you."

Laena smiled. "I would not have thought people would care so much. I've only been in the kingdom for a short while."

Emilia huffed out a breath. "Of course they care. A lot of us thought Hawk would never marry, you know."

"Really?" Laena said, surprised.

Laena glanced at Gretchen, expecting her to shake her head, to dismiss Emilia's comments. But Gretchen was nodding. Emilia clearly did more on her escapades out of the palace than dig into ancient basements. She talked to the people who owned them too. Laena liked her even more for it.

And she clearly wasn't the only one. Gretchen was giving Emilia an assessing look. "It's true," she said slowly. "Even out in the country, it worries people."

"And why is that?" Laena asked. "Why would the king's reluctance to marry make them nervous?"

Emilia pressed her hands to her belly, as if the conversation made her nervous. "We live in Silerith's shadow. With a weak royal family, what's to stop the Ruthless King from swooping in and claiming our lands?"

"If that's what the Sil king wants," Laena said, "I don't see why your brother's taking a queen would stop him."

"Perhaps she wouldn't," Emilia said. "But an heir might."

To Laena's surprise, Gretchen was once again nodding. Laena supposed that, to a point, it didn't matter whether a queen or an heir would actually stop Silerith's king from invading. It mattered that the people believed it would.

It was funny, but she hadn't given much thought to the issue of an heir. It was implicit, of course, and so ingrained in the point of a royal marriage that in some ways it was little more than a word in a contract as far as she was concerned. But Silerith or no, Hawk would be concerned about furthering his royal line, the security of future power transitions. Of course he would be thinking of an heir.

Perhaps Laena simply hadn't wanted to imagine accepting Hawk into her bed. She looked at Gretchen. "And you agree with this assessment?"

Gretchen shrugged. "They allow heart-tithers to roam freely within their borders. It scares people."

Laena had been gone from the pressures and pulls of public life for some time. But she had not forgotten what it was like to hear directly from the people about what concerned them. Hawk's marriage was about the safety and security of their country, their fear of Silerith and all it represented.

What would they say if they knew their king, and their

soon-to-be queen, could both work magic? Would they feel comforted, protected? Or would they riot?

And what would they say if they knew that she would soon be entering Silerith herself to beg for aid from the very country they feared?

Before Laena could formulate a response, Emilia paused, gesturing at a staircase identical to the one they'd used to access this hidden layer of the castle. "This will lead us up to the second floor, with no one the wiser."

CHAPTER 6

LAENA

When it came time to leave her rooms the next evening, Laena was so fully cloaked and hooded that she could not help but feel like a fugitive. Brin was nestled snugly on a handkerchief in her satchel, though the narrow-eyed glare she'd given Laena at being uprooted from her spot on the bed said she wasn't pleased about the late-night excursion.

Laena had been declared healthy by a total of three physicians, though each had prescribed a great deal of rest before she might be allowed to attempt a wedding again.

She couldn't help but wonder what they would say if they discovered that 'plenty of rest' would amount to less than a day.

It was Edmun who came to escort her to an unguarded gate in the back part of the gardens, the old soldier grinning as soon as she opened the door. He must have been off with Callum, wherever he'd gone, for Laena hadn't seen him since reaching Vunmore. Perhaps even before that.

"You gave everyone quite the scare, I hear," he said as he offered her his arm. Though his words were mild, his smile genuine, she couldn't help but hear an accusation within them.

Then again, perhaps she'd have heard an accusation in any

words he said. Edmun was too sharp-eyed not to have noticed the attraction between herself and his captain.

"It's good to see you, Edmun," she said, joining him in the hall. They were the only ones about, the corridors deserted for the evening.

No doubt Hawk had seen to it that the servants and other guards be elsewhere, at least for this brief window of time. The king planned to tell everyone that she was ill, bedridden but improving slowly. Her stomach twisted at the thought of yet another lie, but she understood why they couldn't simply explain what had happened.

They would have to reveal their magic to the people, and soon. But such an announcement… it must be dealt with cautiously. It would take planning, and care, to decide how best to proceed.

"It's good to see you, too, Princess." Edmun leaned in conspiratorially as he ushered her toward the end of the hall. "Young Godfrey wanted me to pass on the news that he received a letter back from young Naomi."

Laena raised an eyebrow. The young soldier had been lovesick for the Etran maid since leaving the country, many weeks ago now. "And?"

"It would appear she loves him, too."

"That's wonderful."

Of course, their countries were technically now at war. Would Naomi be safe, trapped in Etra with Katrina ruling the country? Would anyone?

She only hoped it would not be a very long time before Godfrey got to see her again.

Edmun led her through the halls, pausing at each corner to ensure they weren't sighted. But no other footsteps interrupted their passage, and they were soon stealing into the garden, moving swiftly toward the section of old growth she'd discovered when she arrived here. Crickets chirped their late-night serenades as she and Edmun made their way among the knee-high grasses, finally pausing when they reached a small stone archway with a closed iron door.

Laena had discovered the place before; it had been shut fast, and no doubt guarded from the other side. The back garden of the palace ran alongside a deep stretch of forest, which she'd always found somewhat strange, as that made it more difficult to defend. Especially given Vunmore's proximity to the Sil border. Thick walls could only do so much when your enemy could sneak through the woods and surprise you.

For whatever reason, the Aglyeans kept the forest thick. And no doubt watched by many eyes.

Edmun put his hand on the latch as if to open it and let her out into the forest. But then he paused, the corners of his eyes crinkling as he met her gaze. "Princess Laena," he said. "Before you go, I just wanted to say that your mistakes need not define you forever."

Laena's heart flipped, heat rushing into her cheeks. She looked at her feet, as if she might pretend that she didn't know what he was talking about. Mages, but she hadn't expected him to address the issue so directly.

"If you'll forgive my boldness," Edmun went on. "It's just, I'm an old man. I know the look of someone who replays every imagined misstep on repeat and only sees the ones they think they've let down."

Laena took a shuddering breath. "I don't—"

But Edmun held up a hand. "I'm only saying it doesn't need to define you, is all."

Before she could reply, or even fully register what he'd said, the old soldier opened the door and ushered her through.

Even in the darkness, with only a sliver of a moon for light, there was no doubt about who waited for her on the other side. She would have known Callum's profile anywhere, would have recognized that alert stance from miles away, even if he were standing upon the highest parapet. He stood with his back straight, his hand on the sword at his belt in case he should need to draw it quickly.

When he saw her, he drew in a sharp breath that went straight to her core. As if he hadn't taken a full breath since their last parting.

Belatedly, Laena realized she'd expected Hawk to see her off. But the door shut behind her, Edmun disappearing back into the grounds and leaving her alone with Callum.

A relief. A danger.

Callum cleared his throat. "Are you well?"

The question was stiff, distant. As if he could take back the truth that had been in that breath. Would it be like this between them from now on? Polite exchanges, barely more than civil, yet punctuated by all-too-truthful sighs?

This was her doing, she reminded herself. Her choice.

And perhaps that was why she found herself answering truthfully. "Not really."

It wasn't enough. It never would be. She forced herself to look at him, to meet his eyes. He deserved that much. Her respect. "Thank you. For catching me."

The leather of his gloves creaked as he gripped his sword tighter. "I almost didn't."

"But you did."

Callum stepped closer, too close, bringing with him that intoxicating aura of woodsmoke and leather. A touch of whiskey, though less than she would have expected, today. "Laena," he said, his voice rough. "What happened?"

Ghosts. Poison. Darkness. And pain. She blinked them away. "I was merely overcome."

Too close. He didn't even move, but he still felt too close. And she couldn't back away, as though she was held in place by some invisible tether.

"I have seen you defeat an army of wraiths with your

power." His voice was a near whisper, one that set off a prickle of sensation up her spine. "I don't believe you were 'merely overcome.'"

He knew her too well by now. He could see through any lie.

Laena glanced toward the gate, as much for an excuse to look away from him, the intensity of him, as anything else. "Did you see anything… strange? In the throne room?"

She could feel him watching her, as if he feared she would collapse again. "No," he said. "Though I admit I was looking only at you."

He said it like he was reporting the weather. A straight fact rather than a gut-wrenching truth.

"Don't do that," she said. Breathed, really. "Don't make it worse."

He grimaced. "No? Perhaps I should make up a story about why my eyes would not acknowledge any other sight. About why the moment you appeared, nothing else existed. I'll make it sound honorable. Even convince myself to believe it."

Anger leapt into her throat, quick and hot. "You have no right to interfere in my choices."

He wasn't even touching her, didn't move to do so, but she could feel the heat of his body, the warmth of his breath mere inches away. "Tell me you want this, truly, and I'll believe you."

"You would be an ass not to."

"Agreed."

She swallowed, grasping for her equanimity in the face of that steady gaze. "It's not about what I want."

It never was.

Lightheadedness slammed into her, sudden and startling, and she wavered on her feet as the magic in her gut stirred. Of all the times to show weakness. Honestly.

Callum's gaze darkened with concern, and he touched her upper arm. A steadying touch, but one that sent fireworks of heat coursing through her body.

He gave his head a shake, like he was sorry he'd prodded her. "What did you see, Laena?" he asked softly.

"Nothing."

Her answer was too quick for truthfulness, and she expected him to push, to argue. To insist. Instead, he just backed away. "As you say, my lady. The journey is long. Shall we be on our way?"

CHAPTER 7

CALLUM

*C*allum didn't know how he'd managed to fuck things up so quickly. He'd had a night and a day since the wedding to berate himself into some semblance of calm, and to plan for the moment when Edmun would usher Laena out the door and he'd be alone with her again. He was a grown fucking man. He should be able to keep his emotions in check.

One look at her, and it all crumbled. She looked strong enough, standing there with that hood draped over her curls— no longer a breath from death, no poisonous lines on her skin— and none of his preparations had mattered.

So he'd gone and made it awkward.

They'd passed the last hour in silence. Not the furtive silence of leaving the capital in the dead of night and hoping no one would see, though certainly that ought to be their goal; no, this was the silence of two people who had far too much to say to one another.

Or perhaps that was only the ghost of hope talking. Perhaps it was the silence of people who had nothing left to say at all.

Callum always thought Vunmore's palace was strangely situated, for a place its founders would have wanted to protect. It was placed at the apex of the city, with Vaelthorne at its back, the streets fanning out from it as if to flee the mountain and make for the rivers, resulting in a city that bore the distinctive shape of a clamshell.

And so while the front gates opened into a lively city plaza, the volcano-facing side of the palace led directly into the woods.

In other words, the visibility back here was absolute shit. There were still guardhouses—more since Callum had taken the role of captain—plus watches set in the towers and trees, and staggered patrol rotations. Still, this section of wilderness always set his teeth on edge, as if enemies waited behind every tree. The trees weren't overly tall, but they were dense, their twisted branches casting strange shapes in the moonlight.

With Silerith so nearby, it hardly seemed prudent to allow the vegetation to interfere with the defensibility of the palace. In fact, Callum had argued for razing the whole forest to the ground. A suggestion that had been met with disbelieving stares and, when King Magnus realized Callum was serious, a firm denial.

And even after Magnus's assassination, Hawk still would hear no talk of destroying this place.

Princess Emilia would know the why of it, no doubt. She'd know if some extended time of peace had led the palace builders to neglect the basic tenets of defense, or if fear of the volcano made them turn their backs on it, both literally and symbolically. Or if there was some ancient religion that had required everyone to face the rivers. Callum certainly didn't know.

Though now that he was escorting Laena, it occurred to him that perhaps it had been left this way for the precise reason they were using it now: to sneak royalty out of the city. To protect them.

And to reach the secret roads without drawing notice.

For once, he was thankful for the closeness of the trees, and the moss underfoot that silenced their footfalls. If it meant protecting Laena, it was worth more than he'd given it credit for.

She held her cloak tightly around her, careful to keep it from catching on any branches. Though there was no one to see them, she kept the hood raised, her eyes focused on each step she took. She was sure-footed in the forest, as though she'd lived her whole life traipsing through wilderness.

She hadn't looked directly at him once since they'd left the gates. His own damn fault.

They made their way through the grove that Callum had ensured would be guarded by only his most trusted soldiers, down a slight hill and straight for Vaelthorne, though its crags were hidden behind the trees. They would branch north when they reached the woods that ran along the border between Aglye and Silerith, cutting away from Vaelthorne's ever-present eye.

And for weeks, they would be on the road together, just as they'd been before. Instead of easy conversation, would there be silence the whole way?

He couldn't fathom the idea of only speaking to Laena out of necessity. He couldn't bear the thought of that cold distance between them.

He was just going to have to step up and be the protector, the escort that she needed him to be, instead of fussing like a child because he wasn't getting his way. They could still be friends, could they not? The thought stuck in his throat like a bad piece of meat, but he was going to need to swallow it if he hoped to help her.

As for Hawk's mission, he'd take care of that, too. Though he hoped it wouldn't be necessary.

A twig snapped off to the left, wrenching him out of his thoughts. Moving on instinct, he threw one arm around Laena, dragging her behind the nearest tree. He drew his sword, scanning the woods as he kept his free arm around her shoulder, hoping she would know to stay quiet.

Just over an hour on their way, not even halfway to the secret roads yet, and already they had company. Whoever it was, they were not adept at moving covertly through the forest. He was thankful for that much, at least.

Laena tugged on his sleeve, pointing back the way they'd come. It took him a moment to make out the figure slinking along the path they'd forged through the grasses and the underbrush. Just a lump of shadow among the trees. But that was enough.

Callum lifted a finger to his lips, and Laena nodded. She still trusted him, at least. That was something.

They waited, so quiet he could practically feel her heartbeat against him.

The shadow passed in front of their tree, and Callum darted into the person's path, grabbing them by the shoulder before they could draw a weapon. The person was small, and they struggled against his grip, but it was easy enough to hold on. If he had a free hand, he'd pull the hood down.

"Why are you following us?" he demanded.

His captive huffed out an annoyed sigh. "Let me go, Callum Farrow, unless you want Gretchen to turn you into a pin cushion."

He would have known that voice anywhere.

"Emilia?" Callum let go immediately, lowering his sword as he took a step back from Hawk's younger sister.

He couldn't quite reconcile the sight of Gretchen standing behind her, an arrow nocked in her bow, its point aimed directly at his face. She was one of Maynard's bandits, was she not? What was she doing here?

"What the fu—" Callum cleared his throat. "That is, what are you doing here, Princess?"

"Good catch," Gretchen said. She was still holding the bow. She, at least, had moved through the forest in complete silence.

Emilia tilted her nose up, a gesture she'd mastered since her diapering days. Which he remembered, all too well, having been like a third brother to her. "I could ask you the same."

Laena stepped out of her hiding place and lowered her hood.

Emilia didn't even have the grace to act surprised. "So it is true, then," she said. "You're taking her away. Why?"

When Callum found out who'd spilled that secret, he'd have their head. Though it was entirely possible Emilia had done the spying herself. She always seemed to know everything going on in the palace. A fact he'd do well to remember.

He squeezed his eyes shut as the beginnings of a headache began tapping on his skull. "Because she needs... will you tell your bodyguard to drop the bow, please?"

Gretchen was still standing like a statue, that arrow aimed right at him. It was setting his teeth on edge. Even he wasn't fast enough to duck if she decided to let it fly.

"She's not my bodyguard," Emilia said, though her words were almost drowned out by Gretchen, who said at the same time: "She can ask, and see if I listen."

Laena lifted a hand to cover her mouth, and he thought she might be hiding a smile. But he couldn't see what there was to smile about. Emilia had her arms crossed over her chest, while Gretchen remained stock still. As if she still thought he might attack the princess.

"Please." Laena was still smiling, and it looked genuine. All well and good for her; she didn't have an arrow aimed at her head. "We'll tell you everything, if Gretchen will lower the bow. You're making the captain nervous."

Callum bristled. "I'm not—"

Gretchen lowered the bow. "All right. If you say so, Princess Laena."

For some reason, that made Emilia frown.

Callum had no idea what was happening.

"Captain Farrow is taking me to someone who can... help. With my ailment," Laena said.

Emilia fluttered forward, taking Laena's hands and peering into her face, her brow crinkled with worried lines. "Why can't our physicians help you?"

Laena drew in a long breath, and for a moment Callum was afraid she would tell Emilia the truth. Callum didn't know how the princess would react, though truthfully he was more concerned about the bandit-performer-bodyguard who'd accompanied her.

"You'll have to trust me," Laena said. "I can't tell you the whole truth, but trust me that I need help beyond what Vunmore can offer."

Callum's chest went warm as Emilia nodded, some unnamed emotion rising into his throat that he couldn't quite swallow.

Emilia let go of Laena's hands, spinning to face Callum. "We're coming with you."

Callum shook his head. "Absolutely not."

"Yes. Please, Callum. I want to make sure she's safe."

Callum raised an eyebrow. Third brothers, even unofficial ones, knew bullshit when they heard it.

Emilia clasped her hands in front of her chest. "Oh, all right. I mean, of course I want to make sure you're all right," she said, directing these words to Laena, "but I need to leave Vunmore. Hawk keeps me cloistered there like some kind of poisonkeeper novice. I'm half afraid he'll send me off to Inasvale and lock me behind their walls forever! I want to see places."

"You don't even know where we're going," Callum pointed out.

"Well, why don't you tell me?"

Callum looked at Laena, who shrugged. Amusement radiated from her like a damned drug, her lips still curled into a pretty smile. "We're going to Silerith, Em," she said.

Gretchen sighed. Emilia's eyes widened. "Silerith?"

Callum looked at the bandit—former bandit?—who appeared far less surprised than the princess. Though, she had more reason to suspect the existence of Laena's magic. And where they'd find the cure. "And you?" he asked. "Why are you here?"

Gretchen shrugged. "Someone has to make sure Princess Emilia doesn't break her royal leg traipsing after you."

He didn't know how these two had become friends, or what had possessed Emilia to come after them. Or how she'd even learned they were leaving—a point he should interrogate her on, in case anyone else had heard the same whispers.

Oh, he knew that Emilia had a penchant for sneaking out of the palace. In fact, he'd allowed it on more than one occasion, setting a trusted guard to trail her at a distance to ensure her safety. He hadn't felt it necessary to tell the king.

She wasn't wrong. Her brother sheltered her too closely, as her father had. Perhaps more. Hawk seemed certain that the tragedy that had befallen King Magnus would be repeated with his sister.

Callum felt for her, he really did. But he couldn't allow her to accompany them.

"I have to get you back to Hawk," Callum said.

Emilia's face fell, like he'd crumpled every hope she'd ever had. He was sorry, truly he was. But the king would be beside himself. This would delay their trip by a day at least; it would take an hour to get back to the palace, and they were short on time as it was. He wanted to reach the border forest and the secret roads before dawn, if at all possible.

He didn't want to delay the quest by another day. But he couldn't see another option.

And then Laena put a hand on his arm. He looked down at her, meeting her eyes for the first time in what felt like an age, though truthfully it couldn't have been more than an hour. He suspected he might look her in the eye fifty years from now, and it would still feel brand new.

"Let them come," Laena said, her voice soft.

It took every ounce of restraint in him not to lean in closer. Only Emilia's presence prevented it. "It is dangerous."

"All the more reason to have two more people to watch our backs."

She said it like it was the most reasonable thing in the world, like a sheltered princess and an archer with an acidic tongue would be the best allies they could hope for.

The truth was, he didn't think he could deny the woman a single mages-damned thing she ever asked of him. Callum sighed. "Demons take me. Fine. But they will do what I say. That means running if I say to run. Understood?"

Emilia was already dancing, clapping her hands. "Yes, understood."

"First order is to stop making a scene, before everyone in Aglye knows what we're about."

The princess froze, though she was still grinning. "Thank you, Callum. Thank you."

Hawk was going to have his head. Callum would have to contact him using some of the crystals as soon as they stopped somewhere to make a fire. He didn't want to imagine the king's panic upon finding his sister gone.

One look at Laena, who immediately hooked her arm through Emilia's, and any regret he might have felt faded. Any mages-damned thing she asked, and he'd make it happen. Even if it killed him.

CHAPTER 8

CALLUM

*T*hey barely made Callum's dawn deadline, passing across the narrow plain and into the border forest just before the sun sent its first beams rising over Vunmore, giving Vaelthorne the look of an emerald rising graciously out of the land. Which only made its long shadow more ominous, as if it were the dark side of a very dangerous coin. Callum couldn't shake the sensation that the shadow was reaching for Silerith, as if it, too, wished to get over the border.

It was a relief to dip back between the trees and obscure the sight of the mountain once again.

"Is all of Aglye made of forest?" Laena asked as they paused in a clearing to rest. She offered her canteen to Emilia, but the princess shook her head, holding up one of her own. Why in the Miragelands the princess would even own a canteen, Callum didn't know. Perhaps in anticipation of a trip just like this one.

"We do have a lot of them," Emilia said. "But I'd say your travels have been concentrated there. Though there are the plains between Inasvale and Vunmore."

Laena grimaced. "I did see a bit of those."

They'd only ridden a short way across the plains before

they'd been attacked. The battle was locked in his mind, the sight of her taking out an entire shadow army.

And of course, that was where she'd fought Katrina, her fresh winter magic mixing with the noxious signature of her sister's heart-tithe.

Emilia patted her hand. "There'll be time," she said. "You're to live here, after all. The plains villages make the most incredible honey, Laena. You'll have to try it."

Laena met Callum's eyes, and she offered him a small smile. He nodded, his head still swimming with too many unpleasant memories to match it. Instead of trying, he busied himself with rummaging in his pack for a bite of breakfast.

As if summoned by the sound, Brin poked her head out of Laena's bag, tongue twitching.

"Oh!" Emilia cried. "How sweet!"

Laena startled, reaching for Brin as if she expected Emilia would try to crush her. But when Brin skittered up Laena's arm and perched on her shoulder, Emilia leaned closer, eyes bright. "A shimmerling," she breathed. "I thought they were extinct. What does she eat? Did she bond with you? Are there a lot of shimmerlings in Etra, or is she the only one?"

Laena laughed. "She's the only one I've seen, but I think there must be more. She appears to have bonded with me. And if you feed her a beetle, you'll be her best friend for life."

Emilia glanced toward the underbrush, as if she planned to do that very thing. But Callum rose, brushing his hands on his pants. "Lady Brin will need to be content with a bite of dried meat," he said, offering the lizard a sliver of his breakfast, which she snatched away as if sure he meant to withdraw it again. "We must be on our way."

"Brin," Emilia said. "I love her."

The shimmerling stayed on Laena's shoulder as they started off again, munching her breakfast and watching their passage with bright, curious eyes. Though Emilia was practically skipping with excitement, Laena looked like she was continually stifling a yawn.

"We'll stop to sleep after we cross the border," Callum told her. "There's a safe… space. It's not much farther, truly."

She blinked at him. "How can that be?"

"It can't," Emilia said. "My geography tutor says there are two border crossings. One is on the coast, which is behind us. So that has to mean we must be headed to the northern one. It must be more than a day's walk."

"Your geography tutor does not know everything," Callum said.

Every once in a while, timing could be a wonderful thing. Emilia was just opening her mouth, no doubt to defend the honor of her poor geography tutor, when the trees thinned suddenly, revealing a pile of craggy boulders in the middle of the forest.

Callum headed straight for them, while the women hung back, no doubt exchanging glances that suggested he'd lost his mind. He braced his shoulder against the rounded boulder with the triangular cap—or so it always looked to him—and then shoved.

The rock moved aside, revealing a set of stairs that led deep into the dark. "Don't worry," he said. "If your tutor knew about this place, I'd have thrown him in the dungeon and had him questioned. At length."

Callum had been like an add-on big brother to Emilia for the majority of her life, and it was still amusing to see her jaw fall open in amazement.

"Still want to see the world?" Gretchen asked, but there was definitely a note of awe in her voice, too.

"Even more," Emilia said. "By any chance, are there any frescoes down there? Paintings?"

"I know what a fresco is, and sadly, no. It's just a cave."

A deep, dark cave. With even darker secrets. Emilia was

staring at it like she wanted to crack open the rocks and peel them apart layer by layer, while Gretchen frowned as if expecting a monster to rush out at any moment.

Only Laena remained silent, studying the opening as if its existence told her a deeper story.

Callum moved inside, grabbing a torch from the wall and lighting it as he always did to check for any signs of an ambush. As far as he knew, no one else was aware of these roads, but he never assumed that hadn't changed since his last visit.

When he was sure all was well, he gestured for the rest of them to follow, sliding the door shut after them.

Firelight glinted along the walls as they descended, their footsteps scraping and shuffling against the stones. The air was cool here, and it smelled of damp rock and untilled earth. Somewhere in the distance, a drop of water hit the floor with an echoing splash.

When they reached the bottom of the steps, Callum raised the torch to illuminate the passageway ahead. It was a tunnel, wide enough for two people to walk side by side.

"Tomorrow, we head that way," he said. "For now, though, we rest."

"Rest," Gretchen repeated. "In the creepy cave."

Callum led them to an alcove that someone had carved behind the stairs. A small, circular chamber where he and his soldiers kept a stash of food—dried fruit and meat, plus a good amount of hardtack, mostly; soldiers' fare—plus a lantern, a circle of sleeping pallets, and the makings for a small fire. It had been several months since he'd been here, but their things lay undisturbed.

Not that he trusted it. Anyone who passed this way might leave the items alone for fear of announcing their presence.

"Actually, this is cozy," Emilia said, plopping down on one of the pallets. "What are the origins of these roads, Callum? I assume Hawk knows of them. Did Aglye build them, or did you simply discover them?"

Callum shook his head, dropping his bag beside the pallet by the door and unbuckling his sword belt, though that he kept close at hand. He had no wish to discuss the secret roads. He had no wish to know more of them than was necessary, so he'd never asked. "All I know is where they lead, Princess. Now I suggest you get some sleep, while you can."

He sat on his pallet and leaned his back against the wall, hoping that would silence Emilia's questions. With her sitting directly across from him, Gretchen and Laena speaking in soft tones as if they'd entered some kind of sacred space... it was impossible not to remember the last time he'd shown someone this place for the first time, and the disastrous consequences of it.

—*—

BEFORE THE BOOKS and the magic, King Hawk had been a soldier. A prince, yes, but a prince expected to understand military movements. He'd trained with the King's Guard, and for a time he'd even stayed in the barracks, determined to live fully as a soldier.

Callum had already been leading a unit for several years by the time Magnus sent his son to Silerith for the first time.

At nineteen, Hawk had been young and arrogant. His chest puffed so much that Callum half expected it to burst. They hadn't stopped here on that first trip, instead moving straight on through the tunnels. But the musty, damp-rock smell of the place was the same. The flicker of the torchlight, and the darkness so heavy that it made this place feel like it was set outside of time.

Hawk still had a temper, it was true, but he'd come a long way since his youth. Still, Callum remembered all too well how blustering the king had once been. "The heart-tithers have no chance against us," he'd said. "They think they can flee over the border and escape us."

Callum remembered nearly snorting a laugh at that. The prince had known of the secret roads, and the illegal border crossings, for less than a day. Callum had told him it was just a scouting run. Their job was to track down the runaways, and to let them feel safe while the Guard closed in tight around them.

"They've got no chance against us," Hawk repeated.

But Hawk had never faced heart-tithers.

Once beyond the roads, they'd found the encampment without difficulty. Heart-tithers so often thought themselves safe once over the border, an assumption King Magnus worked hard to reinforce. Whenever they arrested someone, he announced the news far and wide, making it clear they'd been caught inside Aglye's borders. Even when that wasn't strictly true.

Callum had never minded the lie. If Silerith knew of the fugitives, then they were going against the law as much as Aglye; if they didn't, then he figured he was doing them a favor by scouring the criminals from their lands.

These particular heart-tithers hadn't been in Silerith for very long. They'd risked a fire, which was bad enough if one wished to stay hidden.

More damning than that, though, was that they'd risked working magic. Once the wind caught the scent, it was merely a matter of following it until the acid burn grew strong enough to taste. He'd stationed his soldiers at intervals around the camp—Edmun and Riv had been with him, in addition to Hawk—and ordered them to watch.

Heart-tithers could be deceptive. They set traps, laid ambushes. Callum's superior officers had trained him to wait, to watch, and to return with reinforcements. Especially with a group like this one, which was known to have used magic to hijack nobles in their coaches as they left Vunmore for their country estates.

Which was why Callum had startled in alarm when Hawk, having abandoned his assigned post, appeared at his side, crouching awkwardly in the underbrush beside him. "We should attack now," he said, barely bothering to whisper. "They are unarmed."

"Heart-tithers are never unarmed." Callum hardly dared to breathe the words. "Or have you not been paying attention to your nursery-school classes?"

That, in retrospect, had probably been the wrong thing to say. Instead of making Hawk stand down, it'd inspired him to do the chest-puffing thing. Again. "My father would want us to make a good showing."

"Your father wants us to make no showing. That's the whole fucking point."

"I say we go in. And I outrank you, Farrow."

"Not out here, you don't."

The mages-damned kid unsheathed his sword. Callum reached for his sleeve, but he was too slow—mostly because he hadn't expected the prince to be such an idiot.

Too slow to stop Hawk from charging right into the group of heart-tithers.

Who, as they were wont to do, had hidden their numbers behind a shield. Where Hawk thought he was going in for five, maybe six heart-tithers—still too many—he was suddenly faced with twice as many.

The element of surprise gave him the first cut as he took down a man on the edge of the circle, one who'd just turned to face him as the others shouted in surprise.

"Aim to capture, not to kill," Callum called as he ran after the prince, Edmun and Riv closing in from the other sides. But they knew as well as he did that violence couldn't always be prevented.

It was far too late to hope for a bloodless encounter. Nausea punched Callum in the gut as the rotted, burning smell of heart-tithes filled the air, clogging his nostrils and collecting in his throat. He managed to roll beneath the first wave of power—a technique Edmun had taught him—as the heart-tithers cut lines of blood down one another's wrists and arms, sacrificing one another's pain so they could call to the well of magic the mages offered in exchange.

Heart-tithers were strong, but they weren't soldiers, and Callum had been fighting magic users for a long damn time. After ducking a flying tree branch wielded by a woman in a kerchief, he saw Hawk facing off against a pair of heart-tithers. One of the last remaining pairs, as far as he could tell.

The couple were holding hands, blood leaking from their clasped palms, and they were focused directly on Hawk.

Callum dashed for the prince even as Riv appeared from behind them. Riv slashed the woman's legs out from under her with a clean swipe to the calves. The man screamed, falling to his knees, as if he could feel the agony of his lover's injury.

If he could, it didn't stop him. He lunged for the prince, hands extended, the gash on his palm gushing blood. And power poured from him like a fountain.

He couldn't channel the pain Riv had caused. But he still clenched his crying lover's hand.

"Hawk," Callum called. "Take him down!"

But Hawk just stood there, frozen, staring in abject terror as the man whipped arm-length thorns out of the treetops—whether natural or exaggerated by magic, Callum didn't know—and lobbed them directly at the prince.

The woman cried out, and for a brief moment, the man lost his focus and looked down at her, giving Hawk a window to capture him. To disable him, as Riv had disabled the woman.

But Hawk's sword trembled in his hands. He couldn't make the kill.

And then the moment was gone. The man regained his focus and lunged for Hawk.

Callum swept in front of the prince, knocking him aside, and slashed his sword across the man's throat as his lover screamed and wept.

They'd managed to bring only three of the heart-tithers back to Vunmore alive. Three, of more than a dozen. It'd been six years, and still their hatred, their grief was burned into his mind.

That, and the look of fear on Hawk's face as he'd nearly been skewered through the heart.

—*—

CALLUM TRIED NOT to think of that day. The screaming and the carnage, certainly the worst disaster he'd witnessed in his years of chasing heart-tithers over the border. If he allowed it to fester, to bubble up in his mind, he would never have been able to take these roads again.

Now that he was back here and showing these tunnels to new eyes, the past returned with a force that nearly stole his breath, the feeling so strong that it leaked into the present. It was hard not to feel that the others must know instinctively, just by looking at him, that he was a murderer. That they ought to maintain their distance.

But instead of avoiding him, Laena settled herself on the pallet beside his while Emilia continued to whisper to Gretchen. No doubt full of informed guesses and history lessons. She'd have a detailed theory of the place before dawn.

"You've traveled this road often," Laena said softly. He could feel her gaze on him, but he couldn't bring himself to meet it. Not when his knowledge, his facility at traveling these roads was so deeply connected to the awful things he'd done. To the awful things he would still need to do, if Hawk's fears about the Ruthless King proved true.

Emilia might be concerned with the ancient history of this tunnel, but it was the more recent past that haunted him.

"Yes, my lady," he said. "I have."

He was acutely aware of her hand resting on the edge of the pallet, fingertips brushing the stone floor. It was close enough to his own fingers that he could nearly feel it, like a phantom. A mere twitch of his thumb and he'd be touching her.

What would he do, if she asked him? If she demanded an explanation? But she must know he couldn't speak of it here. He wasn't sure he could speak of it anywhere.

If he started, he didn't think he'd be able to stop.

"Edmun said something strange to me as we were leaving the palace last night," Laena said.

Callum grunted, unsure whether or not this was a change in subject. "Something simultaneously wise and impossible, no doubt."

She gave a small laugh. Rueful, as if for her Edmun's advice had come too late. "Yes, actually. I think... I think he'd say it to you, if he were here."

Callum still couldn't look at her. Not when the very rock and earth of this place collided in his memory with the acid burn of a heart-tithe, the copper tang of blood. The echoes of those anguished screams. Criminals or not, they hadn't deserved to be treated that way. They'd deserved a fair trial.

"Edmun told me we shouldn't let our mistakes define us," she said. "I imagine you're not the same man you were even the last time you used this road."

She wouldn't say that if she knew what Hawk had asked of him. He hadn't said a word, and she truly had guessed it all. But he hadn't changed; he was, in every way that mattered, the same heartless bastard he'd always been.

Callum swallowed, throat so dry it burned. "And what of your mistakes, then?"

"I am doing what I can to rectify them."

Before he could organize his thoughts into a worthwhile response, she brushed her thumb lightly along his. So soft, so light that he might have imagined it, if not for the fact that her touch was like a bolt of lightning, electrifying his entire body.

"Good night, Callum," she said softly. Then she lay down on her pallet and closed her eyes, leaving him alone in the dark.

CHAPTER 9

LAENA

*L*aena didn't understand how these secret roads could possibly exist, or who could have dug them. This was not simply a short jaunt to avoid the Sil border, but miles and miles of rock-walled tunnels. The ground was rough underfoot, the air earthy and damp, and even though Callum had handed lanterns around so they would not have to rely on a single torch to show the way, the light remained flickery and dim.

Callum had taken the lead, while Gretchen fell back to walk at the rear and Emilia walked next to Laena. Occasionally they had to split into single file to squeeze through a tighter section, but generally it was wide enough for two people to walk side by side.

That was unnerving in itself. With some planning, one could move an army through these tunnels.

"Are you well, Laena?" Emilia asked after they'd been following Callum for over an hour. "Are you feeling all right?"

A more complicated question than the princess could possibly know. "I feel like I've been down here for an age, but otherwise yes, I'm quite well."

Emilia nodded, then glanced at Callum. He was well ahead of them, his lantern casting a wide glow around his large form.

"He's not so bad, you know," Emilia said. "Once you get to know him."

Laena glanced at her, surprised, and Emilia laughed softly. "It's obvious you two are uncomfortable around each other. And honestly, he rubs us all the wrong way. He can't help it. But he's a good man, if you give him a chance. I think you two could be friends."

"Friends," Laena echoed.

"He's very loyal," Emilia went on. "He doesn't show it, but he notices things about people no one else does. And then he doesn't judge you for those things, even if they're silly."

Or terrible. Like secret magic. "I can't imagine what silly things there would be to notice about you."

Emilia waved a hand. "Oh, you know. I'm fascinated by the history of Aglye, and the Vales. I want to understand more about how it all came to be this way, and what happened before the mages. Even during that time, we have so little information. It's a silly obsession."

"I don't think it's silly at all."

Emilia nudged her shoulder. "And that's why you and Callum should be friends, rather than enemies."

Enemies. She knew she'd surprised him by going to sit beside him last night, that he'd expected her to leave him alone. She could tell by the set of his shoulders, the veins of tension in his neck, that this place made him uneasy.

No, that was an understatement. This place was torturing him. She could only make guesses as to why.

Emilia sighed. "But you must miss Hawk. It's all right. We'll be back to him soon."

Laena merely nodded, not trusting her voice with a response. The princess wouldn't be so friendly with her if she knew the truth.

The tunnel wound on, and Laena's feet grew tired. She'd already lost track of the time, though given that the sun had been rising as they'd stepped into the passage, and the hours they'd rested, it must be well into the day.

"Is there always water in this passage?" Gretchen asked. "Or some kind of... waterfall?"

Laena looked down. A trickle of water rolled along the wall. Small, but ever widening, going from a sliver to a hand's width as she watched it. Still, caves and tunnels were bound to have water from time to time. Perhaps it was raining outside.

Then she heard what Gretchen must have. The unmistakable rush and roar of a waterfall. As though they would round a corner and find it running off an entire wall and into a hidden pool.

Callum paused. "No. There isn't a waterfall."

That wasn't particularly comforting.

They'd been talking for a minute, maybe less, yet the water was already lapping at Laena's ankles. She could feel the rush of a current within it, the promise of more to come.

"It's nearly a mile to the exit," Callum said.

An hour ago, she'd have sagged with relief at how close that was.

Now, with the water rising ever higher, she heard it with dread. They wouldn't make it another mile before the water closed in. She was a strong swimmer, but the others might not be. And it wouldn't matter how well they could swim if the water closed in over their heads. If it left them no pockets for breath.

"Run," Callum commanded, and they did, though it wasn't long before the ankle-high water pushed to Laena's calves and then her knees, forcing her to slow. Even bunching her skirts to her waist did little to help as the current tugged at her legs, urging her in the other direction. The others weren't faring any better, though Callum and Gretchen were both fortunate enough to be wearing trousers. When Emilia went to follow Laena's lead by hitching her own skirts, she dropped her lantern. The light was immediately dowsed by the flood.

The stink of the heart-tithe thickened in the air. The water rose and rose.

Callum dropped back to Laena's side. He'd managed to keep his lantern, and he held it over his head, the water scattering its light in eerie ripples off the sides of the tunnel. His dark curls were plastered against his forehead. He leaned toward her, his arm brushing against hers beneath the water.

"You can stop this," he shouted over the roar of the oncoming storm.

But did she dare reveal her power?

Emilia gasped, and Laena wrenched her gaze from Callum in time to see the oncoming wave. Whoever was causing this meant for them to drown.

And there was no doubt, with the heart-tithe writhing in the air, that someone *was* causing this. And that Laena needed to act.

She reached for her magic, and ice uncoiled from her body like a long exhale, rushing to meet the approaching tsunami. Like it had been shoved up against a dam of her making, ready to erupt.

And erupt it did. The temperature spiraled as she shoved her magic out and into the water.

She raised her hands, hardly noticing when her lantern spun out of her grip. It was only Laena and her magic and the ear-splitting cracks that exploded through the tunnel as the water transformed into a mountain of ice.

And yet... there was something else. A touch of nausea. A shard of pain that curled between her ribs, like the slow onset of rot.

Laena gritted her teeth, focusing on her power. On her magic. And on ensuring she didn't trap herself and the others in ice, which would most definitely defeat the purpose. It was a delicate dance, especially with the sourness of her stomach, the bile that wanted to rise into her throat. But she ignored the discomfort, delving into the water, ensuring that it was thick enough to climb.

As she lowered her hands, she stared at the sloping wave of ice, the water around her feet lapping at it like a frozen shoreline. Frost coated the walls and the ceiling, and a few snowflakes drifted along the edge of the ice, appearing as if from nowhere.

Well, not from nowhere. From her.

Emilia and Gretchen weren't looking at the snowflakes, or the frost, or even the ice that had saved their lives. They were staring at Laena. Emilia was shivering, her skirts still clutched in her hand even though the water had receded back to her ankles.

Gretchen's frown said she wanted answers. And she wanted them now.

"Not now," Callum said. "We need to go."

Gretchen nodded, though the tight press of her lips said the reprieve would be a short one.

Callum led the way out of the water and up onto the glacier-like slope. Laena followed, swallowing back a fresh wave of nausea.

They ascended slowly, carefully placing their feet so as not to slip. When they reached the top of the rise, Laena had to drop to her hands and knees to shimmy through the tight gap between the wall and the ceiling. As she did, she found herself looking at thin veins running through her ice like rotting threads.

She'd never seen her magic do that before.

It wasn't corrupted, or at least it felt as strong as ever. But her uneasiness turned to fear as the veins continued all the way to the end of the downward slope.

If the others noticed the marks, they didn't say.

After far too many minutes spent slipping and sliding along the ice, they stepped back onto the flat tunnel floor. Pure rock. The tunnel ended a few steps later, and Callum shoved another boulder aside, leading them out into yet another forest.

Though it must be the same forest they'd left in Aglye. Political boundaries meant nothing to the trees, after all.

It was almost a shock to leave the ice-chilled air of the tunnel and step out into the early-autumn forest and the smell of fallen leaves. The sun had already set, and she could make out a few stars through the thick foliage.

When she dropped her attention back to their surroundings, she thought she caught sight of a figure retreating through the trees. A figure with long hair, and skirts swirling as she ran.

If Katrina had been the one to attack them, why not finish the battle now, when they were completely spent?

Emilia was shivering violently, arms wrapped around her upper body. Emilia just stared at her, her expression a mixture of hurt and fear.

Gretchen, on the other hand, had notched an arrow in her bow. She wasn't quite aiming it at Laena, but she wasn't quite *not* aiming at her, either.

It was Emilia who spoke first. "You can do magic."

Laena nodded, her throat dry.

"And Callum knew."

It wasn't a question. He very clearly knew. Right now, he was angling his body between Gretchen and Laena as if to protect her from attack. "It's a different kind of magic, Em."

"I'm not a fool," Emilia replied. "I smelled the heart-tithe back there."

"That was the source of the water." Laena's protest sounded feeble even to her own ears. But it was all she had. "I swear it."

She could see, in the crinkle of Emilia's brow, in the clench of her fists, that the task of sharing the truth of her magic—and Hawk's as well—was one to be approached with abundant caution. Emilia knew her, trusted Callum, and still she was frightened of the magic.

As she'd been raised to be. With only knowledge of heart-tithing, one could hardly blame her.

Goosebumps prickled on Laena's arms, and she glanced around, trying to suppress a feeling that they were being watched. The cold didn't typically affect her, but it had been a long trek.

"Does Hawk know?" Emilia asked, recapturing Laena's attention.

Laena looked at Callum, who nodded. There was no sense in keeping more secrets now. "Hawk knows," Laena said. "My magic... it's making me sick. That's why we had to come to Silerith. To search for someone who might have a solution."

Emilia nodded slowly.

"There's one more thing." Laena hesitated, but it had to be said. "Emilia, Hawk has magic, too."

Gretchen cursed under her breath.

Emilia opened her mouth to respond. Before she could, someone else did.

"I don't wish to alarm you." The voice spoke from somewhere deep within the woods. "But we do have you surrounded."

CHAPTER 10

LAENA

*S*urrounded.

As soon as the voice spoke, Laena felt as if she'd been willfully ignoring the obvious. The trees were practically alive with movement—the glint of steel peeking out from between green boughs, the bob and rustle of the branches as their observers shimmied along, barely more than shadows.

She had the distinct impression she was only seeing them now because they'd decided to allow it. How long they'd been there, she couldn't guess. Had they heard the argument, the explanation? Or Hawk's secret? Had they seen her use her magic?

One man sat directly above them, legs dangling so near her head that she might have reached up and tugged him down by his boots.

By the look on Callum's face, he wanted to. Part alarm, part rage, his eyes scanning the woods with narrow-eyed focus as if he hoped to catalog every single threat. He stood close enough that she could feel the heat of him, the tension that said he wasn't sure whether to attack or drag her down and cover her body to protect her.

When Laena glanced over her shoulder, Gretchen's bow was now pointed toward the woods, her expression as grim as Callum's. Emilia merely looked around with wide eyes, her face pale with surprise. They'd been so engrossed in their argument that they'd failed to remember they had crossed the border into Silerith.

A dangerous oversight. She hoped it wouldn't be a deadly one.

The man in the tree slipped off his branch, catching hold of it briefly before swinging down to meet them on the ground. Two other watchers melted out of the woods to flank him. They all wore pants of mottled green, clothing that allowed them to blend into their surroundings.

But this man, the one from the tree, was clearly their leader. Tall and slim, handsome, with brown skin and a bold nose, he wore an amused half-smile the way the others wore their cloaks. Like camouflage. "Well met, I'm sure," he said, stepping toward Laena.

Callum moved to block his path. "Who are you?"

The man paused, leaving a short gap between them, as if that had been his plan all along. Ignoring Callum, he gave Laena a small bow. "I'm Adrian." He offered the information like they were meeting in a ballroom. Or perhaps at a garden party. "And you are King Hawk's betrothed."

Laena nodded, unable to hide her surprise, though he hardly seemed to need the confirmation. She could feel the tension rippling from Callum, like he was ready to attack if this man touched her. Which would not go well. Not with the trees full of Adrian's allies.

Adrian tilted his head to the side, regarding her with curiosity. "Are you not meant to be ill?" He didn't pause to give her a chance to answer. Perhaps he knew she wouldn't. "Yet here you are, prowling the woods with Hawk's pet... raven. How fascinating."

"How many spies do you have in Aglye?" Callum growled.

Adrian put a hand to his chest, splaying his fingers. "Oh, I wouldn't know. I'm but a simple villager."

"Well that's obviously not true," Gretchen muttered.

Adrian's gaze skipped past Laena to the women behind them. He never dropped that easy smile, offering them both the same bow. Laena had no doubt he was cataloging the princess's presence here. If he knew Laena's face, he surely knew Emilia's.

He tapped his finger against his bottom lip, as though considering a great mystery. "But why would Hawk's raven cross the border with such an entourage when he is famed for his silent comings and goings?"

Laena only just managed to keep from glancing Callum's way. He stood silent, and she couldn't quite tell if he didn't know how to respond or if he was simply used to keeping the truth close. He'd admitted to traveling those secret roads often, though he had not volunteered the reason for it. Certainly it must have something to do with his reputation for magic hunting, though she hadn't been aware, before yesterday, of his crossings into Silerith for such purposes. The reason, she assumed, for the secret roads.

Not so secret after all; clearly someone knew where to watch.

Right now, she was afraid Callum might leap forward and attack this man, who was clearly trying to goad him. But they'd come to Silerith for help, and none of them had expected it to be easy. Perhaps Adrian would be able to help.

Best that she speak first. "Captain Farrow is escorting me into Silerith," she said. "We want to see the king."

Adrian's eyebrows shot up, and Laena had the impression she'd truly surprised him. But he seemed like the kind of person who might be well practiced at acting, so it was difficult to be entirely sure. "As would I," he said slowly. "Why not add a winged lion to your wish list?"

Callum opened his mouth to speak, but Laena set a hand on his arm. When it came to negotiations, she was well practiced. A bit rusty, maybe, but at least she would not bite the man's head off. Especially when it was obvious that this Adrian wanted to prod them into saying more than they wished to.

She'd give Adrian a sliver of the truth, but perhaps with fewer expletives than Callum would no doubt be moved to add.

"We need to see him," she said. "It's important. It's about... the ailment you referenced."

Adrian rubbed his chin, thoughtful. "Would you not have done better to go through your paramour, instead of sneaking over the border in secret?" He glanced at Callum. "King Hawk, I mean."

Laena felt as if this man could somehow see right through her, see the truth of everything. As though all their secrets were out in the open for him to read and rifle through, no matter how carefully she spoke. As if he'd known what they were after, and what was between them, from the moment they left Vunmore.

Whoever this man was, he was obviously more than a 'simple villager.'

When neither Laena nor Callum responded to his question, he pursed his lips, studying them like they were a particularly difficult arithmetic question. But the sharpness in his gaze said he would figure it out, and that he'd triumph when he did.

"May I ask, then, what kind of ailment has you seeking to see our king, of all people?" he asked. "What could he possibly do about it that your own physicians could not?"

"You can ask," Gretchen said. "Doesn't mean we'll tell you."

Laena had to appreciate the woman's loyalty. Gretchen herself had just learned the true reason moments ago, hadn't even known they'd come to Silerith in search of the king until this very moment. Gretchen might just as easily have erupted in horror at the idea that they were looking for the Ruthless King.

Adrian pointed a finger in Gretchen's direction. "I like this one. Maybe I'll convince her to join our village."

"No, thank you," Gretchen said.

"You wouldn't be the first Aglyean we've converted." Adrian looked to Laena, then Callum. "You won't assuage my curiosity? All right, I understand. We just met, after all. Unfortunately, I'm not able to help you access our elusive leader. However, I can offer you shelter. I hope you'll forgive me for saying so, but you all look terribly bedraggled."

—*—

DESPITE ADRIAN'S promise of shelter, Laena fully expected a long trek through the forest. The trees were so thick, she couldn't imagine what kind of village could possibly be nearby. Yet they'd hardly taken a dozen paces through the woods before she smelled cook fires, the scent quickly joined by the burble of murmuring voices, dishes clanking, and even the rhythmic sawing of a fiddle. Water rushed in the background, joining the music like a second melody.

And then they were stepping between the trees and into... well, she supposed it *was* a village, though it was unlike any she'd ever laid eyes on. The trees were hardly less dense here, but the trunks were much, much larger, as if forced to grow closer by leaning and twining into one another until they'd melded together—leaving more space between them as they formed the most gargantuan trunks she'd ever seen.

And these people had made good use of them. Staircases twined around the trunks, leading to lofted platforms, some spanning across the air between the trees. Lanterns hung from the undersides of the foliage, lighting the street—if it could be called such—with a cheerful glow. As Adrian led them in further, Laena noticed some of the trunks had been hollowed out, creating alcoves for what looked to be shops and perhaps even some small homes.

"A simple villager, did you say?" Emilia's voice was breathless with the question, her eyes wide and unblinking, as if she feared missing something crucial if she closed her eyes for even an instant.

"Perhaps it's more of a... sizable town," Adrian said. "But I find hair-splitting so tedious, don't you?"

"And you're what, the mayor?" Even Gretchen, it seemed, couldn't hide the note of awe in her tone.

Adrian's lip twitched. "Something like that."

Laena shivered, unable to shake the sense that she should have seen or at least noticed the commotion of this place much sooner than she had. Perhaps even from the moment they stepped out of the tunnels. It felt as if it was hidden by magic. Callum, too, had his hand clasped around the hilt of his sword like he expected to encounter evil magic around the next corner.

But the village smelled of pine needles, of savory spices and roasting meat. No acrid tang of a heart-tithe. Children dashed through the trees, colorful ribbons streaming out behind them as they chased each other. The deeper they went, the more of the ribbons Laena saw, splashes of color thrown from balconies and woven among the foliage.

When they entered a small clearing, they found several crooked trails leading between the trees—no cobblestones here, only well-worn footpaths—where people were hanging more streamers from the branches and hooking up additional lanterns there, too. The cook fires were all staffed with laughing groups of people.

No magic in sight.

In a way, she didn't know whether to be glad or disappointed. They *did* need to find more Vales magic here. Her own magic twisted in her gut at the thought, the familiar knot of cold twining with the sickly darkness. It writhed against the idea of intervention.

All the more reason to pursue it. Still, she didn't know what Callum would do if they encountered heart-tithers in their midst. Surely he would understand that even a heart-tither in Silerith might be able to help them. Not that she liked the idea, either, but they knew so little about the place.

"You've caught us in the midst of preparing for our autumn festival." Adrian nodded toward the people who sat around a nearby table, arranging wildflowers into colorful vases. "It begins tomorrow, officially. But I find the preparation is nearly as much fun as the party itself. Sometimes even more."

"Can we help?" Emilia asked.

"Princess," Callum said, a note of warning in his tone.

"Oh, I don't know," Adrian said. "The baking of pies might be too dangerous for a princess of Aglye."

Emilia rolled her eyes.

One of the men, who'd not left Adrian's side since he'd dropped out of the tree back by the secret roads, now raised a hand to greet two people who came rushing out from between the trees.

"Oh, good," Adrian said. "Reinforcements."

A woman with short red curls came barreling toward them, a grin rounding her cheeks. She was reaching for Laena from the moment she saw her, from far enough back that Laena, thankfully, had time to prepare. The woman squeezed Laena's hands like she was welcoming a beloved cousin to her home, rather than a stranger. "Who did you find?" she chirped. "Oh my goodness, you got here just in time for the festival!"

"This is Maren." This came from Maren's companion, who stood back a few paces yet looked amused at Maren's bubbly enthusiasm.

"And they're Remy," Maren said brightly. "We're siblings, but we look nothing alike."

Where Maren was petite and curvy, Remy was taller, slim, with short black hair and a sprinkle of freckles across their face. Though Laena thought she could make out some similarities in the lift of their noses and the set of their cheekbones. Maren wore a dress of bright blue gingham, while Remy had on the mottled green-and-brown garb of Adrian's companions.

"Obviously," Remy said amiably.

"Who's older?" Emilia asked.

"I am!" Maren said. "Remy tries to keep up with me as best they can. Don't you, Rem?"

Remy rolled their eyes, but they didn't drop the smile. Laena laughed, charmed in spite of herself by Maren's enthusiasm. When they'd talked of entering Silerith, she'd expected... well, she supposed she wasn't precisely sure what she'd expected. Dark-clothed assassins. Cold, stony castles. Perhaps a bid to arrest them before they could reach the king.

She certainly hadn't expected treehouses, festivals, or bubbly villagers. If that was truly who these people were.

"Come." Maren tugged on Laena's hands, clearly ready to drag her away into the treetops. "We want to show you everything."

What Laena wanted to see most was a bed and a pillow. The very thought made her yawn, her jaw creaking with exhaustion. Her skirts were still damp and clinging unpleasantly to her legs, and her hair was a mess of tangles.

She felt like she'd been traveling for weeks rather than a single night and day.

"Or," Remy said, "we'll let you rest and then show you every-thing tomorrow."

Callum took hold of Laena's arm, drawing her away from Maren, who paused, tilting her head in surprise. Laena wasn't sure she'd even registered his presence before this moment.

"I don't think we should separate," Callum said.

Laena turned to face him, wishing she could press a hand to

his cheek, rub a thumb along those careworn circles collecting beneath his eyes. She held his gaze instead, willing him to understand. "We need to find help," she said, as softly as she could manage. "This is how we get it."

"I should stay with you."

She didn't blame him. These people were strangers, and it was difficult to imagine separating.

And yet, it was equally difficult to imagine that Callum would feel comfortable in whatever accommodations Maren and Remy had planned. There was likely to be quite a bit of giggling. And probably a fair bit of lace.

"Don't worry, Callum," Emilia said, practically skipping over to join Maren and Remy. "Gretchen and I will go with her. Won't we?"

Callum narrowed his eyes. "That does not make me feel better, Princess."

"Don't worry, grumpy captain," Gretchen said. "I'll make sure only the right people get murdered."

"I'm going to pretend I didn't hear that," Adrian put in.

Laena gently tugged her arm away from Callum's grip, giving him what she hoped was an encouraging smile. "I'll be all right."

Adrian stepped over and rested his elbow against the side of Callum's arm. An incredibly bold move. Callum just shook his head. "You'll be all right. But will I?"

Laena laughed. "I believe in you." And then she let Maren drag her away into the trees.

CHAPTER 11

CALLUM

*C*allum watched the group go, trying to decide if he was being intentionally separated from Laena and the others. Maren and Remy certainly seemed harmless enough, and they *were* in a group, but these people might do anything. They might poison her or slit her throat once she fell asleep, which she seemed likely to do very soon. Even Gretchen could not stay up all night and protect her.

Though, he had to admit, neither could he. His eyes felt heavy with sand, the buildup of sleepless nights catching up with him.

Still, he couldn't fight the worry that pooled in his gut. This place might be pretty, but it could not have remained hidden like this without the aid of magic. He had traveled the border into Silerith countless times, had traversed this very area time and again. He would have encountered it before.

And yet, he didn't smell the telltale burn of a heart-tithe. Not so much as a hint of it.

Perhaps these people did have Laena's kind of magic. And if that was the case, he needed to let her pursue the help they'd come for.

"Does this look like a place you'd enjoy raiding, Captain Farrow?"

Callum startled. He'd forgotten that Adrian was still standing beside him, along with that sure-footed guard of his. Sure-footed and large. Back to back, Callum thought he and the guard would be about the same height.

"There are elderly people here," Adrian went on. "And children. Quite tempting for you, I'd imagine."

Callum winced. "I never put children in chains."

"But you have orphaned them."

Callum squeezed his hands into fists. "From parents who would bleed them in order to gain corrupt power."

Adrian scrunched his nose. "Ugh, you're right. Corrupt power. So terrible."

"Oh, leave him be, Adrian." A woman joined them, coming to stand beside the blond guard. She had the look of a guard herself, with her hair shorn close to her head and a belt of knives strung around her waist. "You wouldn't have let him into the Grove if you truly thought he'd burn it to the ground."

She said it so carelessly, as if it were the most obvious thing in the world. Where Callum Farrow came, destruction followed.

They knew who he was. They'd let him in anyway.

"This is Saria," Adrian said. "She likes to ruin my fun. And this is Felix, who also likes to ruin my fun, only in different ways."

Felix grunted. "I live to serve."

"Come." Adrian gestured to the nearest cook fire, where several birds were roasting on a spit. Callum smelled potatoes, too, and freshly baked bread. Were they thinking to feed Laena, wherever they'd taken her? He glanced to where she'd disappeared through the trees, but there was no way he would be able to see where she'd gone from here.

"I promise no harm will come to her, Captain," Adrian said. "Nor to the others. Please, join us at the fire."

Callum met his dark eyes, but he saw no hint of a lie. In fact, Adrian looked serious for the first time since they'd met—though Callum had the feeling that the easy smile hid a very serious mind indeed.

And secrets, certainly. The only way to root them out would be to have a conversation with the man.

Besides, the travel truly had left him famished, so Callum followed Adrian to one of the fires, where two benches sat empty. Saria dropped down on one while Felix plucked food onto tin plates, handing the first one to Callum like he was an honored guest. Or, perhaps more accurately—and more alarmingly—a casual friend.

Their acceptance made his back tingle, and he couldn't understand why they would have allowed him to come here at all.

Were their places exchanged, Callum wasn't sure he would do the same.

—*—

WHEN HIS UNIT had returned from Hawk's disastrous introduction to the secret roads, King Magnus had called him directly to his private study. Callum had been settling Riv and Edmun into the infirmary, the older soldier grouching that he'd only suffered a few scratches, the younger one eerily pale as the physicians swarmed him. He'd hidden the extent of his injuries until they reached the Vunmore gates, at which point he'd collapsed in a puddle of blood.

The messenger had appeared, and Callum had been loath to leave his men. But one didn't ignore a summons from the king.

Callum still didn't know how Magnus learned of the incident so quickly, unless Hawk had gone straight to his father to relay the story. Callum made his way to the king's private quarters, his feet heavy as lead, certain the king would be unhappy with the low number of heart-tithers who'd survived.

They were meant to be arrested and tried. Because of Hawk's actions, Callum had essentially been forced to execute them on the spot. The king wouldn't be pleased, and nor should he be.

He steeled himself as he entered the study.

The king was a stern man, with thick shoulders and a lion's mane of reddish-blond hair. He had Hawk's brown eyes and well-sculpted chin, their looks so similar that beholding the king sometimes felt like looking into Hawk's future. Though, it had always been hard to imagine Hawk's face with such worry lines carved into his forehead, and dragging deep ravines down his cheeks.

Callum shut the door behind him, braced for a lecture or worse.

And King Magnus handed him a drink.

"Prince Hawk will not be returning to the border," he said. "He told me what happened. I owe you a great debt."

Callum bowed, the weight of what he'd done pressing between his shoulders. "I know the heart-tithers were supposed to be arrested, sire. Not many of them survived."

He could still remember the weight of their deaths, the effort he'd taken to catalog their faces. Even now, after so many years had passed, he still remembered that group. Still remembered how he'd been responsible for their slaughter.

"They were criminals," the king replied. "Their trial would have shown as much. They tried to murder my son."

Callum knew it was because Hawk had rushed in against his order, but he kept that to himself.

"Hawk tells me he was unable to make the kill when one of them came at him."

Callum blinked. He'd known Hawk long enough to appreciate the prince's honesty. But the past few years had seen Callum's time absorbed by the King's Guard, and Hawk's with the business of learning to rule.

Some part of him hadn't recognized the blustering young man who'd spoken so arrogantly on the secret roads. Some part of him had feared that this was Hawk now, his honest nature a thing of the past.

But Hawk had told his father the truth. Still, Callum pressed his lips together, unsure of how to respond. He had no wish to dishonor Hawk by agreeing, even if Magnus knew the truth.

Magnus stepped forward, clapping a hand to Callum's shoulder, and Callum swallowed hard as the king looked him in the eye. Callum didn't remember his own father; the man had died when Callum was a child. His earliest memories were from living among the young kids of the military academies.

He never thought he'd missed anything growing up, with plenty of adults to guide him. But as he absorbed the approval in Magnus's eyes, he felt an unmistakable glimmer of what he'd missed. Like peering through a window into a world that could never be yours.

"I trust you, Callum," King Magnus said. "I'm promoting you to captain of the guard."

Callum shook his head. "I haven't been commanding my own unit for long enough, sire."

"You've shown yourself to be the equal of any officer in the ranks. They need a strong leader." Magnus released his shoulder and poured himself a second glass of whiskey. "And I need a man who understands that it's sometimes necessary to get his hands dirty."

Callum had to resist the urge to look at his hands. They felt truly dirty—he'd only had a chance to clean them quickly in a stream—and he balled them into fists at his sides, as if that could hide the stain.

Was that what he'd done, back in the camp? Gotten his hands dirty? He'd only wanted to save the prince's life. But then, he knew that crossing the border went against the treaty with Silerith. He knew they were not supposed to retrieve runaway magic users once they'd taken shelter there.

Perhaps he had been doing the dirty work all along.

The king settled behind his desk, hands folded across his stomach. "Have a seat, Captain. I've got another mission for you."

—✻—

THAT WAS how it had begun for Callum, how he'd become adept at searching out pockets of heart-tithers. Not only in Aglye, not only runaways *from* Aglye, but in communities so entrenched in Silerith that Callum had known, without a doubt, that Magnus was hunting magic users well outside of his jurisdiction.

Callum had done it anyway. Because he was trusted. Because heart-tithing was evil. Because the king had commanded it.

And now, he was taking a meal with people who knew exactly who he was. What he'd done.

"So, Captain," Adrian said now, wiping grease onto his pants. "What did you say was wrong with the soon-to-be Queen of Aglye? Some sort of ailment?"

Callum let out a breath, thankful enough for the change of subject not to question it. "She's perfectly well." He would not have volunteered as much information as Laena had. No doubt she knew best, but he needed to watch his words. He was no royal and had no training in diplomacy.

"Oh? Because when you emerged from the tunnels, her pallor made me think the moon had risen early." Adrian plucked a potato from his plate and popped it into his mouth, chewing thoughtfully. "Stories of her swooning at the wedding are rippling through even our land."

Callum bristled. "It wasn't a swoon."

"Captain, the woman is ill. Would we fault her if it was? People are lighting candles, praying for her healing. Even here. Why do you think dear Maren was so overjoyed to see her? So tell me, and perhaps we might be able to help."

Callum gripped the edge of his plate, his appetite turning cold. They'd come here for help, but how much truth would Laena tell these people? Callum had to fight the urge to lay it all out before them, little though he trusted them. But then, he was never much for subterfuge. He liked open doors, clear windows. Honesty.

Or so he'd always told himself. What part did secret roads and treacherous missions play in such a belief?

"We need to see the Ruthless King," he said.

"Yes, yes, you said as much," Adrian said around a mouthful of potatoes. "Though not quite so rudely before. King Evren is the King of the Mountain. A mouthful, I know, but he would not appreciate your nickname."

Callum glanced at Saria and Felix. "Does he always talk this much?"

"Yes," Saria said.

Felix just glared at him, though whether it was because he found the question insulting or true, Callum couldn't have said.

"The Mountain King would box our ears if he heard us call him…" He leaned forward, touching his fingertips to the side of his mouth. "The Ruthless King."

He said it in a loud whisper, as Callum had seen play-actors do from the stage.

"That doesn't sound all that ruthless," Callum said.

Adrian shrugged, still grinning. His smile felt easier now than it had in the woods, more relaxed, though Callum still didn't trust it. How many smiles did this man have in his repertoire? Were any of them real?

More important was the question of how long Adrian and

his people had been guarding the secret roads—and why they'd never stopped him before. Truthfully, he'd expected them to lead him and the others to an army encampment or some kind of military base. A place designed to watch the border.

Instead, they'd revealed this picturesque Grove. Why would they do that if they didn't have the power to protect it? There were children here. If Callum were an actual villain—or more of one, anyway—he would burn it to the ground. He would not stop to question how it had been hidden; he would merely assume they'd somehow masked the heart-tithe.

If Hawk knew of this place, what orders would he give?

Adrian was watching Callum now, as if waiting for him to speak. What had he called Callum? The raven? He'd never heard so much of a whisper of that name, yet it had rolled off Adrian's tongue with ease. Callum didn't like it.

"Who are you?" he finally asked.

Adrian swiped a piece of bread around his plate, soaking in the last of the grease. "Just a lowly Sil villager, friend."

"A lowly Sil villager who knows what the Ruthless King would do if he heard us call him the Ruthless King."

"Rumors make it even to the lowliest of villages," Adrian said lightly.

If this was a lowly village, then Callum wanted to see a Sil city. He glanced at Felix and Saria, but Felix was still glaring at him while Saria was smiling at her plate, pretending to ignore the exchange.

Adrian finished his last bite of food, then clapped Callum on the shoulder. He rose, brushing off his hands. "Get some rest, Captain. You need it. Felix will show you where."

Felix grunted, like it was the last thing he wanted to do. Now or ever.

Callum had no wish to sleep here. "What about Laena?" he asked.

Adrian nodded, as if it was the most natural question in the world. "Your... friend?"

He definitely knew so much more than he should.

"She's safe, Captain. I swear it. Now get some rest. I daresay you're going to need it."

CHAPTER 12

LAENA

*L*aena awoke in a tree.

It took a long moment to orient herself. Maren had hustled her here last night—with assistance from Remy—but the place had been lantern lit, the walls masked by shadows. Despite her promise to show Laena everything, Maren had handed her a nightdress and tucked her straight into the softest bed she'd ever touched. Laena had drifted off to the murmur of voices chatting late into the night.

Now that ribbons of sunlight streamed through the leaves, the place looked entirely different. Green shadows fluttered on the platform floor like stained glass, the sun painting strips across the wood.

The room itself might well qualify as the most delightful one she'd ever stepped foot in. The fact that it was in a treehouse only enhanced the feeling. The ceiling was strung with paper stars, and someone had painted an endless fairy tale upon the walls—castles, dragons, fairies, and in one spot right beside the closet, a giant sea serpent.

A child's room, she realized.

It was warm enough that she didn't shiver when she sat up.

The blanket dropped away from her shoulders and arms, the sun promising to warm the day further still. But though it was summer now, Silerith was not known for its particularly temperate weather.

"What do they do in winter?" Laena wondered out loud.

"Oh, we manage."

Laena startled as Maren bustled into the room, arms full of colorful streamers, which she held up to show, excitement rounding her cheeks even further. "It's festival day!"

Laena couldn't imagine how the woman had had much time to sleep, but she looked as fresh as if she'd enjoyed a full night of it. "I hope I didn't chase someone out of their room," she said.

Maren waved the comment away, ribbons cascading from her arms as she did. "My daughter, Jancy. She slept at a friend's house. She'll probably do that all festival week, though no doubt one of those nights will find approximately seventeen thousand fifteen-year-olds giggling and gossiping within my walls. They always hop around like that."

As she talked, Maren moved around the room, the ribbons clutched in the crook of one elbow and falling out of her grasp as she bent to rummage through the trunk at the foot of the bed.

Laena craned her neck, trying to see beyond the doorway into the rest of the treehouse. "Where are Emilia and Gretchen?"

"Oh, they woke with the sun," Maren said. "I imagine they're already finished bathing at the springs by now, but you might catch them if you go now."

"Springs?"

Maren winked. "Hot springs. I'll point the way."

Hot springs. The thought made her want to weep.

Once Maren had her clothed in a simple white dress and armed with a bar of the loveliest honeysuckle soap she'd ever smelled, she walked Laena down from the tree and pointed toward a path that wound through a section of tall grasses and wildflowers. "Just through there. I'll guess you'll have the place to yourself. It's festival, after all."

The flowers shifted gently in the breeze as Laena made her way along, breathing in the light spice of their perfume. Bright orange lilies with spotted petals, tiny purple blooms clustered together into heavy cones, and lacy white blossoms interspersed throughout, their long stems bowing occasionally over the path as if they wanted to leap to the other side.

This place was soothing, and she felt more rested than she had in months. She hoped Callum had managed to rest last night instead of worrying about her. He needed sleep as desperately as she did. Perhaps more.

The ever-present sound of water grew louder, and suddenly the flowers fell away, revealing the most beautiful bathing spot she'd ever seen. She'd pictured the hot springs as a small pool or two, but this was a network of them, tucked into the side of a pile of boulders. Shallow pools melted into larger ones, the impossibly blue waters steaming like an invitation.

A rock shelf had been stacked with fluffy white towels, and someone had carved a series of wooden hooks, presumably for hanging a dressing gown. Laena stepped toward it, feeling suddenly shy about the idea of running into anyone else. But as Maren had said, it was festival day. No one else was here.

She approached where the pool curved away around a corner; that way she could bathe in the shelter of the rocks and would hear anyone coming before they arrived.

Still, she kept her gown on for now. She could dispose of it at the last moment. She rounded the corner, tiptoeing around the edge of the pool, and stepped through a narrow gap in the boulders.

Callum stood in the center of the pool, water streaming down his shoulders and chest, his hair dripping as though he'd just come up from soaking it. The pool covered him to the waist, steam rising all around him, but it was abundantly clear that he was completely unclothed.

Laena was unable to stop herself from gasping.

Callum looked up, his eyes meeting hers across the short distance, and her breath stalled in her chest as she forgot how to draw it. Ridiculous, she chided herself, but there was nothing for it. The sight of him made her ache.

He shook out his hair, sending droplets skimming back into the water, then started toward the edge of the pool. "I'll go."

Laena turned her back on him, facing the rocks she had hoped would be her shelter. She should go back out to the larger pool, but she did still wish to bathe in relative privacy.

She heard the trickle of water, the pad of his footsteps, and she could imagine him pulling a towel from the second stack and dragging it over his muscles.

It was fine. Not a problem. He would go, and she would bathe. And she would not think about the tanned planes of those muscles, or the way the water must be running down them in rivulets.

"It's safe now," he said. Only somehow, his voice was much closer, and when she turned he was standing not two paces from her. He'd wrapped a towel around his waist, but it was hardly sufficient to cover him. He was still dripping wet, as if he hadn't bothered to use the towel at all beyond covering himself. Which, again, he'd done to the bare minimum.

Safe? She'd never been less safe in all her life. "You did a terrible job drying yourself," she said.

His lip quirked. "Are you offering to help?"

Demons, she wanted to. She wanted to be the one to drag the towel over his body, to touch him. To be with him. Even the short distance between them felt like too much. She longed to cross it, to pull him toward her.

The hint of a smile faded, and the familiar wrinkle of

concern reappeared between his brows. "Are you all right?" he asked. "They took you away so fast last night. I was worried."

That much had been obvious. She cleared her throat. "I'm fine. Maren and Remy were very kind."

Either he wasn't convinced or he wanted to touch her as much as she did him. He stepped forward, bringing the heat of his body so close she could bask in it. He reached a hand toward her, hesitating. When she didn't move away, he settled it on her hip, looking into her eyes. Assessing. As if to ensure she was telling the truth, that she wasn't at all injured or hurt.

While moving his thumb back and forth on her hip. The fabric of her gown scraped lightly against her skin, and heat pooled in her stomach, pulling down between her thighs. She swallowed hard, trying to remember... anything, really. Words. Purposes. Her own name would do.

The way he was looking at her, his eyes like icy fire, she knew his mind was straying in the same direction as hers.

"We can't," she said, but she was already stepping closer to him, lifting a hand to run her fingertips over the hard planes of his chest as he rubbed her hip, his fingers drifting lower to cup her ass.

Callum dropped his lips to her neck, sucking gently. "Can't what?"

"Callum."

"How will I know unless you say it?" He nipped her skin gently. "We can't refrain from touching each other. We absolutely can't refrain from doing this—" He ran the tip of his tongue along the shell of her ear. "Or this—" He ran his lips along her jaw. "Or this."

He kissed her, the barest brush of his lips against hers.

"We can't," she repeated.

"We can." His voice vibrated against her skin, an invitation. "We just *shouldn't*."

He ran his hands up the sides of her body, and she shivered

at the contact, inviting him to touch more of her body. He cupped her breast, skimming a thumb over the hardening point of her nipple before dipping his head to kiss her there, sucking hard, teeth scraping over the sensitive skin through the fabric of her gown. Electricity shot through her body, and she dropped her head back, knees weakening at the touch.

"Callum."

"Tell me to stop," he murmured. "And I'll stop."

But she couldn't. She didn't want him to. She wanted to sink into him, to drink him in. She wanted this moment to last forever.

He reached for the hem of her gown, bunching it up over her hips as he gave her breast another nip. And then he dropped to his knees before her, all the while pushing her back against the boulder until she was resting against the shelf of it.

She ought to stop him, ought to end this before it went any further. Instead, she curled her fingers into his hair as he kissed the inside of her thigh, working his way up. He skimmed the side of her body with his hand until he reached her breast, tweaking the nipple again right as his tongue reached the apex of her thighs, making her hips rise to meet his mouth. And mages help her, but she could not stop the whimper of pleasure that fell from her lips.

He licked her in long, languorous sweeps of his tongue as she moved against him. When he pushed his tongue inside her, her hips bucked helplessly against his mouth, and he laughed, dragging the flat of his tongue along her clit. Once, and then again, until there was nothing but the pleasure. No sense, no reason, only his finger inside her, his tongue—oh gods, his tongue—and his teeth all devoted to worshipping her body.

When she came, her climax hit in rippling waves that had her moaning his name.

And for a long moment he stayed there, hands holding onto

her legs while she trembled with the aftereffects of her pleasure, his breath fast and ragged against her thigh.

When he rose at last, his erection pressed into her side. But though he held her close against his bare chest, he didn't move to position himself between her legs. He stroked her hair, his cheek pressed to hers, his breath hot against her ear.

She wanted nothing more than to throw her legs around his waist and drag him inside her, but his own restraint made her pause, returning a semblance of sense to her pleasure-rattled brain.

"Callum," she said.

"Don't say it." He held her almost possessively, his hand caressing her hair. "If you're not going to tell me to stop hesitating and fuck you right here and now, then don't say it."

She swallowed, her throat painfully dry. "Hawk."

He cursed. "I don't want his name on your lips," he said, his voice a rasp in her ear, "when mine still taste like you."

She pressed her cheek to his, breathing him in, filling her memory with the exact feel of him—the heat of his body, the scratch of his cheek against hers, the smell of the pine soap he'd used in the springs.

She had made her choice. Perhaps it might have been reversed, during those first few minutes when he'd begged her to change her mind. Now, though, the choice hung around her neck like a weight. The people of Aglye were counting on her to marry their king, to strengthen the royal family and ensure the next generation.

The Sil people they'd met so far might be kind. But the Aglyeans believed the Ruthless King had designs on their country, and that a strong royal family would prevent him from invading.

Besides which, the problem of her magic—and Katrina's—was not even close to being solved. To help Etra, she needed the strongest political ally she could obtain. And that was King Hawk.

Perhaps if she kept repeating the reasons to herself, she might begin to believe them.

"I need your friendship," she said softly.

Callum pressed a kiss to her cheek. "I'm not sure how much friendlier I can be, sweetheart."

She laughed in spite of herself, in spite of the tears that were stinging her eyes and threatening to spill down her cheeks. In spite of the desire that still pulsed through her like a current, heady and demanding.

But then he moved away, and it felt like the greatest loss in the world. In all the worlds, every world—the Vales and the Miragelands, and all the rest yet to be discovered.

Callum bent to retrieve his towel, though he didn't bother to wrap it back around his waist. It took a concerted effort to keep her eyes on his face. "I know I should apologize," he said. "But frankly, I'm not sorry."

"I'm the one who should be sorry." Her hands were trembling. Her whole body was urging her to pull him back to her, to forget who she was and what she owed the world. "You did nothing wrong."

His lips quirked into a rueful smile. "Best avert your eyes, my lady. Wouldn't want you to see anything… improper."

And with that, he turned and walked away, leaving her to bathe alone.

CHAPTER 13

LAENA

*L*aena took her time at the springs, trying her best to
luxuriate in having a few moments to herself when all
she wanted was to summon Callum back to her, to
reverse every wretched decision she'd ever made. Edmun might
believe that her mistakes did not define her, but in this moment,
that felt impossible.

When at length she made her way back to the village, Maren
swept her into festival preparations along with Emilia,
Gretchen, and Remy. Even Gretchen's suspicion had relaxed
somewhat, her narrow-eyed watchfulness replaced by an occasional smile. Though Laena didn't miss how she stayed close to
Emilia while they hung the final streamers and ran back to
Maren's treehouse to prepare for the party.

This was not the Silerith she'd been raised to imagine. The
way the stories went, there should be forbidden magic lurking
around every corner. She'd grown up worrying for the people,
who had to live under such an oppressive regime. Yes, Silerith
was an ally—or at least, not an enemy. But it'd always been a
tentative one.

Now, Laena couldn't help but wonder who had spread these

stories to begin with. When was the last time Declan or any of the other Etran council members had visited Silerith personally? Where had the stories arisen?

When the sun at last dipped between the trees, Laena left the treehouse with Emilia and Gretchen. Maren had given her a soft violet gown to wear, and though it was a bit short on her, the fabric felt light and pleasant. She'd pulled her hair back with a simple ribbon, mostly to keep it out of her face. And she found, as she headed back along the twilight-dimmed paths with Emilia and Gretchen, that she did feel a spark of anticipation.

Emilia hooked an arm through hers, practically skipping. If nothing else, at least the princess was getting her adventure. "If only Hawk were here," she said.

"Why?" Gretchen asked. "So he could drag you back to Vunmore and lock you in your tower?"

"No," Emilia replied, dragging the word out in one long, exasperated syllable. "Because it would be so romantic for him to be here with Laena. Wouldn't it?"

Gretchen pursed her lips and didn't reply.

Laena responded with a noncommittal hum, hoping to avoid a straight-up lie. No, she didn't want Hawk here, with the memory of Callum's lips on her skin, on her body, so fresh that it made her shiver. She couldn't let it happen again—even once had been a mistake—and yet she found she couldn't quite bring herself to regret it.

Mercifully, the path skirted between two of the massive trees, ushering them directly into the celebrations before she was forced to reply.

Laena had become familiar with this section of the village throughout the course of the day—or at least she thought she had. Now that the sun had set, tiny lights filtered through the treetops like stars snatched from the heavens.

"How is that accomplished?" Laena breathed.

"You know Adrian," Maren said, bounding over and placing a kiss on her cheek. "He could charm the stars into coming down."

Laena didn't know Adrian, not really. She hadn't seen him since yesterday, in fact; her first impression was of a layered, calculated charm. And she didn't miss the fact that Maren had not answered her question.

The light made everything in the village softer, the lanterns arranged at ground level to keep the shadows at bay. The banners they'd spent the day hanging were silky, drifting in the breeze, and the whole place was filled with the smell of caramelized sugar, baking bread, and the ever-present background note of pine, along with rich soil after a rain. A puppet show played inside one of the massive tree trunks, the audience's laughter filtering through the trees as pleasantly as the lights.

"It would look prettier with snowflakes."

Laena's entire body responded to Callum's presence, her skin tingling with electricity as he appeared at her side. He spoke softly, but his voice was still resonant, a deep rumble that cut through the laughter and the background strains of music. When she turned to look at him, her breath caught in her throat. He'd dressed in a fresh set of black clothes, though she couldn't guess where he'd have found some to fit. The shirt was tight around his chest, but that only increased his appeal as far as she was concerned.

His hair had dried in a riot of curls, and he was actually smiling down at her. Like he could picture the snowflakes drifting on the air.

She could, too.

And she didn't know how she was going to be friends with the man if he insisted on looking like that.

Emilia grabbed Gretchen's hand and ran off, dragging the

archer behind her, and Callum offered Laena an arm. "Are you well, my lady?"

Was she well? Her entire body felt like it was on fire. All she could picture was his wicked mouth between her thighs. The feel of his tongue on her body, his lips on her throat. She wanted to drag him to the nearest dark corner and do it all again.

She swallowed, accepting his arm. "Well enough," she said, fighting for equanimity.

All afternoon, she'd lectured herself on the importance of loyalty and promises. On the duty she'd accepted for herself. She had abandoned her kingdom because she feared her own magic, opening the path for Katrina to take over and mine for more power. If the mages returned to the Vales, it would be Laena who'd given them the opening.

If none of the other reasons sufficed, that one should be enough. She owed it to her country to ally with Hawk and Aglye. And she owed it to him—as well as his people—to keep the promise she'd made.

One look at Callum, and all her careful reasoning unraveled instantly.

"I wonder where our illustrious host has wandered off to," Callum said as they strolled along the winding path through the festival, oblivious to her line of thought. Her wicked, inappropriate line of thought.

"He seems to be some kind of leader," she replied. "Maybe he's preparing a speech."

Callum snorted. "I don't think he needs to prepare. Words flow from his mouth like a waterfall down a cliff. Looks pretty enough, until you realize where it's taking you."

Laena nodded, thoughtful. It certainly seemed that way. But like everything else with Adrian, she had the feeling it was all calculated.

Something moved between the trees to the left of the path,

and Laena paused, gripping Callum's arm. She wished more than expected to see the branches of a bush bending through the darkness. Something to prove that whoever had moved was a real person, made of flesh and blood.

Instead, what she saw was a streak of white fog. As she watched, it coalesced into a figure. A person. A ghost.

"Do you see that?" she whispered.

Callum followed her gaze, but she could tell by the confused furrow of his brow that he could not.

The ghost moved deeper into the trees, and Laena followed, stepping off the path and into the darkness of the woods, the underbrush crackling beneath her feet. Branches tugged at her hair, but she ducked beneath them as best she could, following the subtle glow of the ghost, leading her away.

Callum might have tried to hold her back, might have tried to stop her. But he simply followed, his presence a comfort beside her.

If he couldn't see the ghost, then perhaps it wasn't there at all. Perhaps it was a figment of her imagination, of the ailment that plagued her magic. But that thought didn't stop her from pushing through the bushes and around the branches of thinner trees, following the bluish-white light as it pulsed, always a few steps out of reach. Taunting her with a promise that if she just went a bit further, if she quickened her pace, she would catch up. And all would be revealed.

Laena tripped over a root, and Callum caught her arm before she could fall. She didn't pause to thank him, just kept going, kept pushing, the magic coiled beneath her ribcage pulling her forward. Just as it had at the wedding. The twisted darkness seemed to vibrate in the presence of the ghost, like some kind of resonance. As if it recognized the figure.

That ought to have slowed her steps, but the sounds of the festival soon faded behind them—muffled a bit too quickly as if they'd crossed a barrier—and still she followed, desperate to catch up. As if she could demand that the ghost explain its presence here. Or prove to herself it was real and not a figment of her imagination. A symptom of her shattering mind.

When they broke through into a small clearing of tall grasses, the ghost vanished.

One second there, smoky but visible—a tall figure in a short cloak, a sword hanging from its waist, looking back at her over its shoulder—and then gone. As if it had never been there.

She rubbed her eyes, panic roiling in her gut. "It was there. I know it was there."

Callum placed a hand on her upper arm, turning her gently to face him. He tilted his head, lips pressed together in concern. "What was there, Laena?"

"It's…" She glanced over his shoulder to where the ghost had been. "It was right here, I don't… Maybe I only imagined…"

He regarded her, his blue eyes serious as he reached up to cup her cheek. His fingers were warm and rough with calluses, a comfort. "Just because I couldn't see it doesn't mean you imagined it. If you'd just tell me—" His eyes snapped up, sharpening as he caught sight of something over her shoulder.

Pulling her into the grass, he flattened his body among the tall blades and motioned for her to do the same, pressing a finger to his lips.

Laena didn't know how he'd heard them before she did. But a heartbeat later, Adrian's two guards stalked onto the path through the clearing.

Then, without warning, their leader appeared in a tornado of smoke.

CHAPTER 14

CALLUM

*I*t was rare, in Callum's all-too-extensive experience, for a heart-tither to appear out of nowhere. Or disappear *into* nowhere, for that matter. Katrina had managed it at the end of their battle on the plains because she'd just killed Declan. The woman who'd stolen Laena away from him after they were first shipwrecked had been working with the dregs of her magic, and she hadn't been able to whisk Laena very far.

He'd seen it happen elsewhere, once or twice, a heart-tither fleeing in a twisted band of rancid energy.

Adrian's appearance was nothing like that.

It was not only the absence of the heart-tithe smell, though that would have been enough on its own. It was the pulse of power that accompanied his arrival, the cyclone of dark smoke that writhed around him and dissipated into the air. One minute he was a half-formed phantom, not unlike the shadows they'd fought—Laena had fought—in the battle several weeks ago. And the next, he was solid. As if he'd never been gone.

Lying still as a stone beside him in the grass, Laena's breath caught in her throat. Callum took her hand, lacing his fingers through hers. Mages, but he wanted to hope that Adrian was using the same kind of Vales magic that Laena and Hawk wielded. That he simply hadn't trusted them with the information yet, and that he knew enough about this power to help Laena with whatever was going wrong with hers.

Callum didn't want to think about what he would have to do if it was not.

Adrian paused at the tree line to meet his two guards. Saria approached him with a confident saunter, while Felix continued to scan the woods and the clearing, as if he expected trouble.

Callum willed him to keep those sharp eyes off the grasses.

"It was a pain in the ass preparing for the festival without magic," Saria said, by way of greeting. "But we managed."

"Good," Adrian said. "We can't let them see."

Too late, Callum thought. But Adrian's desire to hide the magic was all too understandable and couldn't condemn him on its own. Laena had tried to hide her magic from Callum, too, and for good reason. If anything, the Sil people had more reason to fear his reputation than she ever had.

"It's terrible timing," Saria griped. "We can't even do the floating light-story. We figured out a way to rig it with strings, but the children are confused."

Cold dread crawled into Callum's stomach. Vales magic was, as far as they knew, gifted only to the royal lines. A rarity. Adrian wielding it alone would make sense; Callum would not have been surprised to learn that the 'simple villager' was in fact the Ruthless King himself.

If he understood Saria's meaning, though, this entire village was not only aware of the magic but able to use it.

Wasn't it possible that these people knew enough about Vales magic to share that power among their people? And wouldn't that be a notch in their favor? It wasn't Callum's place to argue with the will of the Vales, or whatever force had gifted the magic, but it seemed to him that restricting it to the royal lines was a mistake.

"We can have another festival when this is all finished," Adrian said, bitterness staining his tone. "We can have five festivals. We can have a year-long festival."

Callum knew Adrian's casual demeanor had been hiding something more. Still, it was jarring to hear the shift. *When what is all finished?* he wondered.

Saria didn't seem fazed by his tone. In fact, she chuckled. "Conversation went well, did it?"

Where had he been? And who had he been conversing with? It seemed almost as important as the secret of the magic. It seemed likely that he'd gone to inform someone of their presence here.

Adrian jerked his gloves off and shoved them into his pocket. "I take it our guests are enjoying the festival?"

Saria couldn't have missed his evasion, but she just shrugged. "Princess Emilia and her guard are dancing. We lost track of Queen Laena and the raven. But they cannot have gone far."

Laena's fingers tightened around his.

Adrian let out a dark laugh. "They're probably off devouring each other and pretending it's the last time."

Laena pressed her free hand to her mouth, and Callum grimaced, though he was hardly surprised. Only Emilia seemed blissfully unaware of the nature of their relationship. He couldn't bring himself to regret any of it. Not for a second.

Still, it meant these people didn't need magic to take him down. One word of it to Hawk, and they would shatter all trust between Callum and the king. While Laena might have a chance of pretending she didn't care for him, Callum was ill practiced at such lies.

If it came to an interrogation, there was no fucking way he'd be able to keep his feelings from showing.

Mages, but he should put more distance between them. He should unlace his fingers from hers now, just as he should have stepped away from her at the hot springs instead of... well, devouring her, as Adrian put it.

And yet, Adrian and his guards weren't discussing their obvious feelings for each other as a political maneuver. Callum had the feeling that this was about something else.

So he waited, hardly daring to breathe.

Saria held out a hand, and a stream of flower petals stirred from the patch of wildflowers beside her, rising to dance above her palm in a lovely, twisting stream. Like a miniature version of Adrian's cyclone. "As long as they're too distracted to realize we're mages."

It was a good thing Laena's hand was still pressed against her mouth, because it muffled her gasp. Callum tensed, but the others—the mages—must have been far enough away that they hadn't heard. That, or too distracted by their own chatter. They felt comfortable here, that was a certainty; Callum didn't think they even had guards patrolling the perimeter.

Mages. The word echoed through his head like a drumbeat, confusion rattling the inside of his skull. He recalled the strange way the Grove had appeared as if from nowhere, the sudden onset of its sounds. They must guard this place with spells, concealing its existence with some kind of magical barrier.

The mages were supposed to be gone. To be *banished*. Yes, a remnant of their power could be accessed with heart-tithe magic. And yes, Katrina was working to bring them back to the Vales.

But Adrian and the others... they acted as if they'd *been* here. Not for a few weeks or months, but for years. Their entire lives, maybe. Their village, too, had clearly existed for a very long time, and they spoke of this festival as if it'd been going on for years, with their visitors' presence interrupting long-running traditions.

Adrian put a hand over Saria's, and her flowers disappeared

in a waterfall of shadows. "Are you out of your mind? Do you want to call their attention here?"

As if Callum and the others were the ones to fear. When they were actual *mages.*

"Are you really not going to tell us about your meeting?" Saria's posture was casual, her hip cocked to the side, but there was a gleam in her eyes that said she very much wanted to hear the answer.

"I'm parched." Adrian ignored the question for a second time. "There'd better be plenty of mead left."

The roaring in Callum's ears drowned out the rest of the conversation, their voices fading as they made their way back to the village. For a long moment, for longer than was necessary, he lay dead still in the grasses. He didn't think he could have moved even if he'd wanted to; the shock ran too deep.

"Mages?" Laena whispered finally.

Callum could have laughed. She sounded like she was afraid to utter a curse. Their very name *was* a curse.

He turned onto his side, regarding her silhouette against the silvery moonlight. Their hands still intertwined, he brushed his thumb along hers in a slow circle, pressing his lips together. He wished he didn't have to say it, but there was no other option. "I'm overmatched here, Laena. We need to escape."

Laena tilted her head, her gaze still locked on the tree line where Adrian and his guards had disappeared. "Maybe they can help us."

He wished it were so. "They're mages. They held humanity in their thrall for hundreds of years. We'd be fools to forget it."

"They don't seem evil."

No, they didn't. He thought of the smile on Maren's face when she'd greeted them last night, before dragging Laena away to a good night's sleep. A *safe* night's sleep. He thought of Adrian's determination to keep his people safe from Callum.

It made sense now, didn't it?

"We can't risk staying here," he said. "We have to go."

For a moment, he was afraid she would argue. That she'd insist they come up with another plan, that they stay to try and learn more. But they might well be caught in a spider's web, the threads tightening around them with every day they remained. Even knowing the spiders existed might not be enough to save them.

Once you knew you were caught, you had to try and escape.

Please, he thought. *Let me protect you.*

After a long moment she nodded, her bottom lip caught between her teeth. He let out a sigh of relief. His nerves felt raw. He wanted to get her away from them, and fast.

They would have to figure out what that meant for their plan, and for her ailment. But he couldn't do that here. Not when they were surrounded by so much danger.

"Are they back," Laena whispered, her voice barely audible, "or did they never leave?"

He shook his head. For all he knew, this village had sprung out of the Miragelands yesterday, fully formed and weathered like it had existed for generations. But somehow... somehow, that seemed unlikely. "They seem well ensconced."

"I wonder if their king knows."

It seemed impossible that he wouldn't, especially given his notorious lenience toward magic. It seemed likely, in fact, that Silerith had been hiding an entire nation of mages.

And if the king did know—worse, if he turned out to be one of them—Hawk would expect Callum to kill him.

Callum rose slowly, offering Laena a hand. She accepted it, and he pulled her up, relishing the brief brush of her body against his. "Wait here," he said. "I'll retrieve Emilia and Gretchen from the party."

CHAPTER 15

LAENA

*L*aena waited in tense silence, missing Callum's steady presence the moment he disappeared into the trees with a stern instruction that she was to run if he did not return within the hour. Even Brin was restless, wriggling in constant circles in Laena's pocket. She didn't try to peek out, though. As if she knew to remain concealed.

Callum must know she would never leave him, would never leave Emilia and Gretchen here. If they were caught, Laena would come after them.

She had her own power to work with, after all.

But he returned well within the hour, with Emilia and Gretchen on his heels. The archer's stiff-backed alertness said she sensed something was wrong, and even Emilia came quietly, gaze darting around as though she could sense hidden enemies in the trees.

It was well that she trusted Callum and followed him without argument.

Together, they headed away from the Grove, using the moon as a beacon to ensure they didn't walk in circles. Laena and Emilia weren't exactly dressed for travel. Their party dresses caught on the underbrush, their slippers quickly soaked through. Gretchen had on her usual trousers, her bow slung over her back, while Callum wore the same black outfit he'd had on at the party.

"I knew we couldn't trust them," Gretchen said after Laena recounted the conversation she and Callum had overheard. "They were too nice."

Emilia pressed her lips together. "But Maren and Remy were so kind to us. And the children…"

"The children are innocents," Gretchen said. "They'll be raised into cruelty."

"Laena has magic," Emilia protested. "And she isn't cruel or evil."

Laena's heart twisted, and she had to swallow down a wave of nausea. She wouldn't use her magic for cruelty, or to inflict pain on anyone. She couldn't imagine the evil it would take to compel another person to do her bidding against their will—with or without magic—though that was exactly what the mages of old had spent hundreds of years doing to the humans. Holding them in thrall, treating them as slaves. Erupting Vaelthorne to bury their capital, merely because they wanted the place for themselves.

No, she couldn't fathom using her magic in that way. But what if the magic *itself* was twisting into something evil? Something she couldn't control?

"Laena isn't a *mage*," Gretchen replied, echoing her thoughts. "These people *are*."

Emilia huffed out a breath. "Even if Maren and the others did come back from the Miragelands, *they* couldn't have been the ones to do those things. Those mages are long dead."

She had a point.

"That doesn't mean we shouldn't hold them accountable," Callum said.

"And it doesn't mean we can trust them," Gretchen agreed.

Laena exchanged a glance with Emilia, who shrugged. Callum and Gretchen would try to protect them, whatever the circumstances.

Brin stuck her head out of Laena's skirt pocket, her tongue flicking as though she hoped to catch one of the fireflies that flickered between the trees. Either she was oblivious to the danger—which wasn't like her—or she was unconcerned by it.

"All right," Emilia said. "Where are we going, then?"

"We'll put as much distance between us and the Grove as we can," Callum said. "Then we'll regroup and head north again. Try to find the king."

"He's probably a mage, too," Gretchen said. "We should go back to Vunmore."

Callum shrugged, but Laena could see the tension in his shoulders. He wanted to help her figure out what was going wrong with her magic. No one in Aglye could help.

"We'll have to assume he wouldn't hurt a foreign queen," Emilia said. "He'll respect Hawk's position. And Laena's."

Callum crossed his arms over his chest, brow furrowed like he wanted to argue, but Laena just nodded. Perhaps it was naive to think this way, but it was all they could do.

She could only hope they were doing the right thing.

For the first hour, Laena kept expecting Adrian and the others to appear out of nowhere, as they were clearly capable of doing. But they must have been enjoying their mead and dancing, assuming that Laena and Callum—and perhaps Emilia and Gretchen—had snuck away from the party for privacy. The only shadows that moved between the trees were branches bending in the breeze, and the occasional swoop of an owl on its nighttime hunt.

Just as they reached what Laena guessed was the second hour, Brin leapt out of her pocket. She scurried over leaves and rocks to cut in front of Callum, where she stopped in the middle of the path. Emilia gasped as her scales began to glow, giving off a soft pink color.

"Wait," Laena said, though Callum had already paused.

She stepped slowly toward Brin, listening. The breeze rustled the leaves above them, though it was too slight to feel even a hint of air on her skin. Everything was normal, except... except that Brin's glow was reflecting against empty air, as if they'd encountered some kind of dark mirror.

"I think this is the border," Laena said. "The edge of the shield that's protecting the Grove."

"We haven't passed it yet?" Gretchen asked.

Laena stepped forward, holding out a hand. It was like reaching for the first wave of heat from a campfire, the magic brushing gently against her palms. She hadn't known to feel for it before, and it was subtle; if Brin hadn't stopped, she might have passed straight through without noticing.

"I can feel it," she said.

"Will it hurt us?" Emilia asked.

"It didn't hurt us before." Still, Laena reached for Callum's hand as Brin scampered back down the path and hid in Laena's pocket once again, her task of directing the wayward humans apparently complete for now.

Callum wrapped his fingers around Laena's, his calluses scraping pleasantly against her skin, and they stepped forward together.

The moon jumped.

One moment they were standing among the densely growing trees, Emilia and Gretchen mere steps behind them, the moon rising to the left.

And the next, the moon had moved to the right, clouds crowding around it as if drawn to its light, where before it had shone out of a perfectly clear sky.

"It let us out in the wrong place," Laena said.

"Or the wrong time." That one step could have taken them

hours to complete. What if the moon had already peaked in the sky and was now setting?

Only there was no sign of oncoming dawn. No way to guess the time.

The trees were less dense here, their trunks thin and pale. From what she could see in the moonlight, the terrain was more rugged, rocky hills interrupting the creep of the forest at frequent intervals.

And it was far too quiet.

Laena looked back the way they'd come. Instead of dense forest, the terrain behind them looked exactly the same as the terrain ahead.

Wrong place. Wrong time. Perhaps both. She pictured the bubble that protected the Grove as if it were a circular puzzle piece, one that had been pressed into a map and then twisted, the borders no longer aligned with the physical geography of the land.

Perhaps it was always twisting, always turning. Maybe it twisted every time someone came or went. The minutes stretched on, and there was still no sign of Emilia or Gretchen.

Callum called Emilia's name, then Gretchen's. Only silence answered.

And so, hands entwined, they tried to go back through the barrier. But Laena no longer felt its heat, and Brin gave no indication that she did, either.

"The magic won't let us go back to the Grove without Adrian," Laena said. But still, they retraced their path—what should have been their path—and called out for Gretchen and Emilia as rain began to patter the leaves above. The rain fell harder, soaking her hair and the thin fabric of her dress, the drops loud enough to drown out their shouts.

Finally, Callum stopped. "We'll need to wait for daylight. I can't orient myself."

And neither could she. Even had the moon's position offered

a clue—or better yet, the stars—the sky was now hidden behind a thick layer of clouds, turning the night even darker.

Had she not been holding onto Callum's hand, she would have lost him in the darkness.

An impossible shred of moonlight flickered between the trees ahead, and Laena nearly started toward it, thinking the sky must have cleared enough to let her catch sight of the moon's path. The rain seemed too thick to allow it, but there could be a patch of clear sky, to give them a hint of where they'd landed.

Callum's course didn't alter. Whatever break in the clouds might be ahead, he didn't see it.

And then the sliver moved. Not like the flickering moon behind a veil of clouds, but like a person striding between the trees.

Laena's magic lurched, trying to uncoil. As the light flinched directly into her path, she cried out, pulling Callum closer.

Not moonlight, she realized, but a ghost. It illuminated the trees with an eerie light of its own, a smile stretched across its face.

"They're here," she said. "They followed us."

A second ghost joined, then a third. They crowded the woods, watching. Always watching. Even through the steam-like mist that swirled around them she could make out their features, their strange clothing. Two men in half capes and knee-high boots accompanied by a woman in divided skirts, her long hair streaming past her shoulders and down to her waist like a spiraled waterfall.

Callum wrapped his arms around Laena, his body like a shield as he scanned the woods. "Who's here?" he said. "Who followed us?"

The ghosts. The phantoms. They were right there, close enough to brush the blurry mist with her fingertip, had she been willing to loosen her grip on Callum's waist. She didn't know whether to speak to the creatures or to run from them.

She wanted to bury her head in Callum's neck and hide her face from their constant stares.

Instead, she forced herself to step back, though she didn't dare let go of his hand.

She blinked, and the ghosts disappeared. "Laena?" Callum said, squeezing her hand. She could feel the tension radiating up his arm, as if he wanted to draw her close again. To protect her.

"Nothing." Her voice shook. "Just my eyes playing tricks on me."

He frowned. She could tell he didn't believe her, yet he didn't press. "We need to find shelter. I saw some promising boulders up that way before the storm set in. There might be a cave."

"But Emilia…"

"She's smart." He sounded reluctant, but certain. "And so is Gretchen. Chances are they walked out of the barrier and found themselves on the opposite side. We have to trust them to find their way."

Back to Vunmore, Laena hoped.

She nodded, and Callum tightened his grip on her hand, leading her up through the rocky terrain toward where he'd seen the boulders. Laena was shivering so hard she could no longer speak without her teeth clacking together. Her dress clung to her arms, making it difficult to walk. Her legs were so numb she kept tripping, her feet like blocks of ice, but Callum never let her fall.

And all the while, her magic roiled within her, as if it wanted to strike out after the ghosts. As if it could still feel their resonance.

As if it wanted, more than anything, to follow.

CHAPTER 16

LAENA

*I*t felt like hours before they found it: a gap in the rock face. For the first time since Laena and Callum had left the barrier, he released her hand and proceeded into the tunnel to check for unpleasant surprises while she waited outside. She knew it was the wise course, but she was desperate to be out of the rain and the cold.

And after losing Emilia and Gretchen, she didn't want to let him out of her sight.

Callum returned quickly, carrying a small lantern. The tension in his shoulders had eased somewhat. "We're in luck. There's a hunting stash."

Laena didn't think she'd ever been happier to see a pile of dusty blankets and firewood. Not to mention the tin box in the back corner that hinted at food.

Callum set about lighting a fire while she stripped her wet clothes, well beyond modesty now—though he kept his back to her. She spread one blanket on the ground and wrapped herself in another, but she was still shivering so badly that when Callum started the flames up with a sputter and crackle, he took one look at her and gestured for her to make room for him.

"Is that wise, Captain?" she asked, immediately wishing she hadn't. She wanted to banish even the suggestion of Hawk from their presence, just as Callum had banished his name from the hot springs.

Brin had settled by the fire, apparently unconcerned about the threat of wayward sparks. Even she seemed to have no interest in food. Only rest.

"Your lips are blue." There was no hint of flirting or jest in his tone. "I don't think your fiancé will thank me for returning an icicle in the place of his queen."

He unbuckled his belt and laid it beside the blanket as if to keep his weapons close, then fumbled with the buttons of his shirt, his fingers clearly numb with cold. Under other circumstances, she would have watched, drinking in the sight of him, the broad muscles of his chest.

Instead, she averted her gaze as he peeled off his trousers and laid them out to dry beside the fire.

"The cold didn't used to bother me," she said as he settled down beside her, his body pressed tight to hers beneath the scratchy blanket. "Something... something's wrong."

He draped an arm over her shoulder, pulling her closer, and she leaned her head against his chest. "What did you see out there, Laena?" His voice was soft. "What have you *been* seeing?"

At the wedding. At the festival, when she'd gone tearing through the trees. And now, in the woods. In the rain. She knew he'd noticed—she didn't see how anyone could have avoided noticing it—but she didn't want to tell him. Didn't want to admit what she feared would pull them apart even more than they already had been.

"You asked for my friendship," he said, his breath warm against her hair. He rubbed his thumb in a circle on her shoulder, sending a maddening thrill through her body. Friendship? She wanted so much more than friendship from this man.

Yet, he continued, "You must know that you have it. Always. So tell me what you're seeing, so I might banish it to the grave."

She believed him. Mages, she believed that he would do it. She almost wanted to laugh at the irony.

"Ghosts," she whispered. "I keep seeing ghosts. At least, that's what they look like. Spirits. I don't... I don't know if they're real."

His hand stilled on her shoulder.

"I think my magic might be driving me to madness," she confessed, the words coming easier now. It felt good to say them. Like shining a light on a corner of darkness. "You saw the lines on my skin. In the ice I made on the secret roads. What if... what if it becomes something evil?"

Like Kat's. She didn't say it, but she couldn't help thinking it.

"Never." The answer came without hesitation, his faith in her as solid as his arms. Immovable.

"How can you know that?"

"Because I have spent much of my life making sure that magic users are held accountable for their actions." His voice was a rumble against her body, comforting and sure. So very sure. "I know what evil magic looks like, Laena, and yours is not it."

"Even with the dark lines?"

He let out a huff of a laugh. "If a little darkness defined us, then I would already be damned." He hesitated. "Though perhaps it's foolish to think I'm not."

"And why is that?" she asked.

She wanted more of him. No, she wanted all of him. She'd guessed at so many of the secrets he kept close, but she wanted to hear the truth from him. She'd seen so much of his light, but she wanted to see the darkness, too.

For a moment, she thought he would keep his secrets close, even now. But then he shifted, resting his cheek lightly against her hair. "I am the king's dark hand," he said, a note of bitterness entering his tone. "I do what must be done."

She waited, feeling the rise and fall of his chest, the warmth of him. She wasn't sure when her shivers had ceased, but she was glad of it. Glad of the way his skin pressed against hers.

"I kill at the king's command," he continued, "even if not always in his name. You saw the secret roads. Guessed their purpose, I'm sure. I've used them for a very long time to track heart-tithers into Silerith."

Against the treaty. Against the law. Knowing that, had he been caught, King Hawk—and Magnus before him—would deny having given him permission to act.

But Adrian and the others were obviously well aware of the deeds he'd committed. It was reason enough to incite a war.

What did Silerith want in all of this? Where was their king?

"I'm a monster, Laena," Callum said softly. "I would recognize one of my own."

She turned her head to look at him, finding his face much closer than she'd anticipated. Her breath caught, burning in her throat. "You are no monster," she whispered.

His lips brushed hers with such softness, such tenderness, she almost couldn't bear it. A question, and an answer, all wrapped into one. A friend? No. She wanted so much more than that.

And so she was the one to deepen the kiss, to swipe her tongue along his upper lip until he groaned, meeting her stroke for stroke. His hand skimmed down her arm, his touch dragging a trail of lightning across her skin.

"We can't," he said, even as the calloused tip of his thumb scraped across her nipple, sending bolts of desire coursing through her. Her body responded to him like it had been waiting, like it had only ever wanted him.

"We can," she said, echoing his words from the hot spring. "We just shouldn't."

He pulled her into his lap, and she straddled his hips, his hard length pressing into her belly as she arched against him, desperate to feel him everywhere. His kiss was a brand against her lips, the caress of his thumb on her breast practically enough to undo her all on its own. Desire seared a hot line through her body, igniting a pool of heat between her legs. Mages, but she wanted him. She'd never wanted anyone more.

She dragged a hand down his chest, exploring the ridges of his body and reveling in his encouraging moans as she delved ever lower. When she wrapped her fingers around his cock, he growled against her mouth. She smiled as she stroked him, basking in the sounds she could tease from his lips.

In this moment, she could not imagine returning to Vunmore to marry Hawk. She could not imagine forsaking this man, who put so much of his trust in her, insisted she wasn't a monster even if she might well become one.

That alone should be enough of a reason to stop this. Before she turned to darkness, before her corrupted power could hurt him.

But she couldn't stop.

He flipped her onto her back, laying her gently on the blanket as he settled himself between her legs, his cock poised at her entrance. Even that much connection between them, light as it was, made her want to whimper.

She hooked an ankle around his hip, drawing him toward her, but he paused, his muscles taut, his lips a breath from hers, and said, "You want this?" His breathing was ragged.

"I want you," she said. "I want all of you."

He pushed into her and she cried out, muffling her cries against his neck even though there was no one to hear them. And for a moment he was still, eyes open, hands gripping her hair, the intensity in those blue eyes making it impossible to break his gaze, breathing hard, gasping with the exquisite torture of it.

And then he shifted, withdrawing only to slam into her again, hard enough to make her see stars. He groaned, twining his fingers with hers as he fucked her, her skin alive with sensation. He dragged his lips along hers, down her neck, along her collarbone as he rocked into her, again and again. With his other hand, he worked his thumb against the sensitive nub of her sex until light exploded across her vision, her climax nearly within reach.

"Mages, Laena," he said. "You are... you are everything."

She let herself believe it, if only for the moment. If only for this breath of time. Their bodies entwined, joined, their need escalating together.

Her promise, and her darkness, would be problems to solve tomorrow.

He shouted her name as he came, the ragged sound pushing her over the edge into her own climax. They shuddered together, waves of pleasure rocking through her body.

Callum dropped his forehead to hers, their bodies still joined, his cock still pulsing inside her. He kissed her temple, her cheek, the corner of her mouth. His skin was hot against hers, their bodies flush against one another.

When they finally separated, she felt the loss for only a moment before he settled her in his arms, dragging the blanket over them. The fire was crackling enthusiastically now, lighting his face in dancing orange light as he watched her. This had been so long in the making, promised from the very moment they first locked eyes back in Riles. And demons, she should feel guilty—but she didn't. She couldn't. Not when everything about him felt so very *right*.

Now what? She could practically hear the question hanging between them, the weight of it threatening to turn this moment into something dark and bitter.

She didn't want to let it. She reached up and touched his cheek, trailing the back of her knuckles along his golden skin.

"The darkness in my magic," she said. "It's why I chose... it's why I accepted him. If I can't save Etra, he can."

She half expected him to let go, to expel her from his embrace for mentioning Hawk even though she knew they were both thinking of her promise to the king. Instead, his arms tightened around her. "Cleansing by fire?"

"Something like that." She nestled closer to him. "I'm frightened of it, Callum."

His eyes softened. "Laena." He swallowed, throat bobbing, and again she thought he would banish the king's name from their presence. He gave his head a shake, like he didn't know what more to say. "I'll always keep you safe."

She knew that he would. She kissed him again, softly, and it didn't take long for the gentleness to turn to hunger, for the heat to rise between her thighs again. She rolled on top of him and he reached for her, caressing her hips as she guided herself over his body, sliding him inside her again. And for a while, there was no more need to think of anything but each other.

CHAPTER 17

LAENA

*T*here was no way to tell what time it was when Laena woke. It was still raining, and the fire had burned low, though it hadn't died entirely. Callum was sleeping, his lips parted, dark hair splayed across his forehead as his chest rose and fell in even breaths. It was so rare to see him at rest like this. She wondered if he had slept at all in the Grove or if he'd stayed awake the whole time—or most of it—out of fear for her safety.

They hadn't made things easier on themselves with what they'd done last night. She should not have allowed herself to give in to temptation—she knew that. But even as the thought crossed her mind, she couldn't bring herself to regret it. Temptation was too small a word for what existed between them; this was more than lust, more than a passing fancy. It was a searing hot feeling that cut straight to her heart. Straight *through* it.

Cleansing by fire, he'd said. Perhaps he would be the one to do it, rather than Hawk.

Heart aching, Laena disentangled her body from his and wrapped one of the extra blankets around herself, then added another log to the fire. She blew on the ashes, watching in satisfaction as the new piece ignited, the bark curling and crackling in the heat.

The thin fabric of her dress had dried after a few hours by the fire, so she slipped it on, then walked to the mouth of the cave and looked out at the rain. It still fell in sheets, making it impossible to see very far. Had Emilia and Gretchen escaped the storm? Or had they been caught in it, too? She hoped they were safe, wherever they were.

Something writhed in her core, a sympathetic vibration—like the jitter of bronze after the toll of a bell—and she startled, pressing a hand flat to her stomach. She peered into the rain, expecting to see one of the ghosts. Was it like calling to like? A warning system? Or was it this twisted new version of her power, driving her slowly to madness?

A hint of rotting fire hit her nostrils, and she opened her mouth to call out to Callum. Before she could find her voice, a wave of power slammed into her, thick with the acrid burn of a heart-tithe. Her feet left the ground and she plummeted back, breath escaping through her lips as the power lifted her and threw her away like a discarded doll.

Her head hit the wall and blackness strobed across her vision. Her power coiled away from her, slick, but she grasped hold of it with the firmest grip she could manage, fighting the nausea that tried to push up her throat with every breath. The rain turned to ice, shards shattering against the cave walls like glass.

Katrina dropped to the mouth of the cave like a bird of prey coming in to land, the falling ice pattering uselessly against her back. Laena scrambled to her feet, shock coursing through her at the sight of her sister. Not as much at the fact that she'd found Laena here—some part of her had been anticipating the reunion since the flood on the secret roads, perhaps even since their battle on the plains—but because the sister she had known was much changed.

Katrina's ringlets were gone, her golden hair now flying wild and unkempt around her head like the mane of some predatory creature. A nightmare-black dress hugged tight to her curves, replacing her usual puffy pastel gowns.

"I am in mourning for the regent," she said, though Laena hadn't asked about the dress, hadn't asked about anything. Her voice was a grating echo through the cave, too loud to be natural. She said Declan's title with a sneer that Laena didn't know how to interpret, but Katrina didn't give Laena a chance to respond. She lifted her hands, and a rancid breath of wind rose around her, hurtling Laena back against the cave wall as she stalked forward, eyes flashing.

She stopped in front of Laena, until they practically stood nose to nose—or would have, if Katrina had shared Laena's height.

There was no way that Callum was still asleep. Laena let her gaze dart toward the back of the cave, but their camp was nestled deeply enough in the cave that she couldn't make it out. Callum must have smothered the fire.

Katrina caught the look, and rage flickered across her eyes. "I'm going to pick your lover apart, limb by limb," she said. "I'm going to make you watch me do it. He *stabbed* me."

Laena coughed, trying to draw on her power while ignoring the twist of nausea that rose with it. The way it tried to ebb away from her, as if something had coated it in a sheen of oil. "You seem all right to me."

Katrina sneered. "I am far from all right."

Laena willed Callum to remain concealed, to let her fight this battle. There was no doubt in her mind that Katrina would kill him if given the opportunity.

And she would do it easily. Her power had grown, and it surged around her like a hurricane, the wind holding Laena against the wall with ease. Laena's magic felt like it couldn't decide whether to flee in the face of it or rise to meet it. She couldn't believe Kat was still drawing on the remnants of the heart-tithe power of killing Declan. This felt like something more. Something extra.

Though, there was plenty to love—plenty to sacrifice—back in Etra. Laena's heart seized at the thought, her breaths coming in gasps of panic. The people shouldn't have to suffer for Katrina's ambition.

"You clearly have your own power now." It was an effort to push her voice above the howl of the wind, to steady her breaths enough to speak. All the while, she delved for her magic, begging it to respond. "Do you really need to kill me for more?"

"Maybe not. But now I *want* to." Katrina grabbed Laena's chin, her fingers digging in sharply enough to draw blood. "And more importantly, *they* want me to."

But then, a strange thing happened.

Katrina hesitated. Laena wouldn't have noticed had she not been looking directly into Kat's eyes. But she caught the flicker of doubt, the brief flash of the person her sister had once been.

With her free hand, Katrina reached into a pocket and pulled out a vial, then dragged the lip along Laena's jaw to collect her blood.

"What are you doing?" Laena choked.

Katrina pocketed the vial, her fingers still digging into Laena's chin. And still, she hesitated.

Callum dove out of the darkness, surprising Katrina enough to knock her off her feet. She screeched like some kind of wild creature as she fell. Callum jumped to his feet, his sword in his hands. Ready to fight for her. *With* her.

And every part of Laena wanted to protect him.

Her power exploded out of her like a shield, a blast of cold air that knocked Katrina further toward the mouth of the cave. Laena was still on the ground, but the power pushed her back anyway, scraping her hands and knees against the rocky floor as she tried to scramble for purchase. Icicles rained down on her from behind, and she bared her teeth.

"You were never worthy of the power you were gifted," she said. "You never earned it."

Laena didn't disagree. "Neither did you."

Katrina rose to her feet. The air around her shimmered as an army of ghosts materialized from every side. They wore strange clothes—long, shapeless dresses and belted tunics that reached to the knees, as if they'd risen out of some long-forgotten tale. The knot of magic in Laena's core pulled and tightened, as if trying to break free, though whether to fight the phantoms or to join them, she couldn't say.

Laena looked at Callum, but he was entirely focused on Kat. They looked so real, like she could practically reach out and touch them, but he couldn't see them.

More importantly? *Katrina* couldn't see them. She gave no indication that she was aware of their presence.

It was all in Laena's mind.

Her magic faltered. She gritted her teeth, trying to maintain her hold on the shield, but it was melting, and the falling ice was shifting back to rain. Laena grasped for the power, panicked, but it slunk away from her as though insulted by the attempt.

Katrina took advantage of the slip, pushing a blast of rancid hot power at them. Callum's face contorted in pain, and Laena tried to run to him, but Katrina lifted her hand, pushing Laena back with another wave of hot air. It looped around her wrists and ankles until she hung immobilized, until all she could do was watch as Callum fell to his knees, sword still in hand, breaths coming in ragged jerks.

Laena's wrists burned against Kat's restraints. Whatever her sister was doing to Callum, it was killing him.

The ghosts were just watching, their expressions too murky to make out.

"No!" Once again, Laena tried to call her power, and once

again it slipped away, the ice evaporating on a wave of slick oil. It wouldn't rise to meet Katrina's power, wouldn't break the restraints. It wouldn't do anything.

Blood trickled from the corner of Callum's mouth, and she could see the monumental effort it took to lift his head, to look her in the eye. "I'm sorry, my lady. I tried."

Laena struggled, desperate to reach him. Desperate to stop this.

Light exploded into the cave, banishing the ghosts around Katrina in a flare so bright Laena had to squeeze her eyes shut. And even then the light warmed her eyelids, cutting through the gray rain with bright persistence. When she looked up, Kat was shielding her eyes, hands poised to fight, if only she could figure out where to aim.

With Kat distracted, the invisible bonds holding Laena disappeared, and she fell, her hands smacking against the cave floor. She ignored the smarting pain and crawled toward Callum, who was already staggering to his feet. He offered her a hand, drawing her close against his chest as if he still hoped to protect her from the worst. From whatever came next. As if he wasn't the one who'd been near death just seconds ago.

His chest was solid against her, his cheek pressed tight to the top of her head.

Something in her core eased, the tightness relaxing until she could nearly distinguish the original seed of her power from the darkness that encircled it. She breathed into the sensation as the light pressed on, scouring away the rancid smell of Katrina's magic. And obscuring its source.

Another moment, and she would have it—a clean path to her magic. A way to face this new threat, whatever it was.

"You can go now." Laena couldn't make out the speaker, whose voice echoed along the stone walls. They were, she was certain, the source of the light.

Katrina whirled around, hands raised as if to fight the light.

But it only intensified, scattering through the rain until Laena had to shield her eyes once again.

With a screech of rage, Katrina vanished. Though whether of her own volition or because the light had sucked her away, Laena wasn't sure.

She blinked, her shoulder still pressed against Callum's chest. His breaths were coming quickly, his fist still clenched around the hilt of his sword. "Now what?" he muttered.

She would have laughed, but her breath caught in her throat. She only had the strength to hope that whoever had defeated Kat was an ally rather than a new enemy.

The light faded, and Adrian, Felix, and Saria stepped out of the rain. Maren and Remy followed them into the cave.

"Well," Adrian said. "This is awkward, isn't it?"

CHAPTER 18

CALLUM

*C*allum assumed that Adrian and his entourage were bringing them back to the Grove, though no one said as much.

Maren fussed over Laena the whole way, wrapping her in a blanket and bossing Remy into bringing her hot drinks and mittens and towels until they rolled their eyes and dropped to the back of the group to walk with Saria. But Felix made a point of glaring at Callum so intensely that it was a wonder the man didn't trip over his own feet. Callum didn't know if the warrior was unhappy about the escape, the battle, or the simple fact that Callum was back in their midst.

Perhaps Felix would have preferred for Katrina to end Callum back there. For a good long minute, he'd thought she would. The acid burn of her magic had felt like it was dissolving his skin, boring through his flesh and straight into his bones, until he would no longer be capable of drawing breath. The pain had been excruciating.

Worse still had been the look on Laena's face. The grief, and the utter helplessness. He knew precisely how that felt.

The pain might have abated, for now, but he couldn't

convince himself that they hadn't stepped directly into another battle. Adrian strode ahead, his shoulders relaxed yet confident, as though he never doubted that he would retrieve his lost 'guests.' As if he had no qualms about walking them, unrestrained, back to his home.

Perhaps that wasn't where they were going at all. Perhaps Adrian would take them to some fortress, where he'd throw them into an underground dungeon. But every time Callum looked at Laena, wrapped in Maren's blanket and sipping a flagon of something warm and hopefully restoring, he had to admit it would be a strange way to escort prisoners. Felix's glares notwithstanding.

As soon as they passed the protective barrier back into the Grove, the rain abruptly stopped.

Callum nearly missed a step as the storm-obscured sky was replaced by the burnished rays of a late-afternoon sun. Laena, too, was squinting in the light. It was hard to tell if they'd been gone for a few hours or a few days. They couldn't have passed the actual night in the cave—those hours had been spent escaping and searching for shelter—but it was still strange to step out of the deluge and into aggressive daylight, without a cloud on the horizon.

How far had that barrier pushed them?

But that wasn't the most urgent question. With the rain no longer pounding in his ears, Callum picked up his pace, falling into step beside Adrian.

"Where is Princess Emilia?" he asked. They were just coming into the village, the tree trunks thickening bit by bit until they were large enough to hold alcoves and homes. No fortress. No dungeon. Just the village they'd fled mere hours ago.

"Don't worry," Adrian said. "Princess Emilia and her lady exited the barrier on the Vunmore side and headed back into Aglye. Which we allowed them to do, since *we* do not cross the border."

Unlike you. That was the implication. But there was no doubt they had spies working in Aglye, which definitely undermined the mage's attempt at self-righteousness.

Callum's head was starting to spin with all the pretense and politics. He hated it.

And he was poor at it, too. He must have looked unconvinced because Adrian added, "They're safe. You have my word."

The back of Callum's neck prickled. What good could this man's word possibly be? Who *was* he? Not a simple village leader, though Callum didn't know if Adrian had ever truly expected them to believe that he was.

To his knowledge, not even Hawk had ever seen the Ruthless King. He supposedly lived in the northern mountains. But it was impossible to say where the Grove sat on a true map—it might be located in the north itself, for all Callum knew. And the way these people could cross significant distances at will, the Ruthless King might easily take up positions in more than one part of Silerith.

Again, Callum couldn't help but wonder if Adrian and the Ruthless King were one and the same.

"If Emilia and Gretchen exited on the Vunmore side," Laena said, "where did we come out?"

"You nearly made it to the wilds," Adrian replied. "And wouldn't that have been exciting?"

"Not remotely," Callum muttered. The wilds would have taken them beyond the edge of any claimed territory. They were lucky, in that case, not to have happened upon a wild animal. Perhaps the rain had kept predators at bay.

Adrian led them to the center of the village, where remnants of last night's festival still lay scattered about. Streamers hung from the trees, some fallen to crisscross the paths like colorful serpents. The place still smelled pleasantly of fried pastries and honey.

No one was out and about in the streets, though. Whether

because they were sleeping off last night's excesses or because they'd been urged to hide, Callum couldn't guess.

Adrian led them straight to the largest tree, which was located at the center of the village, and started up the long, winding stairs until at long last, when Callum's aching legs were begging for respite, they reached a house.

A house. In the tree. Complete with a flowered wreath on the red-painted door, shutters adorning the windows, and smoke curling from the chimney.

Yes, the rest of the village had treehouses. But those *felt* like treehouses. They had open sides, leaves for ceilings, and vines curling around the windows. This... this was a *house*.

Laena gave her head a shake, as if she thought she might be dreaming.

Impossible. It should be impossible for such a place to remain aloft.

Mages, Callum thought. *They're mages.* What was a lofted cottage to them? Still, as solid as it felt beneath his feet, it made him queasy to think of how high they'd ascended.

"Welcome to my home," Adrian said, and opened the door.

—*—

A MEAL HAD BEEN LAID out on the table, and Adrian invited them to crowd around it. As though they'd just come from a recreational hike through the woods, with no harrowing battles or treacherous queens trying to suffocate anyone with magic. The dining room was suspiciously normal. Cozy even, with red-cushioned chairs set around a dining table of knotted wood. Someone had painted a border of landscapes along the ceiling, green hills bumping against flowery meadows and white-capped mountains.

Whoever had prepared this meal for them was nowhere in sight, and Callum wondered if Adrian might have conjured it from nowhere. Callum tried to recall what he knew of mage magic—rumors, myths, even storybook tales might harbor a clue—but he wasn't sure anyone knew very much. Thaddeus and his poisonkeeper brothers would know something, he supposed. Though their knowledge clearly didn't include mages who'd never stopped living in the Vales.

The one thing Callum did know, that everyone knew, was that the mages had been able to hold humans in thrall, forcing them to do their bidding. What it had looked like, felt like—and whether he would recognize it if they were wielding it on him now—that, he couldn't say.

Though he had to admit that right now, they didn't look like they were working any magic at all. They all simply looked... tired. And hungry.

Callum expected Adrian to seat himself at the head of the table, but instead he left that seat open and positioned himself across from Laena. Felix stuck to Adrian's side like he was anticipating an assassination attempt, and though Saria allowed more distance, Callum could feel the way her muscles remained tense and ready. In case one of them should decide to attack.

Callum squeezed in beside Laena, with Remy on his other side and Maren at the far end.

To his surprise, the mages began to fill their plates. No speeches, no price, no conditions, just... food?

He exchanged a glance with Laena, who gave him a small smile and bumped her shoulder against his before following their lead.

The woman had just made a frantic escape through the woods and endured a battle with her sister. They had not spent a significant amount of time actually sleeping during their time in the cave. Not that he regretted it.

Despite all that, he thought no one had ever looked more beautiful.

He might not regret what they'd done in the cave, but did

she? He'd barely had time to think about it himself, what with all the murder attempts and trekking through rainstorms. She still meant to marry Hawk, still thought his magic could scour away whatever was sickened about hers. Or at least she was still telling herself that. The thought made him want to push his plate away untouched.

Because the cave... that had been more than a mere dalliance. He couldn't believe she didn't feel it, too.

Every time her sleeve brushed against his, every time her green eyes met his—which was often—he had to swallow back the desire to throw her over his shoulder and take her somewhere they could be alone.

When a good portion of the food had been consumed, Adrian propped his forearms on the table. His sleeves were rolled to the elbows, and despite the lightness of his tone, there were dark circles under his eyes. He must have spent a good portion of the last day searching for them. "This is the part, my friends, where we lay our cards upon the table," he said.

"And see who's won the game?" Callum asked.

"And see who still gets to play." Adrian's gaze flicked to Laena, sharp and assessing. "King Hawk's lady love has been hiding secret magic."

Callum fought the urge to launch himself across the table and wrap his hands around Adrian's throat. He wanted to pretend it was out of a desire to protect her, but the words 'Hawk's lady love' applied to Laena made his stomach ignite with rage.

Laena merely met the mage's gaze with a cool one of her own. "Forgive me if I say I don't think you're one to talk."

Adrian snatched a piece of bread from the table and leaned back, tipping his chair onto two legs. All casual again. All friendliness. He bit through the crust with his molars and paused for a few seconds to chew.

"An evasion," he said around the mouthful of bread. "But a

fair one, I suppose. We hardly know one another. But now we've saved each other's lives, yes? I'd say that warrants a bit of trust."

Laena hesitated. Callum didn't want to tell Adrian a damned thing, but he'd take her lead in this either way. It was her power, her magic. Even if these mages clearly knew about it, there was reason to keep the details close.

The silence stretched.

"All right, I'll go first." Adrian opened his arms to gesture to his friends, a heel of bread still balanced between his finger and thumb as he rocked the chair. "We *are* mages. The discovery of which, I suppose, was what prompted you to flee. A discovery you made, by the way, by eavesdropping on our private conversation."

"A private conversation you held out in the open," Callum said.

Laena set a hand on his arm, her fingers pressing gently into his wrist. He clamped his mouth shut.

Adrian ignored his comment. "We are descended from a rather sizable group of mages who never left the Vales when the rest of our people—" He spat the last word like a curse, as if he didn't want to claim association with the other mages. "They were banished back to the Miragelands."

Callum could do nothing but listen in stunned silence. Listen and watch the others—the mages—as Adrian spun the tale. Remy had a small smile on their face, but they were nodding along, as was Maren. Felix was frowning, but with concern now—as if he didn't like the way Adrian was so openly sharing their secrets. With that, Callum could relate. As for Saria, she was still focused on her food, looking for all the world like she was listening to a tale she'd heard a hundred times before.

If they'd been going along with a lie, he'd have expected their expressions to be more guarded.

Unless this was all a complicated ruse, and they the practiced actors ready to enact it.

"Our ancestors," Adrian went on, "helped your ancestors to lock the bad enthrall-happy mages back in their broken world. It might surprise you to learn that we have lines of shared ancestry. Humans marrying mages. All very romantic.

"And yet, those ancestors knew they'd never be accepted by people who'd been enslaved for generations—fair enough, by the way—so our ancestors retreated to Silerith. Where they kept to themselves. As do we."

"Except for the spies," Callum said.

Adrian dropped the front legs of his chair to the floor. "Captain, would you leave us defenseless? We'd seal ourselves away from the rest of the Vales if it would do any good. But like it or not, we're a part of this world. There are times when it would put us at risk to ignore that fact."

Laena's hand remained lightly on his wrist as she watched the exchange, her lips pressed together, her skin pale. Whether with shock or exhaustion, he couldn't say. Perhaps a dose of each.

"What about the heart-tithes?" she asked. "Do you facilitate those?"

Adrian's face remained unreadable. "We do not."

He offered no more than that, then said, "Now, your turn."

Callum wanted to hesitate, to protect their secrets until they could confirm the truth of Adrian's story. But what did Adrian have to gain from lying? If anything, telling Callum the famed magic hunter that they were all mages was an act of trust in itself.

Even now, Callum couldn't say whether it was misplaced trust. Hawk would no doubt expect to be contacted via the fire and debriefed on everything Callum had learned. But what would the king then ask him to do about it?

Surely Hawk would be reasonable. He had to be.

While Callum was still mulling this over, Laena met Adrian's gaze straight on. "I have Vales magic," she said plainly. "So does King Hawk."

Callum grimaced. He might have kept Hawk's magic a secret, for now. But Adrian nodded, clearly unsurprised. He asked for no explanation.

And that gave Callum hope. If Adrian knew that Vales magic existed, maybe he could help Laena. He might know how it worked.

"Mine is the magic of winter and ice," Laena continued. "But there's something wrong. It's... it's making me sick, in a way it never did before. It feels like it's broken, somehow. We came here hoping to see the Ruthle—the Mountain King. We had hoped he might help."

Adrian stood abruptly. "The king can't help you." He grinned, though his words cut through Callum's heart like a blade. "But I know someone who can. Petra. We'll head to her tomorrow."

Laena let out a breath. "Truly?"

Adrian leaned over the table and snagged another piece of bread. "Truly."

"Excellent. Another trek," Felix muttered.

"It's good for you," Remy said. "Builds character."

Saria clapped Felix on the shoulder. "And you could definitely use more of that."

Callum didn't know who the hell Petra was. He wasn't sure he cared. But if Adrian thought she could help Laena, he would break the world to get to her.

Laena was watching Adrian, wary. "You'll help me? Just like that?"

Adrian nodded, still grinning. "Just like that. See you in the morning, bright and early. Better get some rest. We've got mountains to climb."

CHAPTER 19

KATRINA

atrina no longer needed a heart-tithe to carry herself into the heart of Inasvale, to appear at the very lip of the magepool and drop the two poisonkeepers who watched it directly now—the monks had grown more cautious after her attack—into a deep sleep.

She called to the aether, and it answered.

The mages had increased her power, replaced the ever-draining well of heart-tithed magic with a source that did not wane. The wound in her shoulder ached, but she could already feel the flesh rebuilding itself, her skin stretching to close and heal the wound quickly. She wielded shadows and thunder. She wielded the very air.

What would the mages do for her when she opened the door to the Vales for them? What gifts would they provide?

Laena's power, in contrast, had been ragged during the battle at the caves. Tinged with a darkness Katrina hadn't seen before. What could have infiltrated her beautiful, perfect ice like that?

It was almost as though as Katrina grew stronger, her sister grew weaker.

That captain was certainly a weakness. Katrina didn't want

to think of the agony on her sister's face as Katrina had nearly ended him. Katrina had never seen that look in Laena's eyes before, the pure despair. Always the perfect queen, she'd kept her feelings contained in neat little boxes from a young age. Even when she'd approached the council to abdicate, her brow had been smooth, her eyes clear and calm.

For Callum Farrow, she'd become... something else.

And although he'd been the one to stab her in the battle on the plains, Katrina had hesitated. Not once, but twice. First when she'd collected Laena's blood—she might well have stabbed her sister in the gut, yet she'd been unable to make the final cut—and again when she had Laena's lover at her mercy.

That was a mistake she didn't intend to repeat. Because Laena had somehow made mage friends of her own, and Katrina almost hadn't survived the encounter.

Now, she strode up to the lip of the pool, her black gown sweeping around her legs in an elegant billow. She liked the way the fabric clung to her body, the way it appeared to reveal everything while keeping a few secrets in its folds.

Katrina tipped her newly acquired vial over the pool, spilling Laena's precious blood into the water.

A circle of ice crackled around the offering, like a lily pad forged out of frost. It floated for a heartbeat, then two, before sinking beneath the surface.

And again she found herself looking into the eyes of the same two mages. King Valdric and his son Koreth.

During that first encounter, their images had been clear enough, yet they somehow seemed much clearer now. She could make out the fine lines around the older man's eyes, and the black slashes of a tattoo on the son's neck. She wondered what she could make out if the image should crystallize even further. A glimpse of the Miragelands, surely. Of the mage king's palace.

The older man narrowed his eyes. "You did not kill her."

"She *could* not," Prince Koreth spat.

She hated him, she decided. Hate was easy; it came naturally these days. And she definitely hated this mage prince. He would kill her where she stood, were she not useful to him. His disdain for her, for her humanity, was clear.

When Valdric shot him a look of annoyance, however, he pressed his lips together.

"It was six against one," Katrina said. "And you neglected to inform me that the Sils are *mages*."

Valdric picked at his nail, as if she bored him greatly. "Did I? Well. Certainly their powers are nothing serious. Weakened by generations in your lands."

Katrina managed to keep herself from wincing, her shoulder smarting painfully. "*I* wouldn't call their powers nothing."

The mage king snapped his fingers, sending ripples across the surface of the pool, and Katrina gasped as a cool sensation flooded her shoulder.

A breath, and the pain was gone. She knew, without having to check, that if she removed the bandage, she would find the skin completely healed.

"You will see," King Valdric said.

She touched her shoulder, unable to hide her awe. This power could be hers. *Would* be hers, she vowed, as long as she stayed the course.

As long as she didn't fucking hesitate.

"Father," Prince Koreth said. "I smell royal blood. Here, in *this* city."

Valdric tilted his head, as if searching. As if Laena's blood, and those ripples of frost, had opened the door to the Mirage-lands just a little bit wider. "You are right."

"It's Hawk's brother," Katrina said dismissively. "A younger prince. He's a poisonkeeper. He lives here in Inasvale."

If her blood was of no consequence, then Thaddeus's should be just as useless.

"No." Valdric's voice was distant, as if he were feeling for the blood, a hound narrowing in on its resonance. "The brother must keep some of the true king's blood in Inasvale. I smell it, too."

Katrina breathed deeply. Mage-given powers or no, all she could smell was pine, and the loamy thickness of ancient earth. An edge of damp stone, perhaps. Was this some kind of trap?

It seemed too easy. Too simple that King Hawk's blood should already be waiting right here in Inasvale, at her finger-tips, with only inept monks to guard it.

She was tired, her thoughts murky. She ought to have slept before offering the blood to them. They might be empowering her, but they were certainly not to be trusted.

Yet she couldn't think why they would bother to trap her when she was already questing for the blood that would let them back into the Vales. Unless they were secretly allied with the poisonkeepers—unlikely—then Valdric was probably telling the truth.

If there was something else he wanted from Prince Poison-keeper Thaddeus, there was no reason for him to hide it. He might as well just say it outright.

If she were being honest with herself, she'd hoped to face King Hawk before venturing into Silerith to meet with the Ruthless King. Something told her he wouldn't be quite so easy to rob as her sister had been.

But if King Hawk's blood was here, then she would retrieve it.

Katrina withdrew her second vial—the second of three—from the deep pockets of her gown. "Where is it?"

A pinpoint of light materialized at her feet, a tiny reflection that danced across her toes before swinging away, drifting down the shallow steps. It should have been impossible. What was it reflecting, and how, with the trees so thick that the sunlight barely leaked through? But by now she knew better than to reject the impossible.

She followed the light back through the tunnel, back up the secret steps that led into the heart of the monastery. She hadn't come this way, which meant she'd have to surprise two more monks from behind. But it was a simple matter to put them to sleep—a wave of her hand, a twist of magic—as she had with their brothers at the pool.

The light paused at the third door in the corridor. Thaddeus's rooms, or so she assumed. She didn't know why they would allow such a young poisonkeeper to stay so close to the magepool. Perhaps it was meant as training. Or perhaps the others were wise enough to want to put some distance between themselves and the pool.

Thaddeus must be studying it. Studying his brother's mysterious Vales magic and the way it interacted with the pool. Another younger sibling whose life was defined by the older's whims. Under other circumstances, she might have pitied him.

Katrina waved a hand, and the door opened silently. She stepped inside.

The room smelled of books. She should know; she'd been spending hours upon hours in Etra's libraries digging through the oldest, moldiest volumes they possessed. Like her library in Riles, Thaddeus's rooms smelled of leather and old paper, with the oily tang of fresh ink added in. Books lay stacked in corners, open on tables, and, in some cases, open *and* stacked upon any available surface.

Prince Thaddeus was asleep on a cot in the corner, his spectacles askew, his hand splayed across the page of an open book.

She stepped around him, instead heading for a shelf in the corner. Its contents were as jumbled as the rest of the room—quills and herbs and scribbled notes—with the exception of the top row, which held five small vials of blood.

No need to ask whose it was. As if in confirmation, the pinpoint of light landed on one.

Katrina plucked one from the shelf.

Thaddeus gasped, and she whirled around to see him sitting up in bed, his hair wild, his glasses practically falling down his nose. Did he have some spell in place that would wake him should she touch Hawk's blood? Or was it just bad luck?

It hardly mattered.

"You," he breathed.

But he was nothing. And her power was everything. "Me," she agreed. She waved her hand. "Now sleep."

She didn't wait to see him fall. With King Hawk's blood in her grip, she called to her power to whisk her away to the mountains.

CHAPTER 20

CALLUM

The lofted cottage featured, among other things, a balcony, one that Callum found—and took imme-diate advantage of—as the others were saying their goodnights. Never in his life had he needed a breath of fresh air, a moment to himself, more than he needed it right this minute.

The balcony swept out from the main part of the house in a swelling half circle. The floor was decorated with potted plants, though they looked as if they were surviving by luck rather than care; several of them had as many dead leaves as living ones, and their drooping stalks said they were overdue for a watering.

One of the pots bore the unmistakable loops of a child's artwork, the paintings clumsy and colorful. A gift, lovingly created.

Bonfires blazed in the streets below, and Callum watched the shadows of people who clustered around them, laughter and music drifting up through the branches. He wondered if they'd been told they could use their magic. If they'd redo their festival, now that their secret was out.

He should be making his way down to one of those fires now, to make use of the magical crystal shit Hawk had given him. He should be informing the king that Adrian and the others were mages.

It was critical information, and worth the risk to report.

But he couldn't convince himself to go down there. He wanted to believe that Hawk would appreciate this development for what it was—a chance to help Laena. To save her, as Callum was beginning to believe it was.

He wanted to believe that Hawk wouldn't want to hurt these people without reason.

But Hawk's reactions were not always predictable.

———*———

JUST OVER A YEAR AGO, Callum had escorted Thaddeus to Inasvale to join the poisonkeepers. The journey had taken a week, there and back. They hadn't hurried.

But Callum had returned to find Vunmore in chaos.

Rumors ran through the city like cheap ale as he'd made his way up from the gates, dark smoke pouring from the direction of the palace, the scent of a heart-tithe stronger than he'd ever smelled it. And growing thicker with every step.

The only thing he could think, as he'd pushed through the city, was *Don't let it be true.*

Edmun had been the one to meet him at the gates with the news: The palace had been attacked in Callum's absence. King Magnus was dead.

Callum had left orders with the King's Guard, most of which had been unnecessary as Edmun and the other officers had already seen to it. And then, with his own heart shattered, he'd gone to Hawk. His friend. His brother, in feeling if not in blood.

Hawk hadn't been in his own rooms. Instead, Callum found him in his father's study, standing before a broken window with shards of red and green glass still scattered on the floor around his feet. And the scent of a heart-tithe, so thick that it coated the back of Callum's throat, threatening to choke him.

"Your Highness," Callum said. "I must ask you to step away from the window."

Hawk turned, eyes hard. "Your Majesty."

Callum paused, gripping the back of one of Magnus's tall chairs. A draft exhaled through the window, a brief respite from the rancidness of the leftover magic.

"I'm the king now," Hawk said.

Callum swallowed, grief surging into his throat. He didn't know how to comfort his friend, except to tell him how he was taking action. "I've called in some of the reserves to strengthen the guard," he said. "The perimeters—"

"I'm the *king* now," Hawk repeated.

Callum's shoulders slumped. "Too soon," he said. "But your father prepared you well. Your rule will make him proud… Your Majesty."

Hawk stepped away from the window then, finally, glass crunching under his boots. His eyes were rimmed in red, his lips trembling with the effort of keeping them pressed tightly together. "One kneels in the presence of one's king."

Callum blinked. "King Magnus hasn't required me to kneel in private for years—"

"He was wrong," Hawk interrupted.

Anger replaced Callum's sympathy, a wave of red-hot indignation. And hurt. He'd be a fool to pretend he wasn't hurt by Hawk's callousness. "You can go to the Miragelands if you think I'll kneel to you in private. I'm sorry about the king, Hawk. Don't let his death make you someone he would scorn. He was dear to me, too."

Hawk laughed, an ugly sound. "Was he?"

It shouldn't even have been a question. "You know that he was."

"You weren't *here*." Hawk shouted the last word, and Callum had only been able to stare at the prince—the king—as he tried to understand what Hawk was implying.

"You weren't here," Hawk repeated, shaking now. "You're meant to be our great protector, and you weren't here. And now he's dead."

"I was escorting Thaddeus—"

"No one wants *Thaddeus*," Hawk shouted, flinging his arm out to the side. "No one cares about *Thaddeus*. Edmun could have escorted him to Inasvale. Anyone could have escorted him to Inasvale. But it had to be you."

"What—"

"Get out, Farrow." Hawk gestured to the door. "Go now, before I make you."

Callum would have liked to see him try.

Even now, with a year to cool the anger, he still felt a flare of it on Thaddeus's behalf, when he thought of the way Hawk had dismissed him like that, like he was nothing. It was worse now, in fact, knowing that Thaddeus had gone to Inasvale to *help* Hawk. Had exchanged the course of his own life for a studious, celibate one, all for the sake of helping to figure out Hawk's magic.

Hawk had known that then, even if Callum hadn't. And he'd felt so entitled to Thaddeus's sacrifice that he'd had the audacity to say that no one wanted him. To imply that Thaddeus meant nothing to him at all.

—✳—

A CLICK SOUNDED BEHIND HIM, and he startled as the balcony door opened and Laena joined him by the rail. She'd changed into a simple gown, not unlike the one she'd been wearing that day at the hot springs.

"Just me," she said.

He scoffed. "You're never 'just,' my lady."

162

What would Hawk do if he learned of their gut-tearing betrayal? The king wasn't cruel, but he was unpredictable. He might well throw them both in chains.

Laena would ground the man into dust if he attempted that. Or snowflakes, he supposed.

"I thought you would stay the night at Maren's," Callum said.

"I asked to sleep here." She placed her hand on top of his. Her hand was warm, her skin so soft against his. He wanted to pull her closer. He wanted to kiss her until she cried his name, the way she'd done in the cave. Just the thought of it made his cock stiffen with desire.

"What will the king do?" she asked. "When he learns of the mages?"

Callum shook his head. "I don't know."

"What will *you* do?"

Callum met her green eyes. She didn't know of Hawk's request, didn't know that the king had tasked him with an assassination. But that was if they found the Ruthless King heart-tithing. He'd said nothing about mages.

The difference, Callum knew, was negligible. Hawk would likely see none at all.

And Laena knew enough about Callum's past, his reputation, to guess at his conflict. She might not know of Hawk's specific command, but she knew what he expected of Callum.

"You think I'll arrest an entire village?" he asked.

She shook her head slowly. "I think you're more likely to save it."

She had it wrong. The only person he wanted to save was her.

Laena lifted herself onto her toes and brushed her lips against his. She was so damned sweet, like nectar straight from a fucking flower. He ran his tongue along the seam of her lips, dipping further into her mouth until she made the most delicious sound he'd ever heard.

Grabbing her by the hips, he turned her around, backing her toward the wall until he had her trapped against it. Her breasts pressed against his chest, every curve tight against his body.

"Callum," she breathed.

"If you say we can't," he said, "I'll—"

She cut off the rest of the sentence with a kiss, her tongue brushing insistently against his and wiping every thought from his mind. The woman was a damned hurricane, destroying every ounce of control he'd ever convinced himself he had. He'd had lovers before, plenty of them, but not one of them had ever claimed such a hold on his soul.

Hawk could throw him in jail. It would be worth it.

Callum ran his hand down Laena's thigh, scrunching her dress up and baring her legs to the night air. Drawing slow, torturous circles along her inner thigh, he kept going until he reached the heat of her center.

He pushed a finger inside her, and she arched into his touch, rocking her hips and fucking herself on his hand. She moaned, her dark curls splayed out against the wall, and if he hadn't already been rock hard, the sight of her would have rectified that immediately. As it was, his cock was straining against his trousers, as ready for her as she very obviously was for him.

He pressed a thumb to her clit, and she cried out so suddenly that he didn't manage to muffle the noise with a kiss.

He didn't care. She belonged to him. The entire village might as well know it.

Laena reached for his belt and he pushed a second finger inside her, breaking her concentration and laughing as she cursed, throwing her head back against the wall. "I want you inside me. Now."

"So bossy."

She hooked a heel around his thighs, drawing him closer, and he ground himself against her, wanting her, wanting to draw out this moment. "Not making it easier, Princess," he said.

She reached for his belt again, and this time he let her unbuckle it, moving his hand from her heat only to help her free his cock. She angled her hips forward, guiding him inside her.

The pleasure of sinking into her threatened to finish him right there, as if he were some untried teenager. He gritted his teeth, fighting for control as his hand cupped her face, kissing her, nipping at her lips, at her neck, wanting to taste all of her, feel all of her. This was not a momentary fascination, a temporary comfort. This was everything. And he would never be able to make himself leave her.

Yet he would not spend his life as her secret lover, either. He wanted all of her, not only in this moment, with her pussy wrapped around him and her moans in his ear. He wanted her heart. He wanted *her*. Not in secret but out in the open, hands joined, for everyone to see.

And he did not want to fucking share.

Together their breathing grew more ragged, until Callum could not tell her breaths from his own, until they were moving together in an unbreakable rhythm, until the climax was right there, a breath away.

"Come with me, Laena," he whispered.

And she did, throwing her head back and crying out as she shattered. His own pleasure rose to meet hers as he pushed deeper, the night constricting around him until there was only this one moment, this one place. And her. Always, always her.

He kissed her softly as the pleasure ebbed, her legs wrapped around him, the flickers of the bonfires below flowing back into his awareness. The strain of a fiddle. An off-key drinking song. The smell of fresh snow.

"You cannot marry the king." His breath was hard against her mouth. They were still joined, her body wrapped tight around his.

She was panting, too, her forehead damp with sweat. "So bossy."

"Laena."

"My power—"

He gripped her hair. "This Petra person will fix your magic. And then you will break your engagement."

She kissed him, long and slow. His cock was still pulsing inside of her, and damn if he wasn't going to get hard enough to fuck her all over again.

"Is that a command, Captain?" she asked, her voice husky.

"It's a fucking promise."

She sucked in a breath. "Who's going to tell Hawk?"

The fact that she didn't shut down the idea, that she didn't protest or pull away... maybe there was hope, after all. He leaned his forehead against hers. "I vote for Adrian."

She laughed against his mouth. And then she shifted her hips back, breaking their connection. She adjusted her dress, letting it fall back over her legs as she slipped past him and headed for the balcony door. Casual as anything, though it gave him a twinge of satisfaction to see the slight wobble in her step. "Good night, Captain Farrow," she said.

And as he watched her go, trying to collect himself, he allowed his thoughts to articulate what he'd already known: He would not tell Hawk about the mages, nor would he do anything to endanger her recovery. If this Petra person could help her, then Callum would keep the secret from Hawk for as long as necessary.

And if the mages helped them get there? Then he would owe his allegiance to them.

CHAPTER 21

LAENA

This time, the first step beyond the Grove's magical barrier brought them from the middle of a forest to the middle of a mountain. Midway up a steep slope, even, with shrubs replacing the trees and tapering off at the start of a rocky ledge.

In theory, Laena supposed she ought to have been prepared for the change. But the sudden shift in terrain was just as shocking as it had been the first time. They were high enough to make out the ragged peaks of the mountain range. It was a clear day, the sun glinting off frequent patches of snow, though a few bands of mist clung to the furthest peaks as if to maintain an air of mystery.

Laena had known the range existed, of course, had studied her geography. But it was one thing to trace a few zigzagging lines on a map of a country across the sea. It was another experience entirely to stare out at the rugged beauty of them.

And it was cold, too. No wonder Maren had insisted on woolen leggings and heavy cloaks. Laena was glad for hers now.

Callum hadn't left her side since they'd set out at dawn, and he stood beside her now, shading his eyes with one hand to look out at the peaks. A breath of wind curled through his hair, teasing the dark strands around his ears in a way that made her heart flip over in her chest.

She'd just stepped across a magical ward that transported her from a low-lying forest to the middle of a mountain, yet it was Callum who held her attention. She ought to be used to his presence by now, but every time she looked at him, her stomach fluttered with the memory of his hands on her, the way he felt inside her.

It's a fucking promise, he'd said. And she believed him.

He caught her eye, crooking a half-smile at her. As if he knew exactly what she was thinking.

Laena flushed. "Is this your Mountain King's domain?" she asked, making a point of turning back to Adrian. His whole entourage had accompanied them on the journey—Felix and Saria, of course, but Maren and Remy as well. A situation that had reportedly thrilled Maren's daughter, who'd been granted the chance to stay with her friend for the next few days.

They were waiting where the ledge met the scrubby foliage —grasses and bushes here rather than trees—as if they expected their visitors to take a long time gawking at the view.

"It is all his domain," Adrian answered. "But if you're asking where he lives, that particular spot is quite a bit down the range."

He waved a hand toward the mountain range, which was hardly illustrative since the line of mountains must stretch hundreds of miles into the distance. All the way to the sea, if she recalled her maps correctly.

Though that was probably the point.

"How can he rule his people from such a great distance?" Laena asked. She'd known of the Ruthless King's reclusive reputation, of course. It was one of the only things everyone did know about him

Now that she was here in Silerith, she realized she'd never

expected the king would turn out to be reclusive among his own people.

"With great care and attention, I'm sure," Adrian said, his tone a touch too light. "Certainly I would not be privy to such information."

Callum huffed out a breath. "So much for honesty."

Adrian shrugged, wearing his smile like a mask. Though Laena didn't miss the tightness at the corner of his mouth, or the way the others were studying their feet with great interest. All except Felix, whose attention was locked on the thin path behind them. Ever watchful.

After a long pause, Adrian said, "Not all secrets are mine to tell. Come. We should be on our way before night falls."

Laena followed him toward the path, which was nothing more than a deer trail through the tall grasses. A deer trail with a steady incline.

Callum stayed close behind her, so close that she could practically feel the heat of him.

"We saw you smoke into the Grove," Callum said. "Can't you just smoke us there now?"

Adrian laughed. "You think the Grove is warded? Petra's sentries make that look like a child's lesson. No offense, shield-speakers."

"None taken," Remy replied. "But watch your back the next time you need your room protected."

Laena glanced at Callum, who gave his head a small shake. He didn't know the term, either. And judging by the look of warning in his eyes, he didn't want her to inquire any further. But they would not learn anything if they refrained from asking questions.

"What's a shield-speaker?" she asked.

Remy stepped up to walk beside Laena, clearly unconcerned with the way the grasses brushed at their legs. "Mages have categories of power. Some broader than others. Shield-speakers work barriers and wards. But the Grove's shields… they're something special. One of Adrian's powers is to manipulate space, so those wards are a special combination of his abilities and mine."

"And his other powers?" Callum asked pointedly.

Laena frowned at him. Though she supposed, as questions went, it was a valid one.

"My other power is forbidden." Adrian quickened his steps, increasing the distance between them. Taking the lead, though clearly also hoping to put an end to that line of questioning. Which, of course, only increased Laena's curiosity. What type of mage power would be forbidden?

Felix remained by Adrian's side as he pushed farther along the path, while Saria dropped to the rear of the group, presumably to watch their backs.

Callum glanced at Adrian, then at Laena, as if he couldn't decide whether to trust Adrian to lead them safely or Maren and Remy to watch over Laena.

"Go," she said. "I'm fine here. But be nice."

He pressed a hand to his chest. "Me? I'm always nice."

"Be nice to *Adrian*."

He sighed. "I'll try." He touched her arm lightly, brushing his fingertips along her sleeve before heading up to join Adrian and Felix.

"I hope they don't kill each other," Laena said.

"It's all right," Maren said softly. "Adrian's touchy about the poison-speech. It's… not something our branch of mages is very proud of."

A chill trembled up Laena's spine, the question frozen on her lips. She knew the stories; everyone in the Vales knew the stories. During the time of the mages, humans had been held in thrall, their actions not their own. In the presence of a powerful mage, they might not take a single action for themselves in their entire lives.

And the mages had used magical relics to exert lighter control—but still control—over the humans who didn't live in their direct vicinity. Which was why it had taken centuries to oust them from the Vales.

"He doesn't use it," Remy said.

Because it was forbidden. Not only had these mages lived in peace in Silerith for all this time, but they also reviled the magic that their people had used long ago.

No. Not their people. They were their own people now.

"Adrian's lucky he's also a traveler," Maren added. "Otherwise he'd have no usable powers."

She nodded at Felix, the implication clear. Felix had poison-speech, and no other magic. Which, according to their laws, left him powerless. At least as far as the magic went.

Though she couldn't help but wonder what would happen if some of them decided to make use of those forbidden powers again.

Laena swallowed. "What powers does the Mountain King have?"

Remy and Maren exchanged a look. They were willing to explain a lot of things, even Adrian's forbidden magic, but the mention of their king gave them pause.

"It's complicated," Maren said.

They walked in silence for a while, Laena paying attention to her feet to keep from tripping as the path narrowed and eventually tapered off around the stubby foliage. Her breath misted in the air, but the cold felt good in her lungs. She drew it in deeper, held it longer, until the magic in her core unfurled just a little as if to soak it in.

For a heartbeat, it felt as it always had.

And then a flicker of movement caught her eye among the thin trees, and she looked up to see a misty figure watching from between the trunks. He stared at her, jaw tight, eyes dark.

Like she was the interloper. Maren and Remy didn't even glance his way.

In her gut, her magic somersaulted. Restless.

"And what about Callum?"

Laena jumped when Maren spoke, startled. She was still looking back over her shoulder, trying to decide whether she should approach the ghost. Or let her mind wander with its wild hallucinations.

She blinked, bringing her attention back to the path. There was no sense in following what had to be merely a figment of her imagination. A symptom of her tainted magic.

"What about him?" she asked.

"I'm just trying to understand the dynamic," Maren said.

"Nosily," Remy put in.

Maren smacked them on the shoulder, and they laughed. The easy camaraderie of the siblings made her heart twist, just a little. She didn't want to think of Kat, but it was difficult not to.

Laena thought of deflecting, of pretending she had no idea what they were talking about. But she didn't think she and Callum had been all that discreet, and she had no confidence in her own ability to hide what she wanted.

"It's all right," she said. "I'm trying to understand it myself."

"Truly?" Maren said. "It seems to me that you already know."

Did she? Callum had certainly made his wishes clear. First after she'd agreed to marry Hawk, and then repeatedly during this journey. And last night, for the first time, she'd actually felt... a spark of hope. If this Petra person could help fix her powers, perhaps Laena would be able to trust herself enough not to rely on Hawk's balance. On the way he could cancel her powers out, if need be.

There was still the matter of the renewed confidence their engagement had sparked in Aglye. She could not simply retract a decision that would affect so many people. With this trek into Silerith, though, maybe they could come to a stronger pact between the two countries, one that would assure the people that Silerith meant no harm.

Laena was now sure that they did not. Absent though their king might be.

But there was also the matter of Katrina. Callum believed Laena should retake Etra's crown and assume what he saw as her rightful place.

If she could find a road to it, she would.

"I committed to marrying King Hawk," she said.

"But you love the captain." Maren said it like it was a fact. Not only a fact but an argument against marrying Hawk, a clear reason. Laena wasn't sure Hawk would see it that way, if she were to confess it to him.

For Laena, love had been a complicated subject ever since she'd first run away with Ben, and even more since he'd left her alone in her sacrifice to fend for herself.

Maybe love was always complicated, especially among kings and queens.

"Maybe it doesn't matter who I love," Laena said finally.

Maren patted her arm and said cheerfully, "It always matters, strange human. Come, let's catch up before your lover panics at us being out of sight."

CHAPTER 22

KATRINA

*K*atrina's power dropped her in the mountains.

When, on her various travels, she'd glimpsed the peaks from afar, they had not looked like much. A distant range of jagged teeth. That was all.

Now, a pair of those teeth rose before her like giants, as though they'd journeyed a long way just so they could peer at her in disdain. The magic had dropped her in the middle of a crumbling stone staircase, halfway up a third mountain, which gave her an intense feeling of having been caught mid-fall by yet another giant. Who was now weighing the benefit of tipping her over the ledge.

A wall of mist shrouded the landscape beyond this collection of cone-like mountains. It would be easy to feel that the magic had brought her to another realm entirely—out of the Vales, or even out of time—to face the judgment of the mountains. Katrina had never been an accomplished scholar, but even she remembered the maps well enough to know that Silerith's mountain range stretched for hundreds of miles.

Her breath came too quickly here, as if no inhalation were large enough to truly fill her lungs. Spots flirted with the edges

175

of her vision, and she flattened one hand against the cliff to steady herself. The magic must have left her very high up indeed, for the air to fail her like this. She tested it, breathing slowly and wondering if it was a trap set by the Ruthless King to collect trespassing flies in his web.

But *someone* lived here. *Someone* breathed the air, and survived it. Because at the meeting point of the three mountains —their shared base—there stood a castle.

There was no city surrounding it, no bustling marketplace, no military encampment. Just a lonely fortress with black walls, its towers crowded into a mistrustful cluster. No light shone from within. Nothing moved, save for a single purple banner that flew from the highest tower like a forgotten streamer left hanging after a ball. The wind ripped at the fabric, as though frustrated that the castle had given it nothing to sink its claws into, aside from this thin band of cloth.

Katrina started down the stairs, gripping her skirt in her fist to keep it from tangling with her legs. Powerful as she was, she didn't think she would survive a fall over the ledge. It now seemed a foolish choice not to have changed her clothes or taken time to rest before coming to face the Ruthless King. When had she last slept? Or eaten?

It didn't matter. The magic sang in her veins, filling her with strength, pushing her onward. The sooner she retrieved the last drop of blood, the sooner King Valdric would be strong enough to take the Vales.

Etra would be hers, and no one would dare oppose her.

She repeated this promise until her legs had turned to jelly, until the muscles of her hand were spasming from clutching her skirt so tightly. She repeated it until, at last, she took the final step off the mountain—all three giants now looming over her— and crossed the spindly bridge that spanned the width of a deep gorge to reach the castle gates.

She needed no magic to open them; they stood unlocked.

The entrance to the interior walls gaped, the door not merely open but entirely gone, as if it had been ripped from its hinges.

Drawing her dagger, Katrina stepped inside.

There were no boundaries. No wards. And no rugs, no curtains, no tapestries. No decorations of any kind, just an empty corridor with cold stone walls, cold stone floors. And, if the itch in her nose was any indication, a fair bit of dust. The wind whipped through the open doorway and through the hall, making the place feel even colder.

Without any pinprick of light to guide her now, she was left with only her own intuition, like a hook drawing her forward from her ribcage to guide her through the hall. The wind tugged at her hair and skirts, but she ignored it. There was only the scuff of her slippers on the floor, the itch in her nose, the unlit sconces.

She turned a corner, that tug drawing her to the right. On the floor was a triangle of orange light cast by a fire in one of the interior rooms flickering into the hall from behind a half-closed door.

Katrina slipped sideways into the room, careful not to nudge the door.

The Ruthless King—Evren Avery, the mage king had called him—was asleep in front of the fire. Or he was unmoving, anyway; she couldn't make out his eyes. Only his profile as he sat—sprawled, really—in a scuffed wooden chair, his elbow on the arm, his cheek propped on his hand. The only movement was the orange light of the fire, glinting against his raven-dark hair and the soft rise and fall of his chest.

Katrina approached him from behind to keep her shadow from interrupting the light and heat of the fire, careful not to make a sound. With shaking hands, she withdrew her vial, holding it in one hand, the dagger ready in the other.

With a shaky breath, Katrina knelt beside the king, keeping her skirt pooled behind her in case she needed to run quickly—

silly, foolish girl that she'd been, to wear it here. His eyes *were* closed, dark lashes fanned out against the light brown of his skin. His sleeve was rolled to the elbow, the expanse of flesh beckoning her dagger. A quick slash, a swipe with the vial, and it would be done.

Slowly, she reached for him, aiming the dagger's point at his flesh.

The king moved. He grabbed her wrist so suddenly that she dropped both the dagger and the vial.

"What are you doing, little villain?" He held her firmly, and he'd certainly moved fast enough. But when he spoke, the words came out in a drawling baritone. Like he was requesting a tea service rather than catching a knife-wielding intruder.

Katrina struggled, trying to pull her wrist out of his grip. No use; his fingers might as well have been vises. He wasn't hurting her, but he wasn't going to let her go, either.

"Still intent on dooming the Vales, are you?" he mused. "But then I suppose we knew that."

Katrina's heart thundered in her chest, and she reached for her magic, the power the mages had so generously gifted her. It was there—she could feel it, surging, ready for her—but it was like it was trapped behind a wall of glass. She threw herself at it, but the king chuckled, and the magic skittered away. Just out of her reach.

How was that even possible?

"Are you going to kill me?" she choked.

He sat back, holding her wrist as some might hold a glass of wine. Unbothered. "That sounds like a lot of effort. And if there's one thing I'm opposed to, it's effort."

Katrina paused her struggling, replaying his words in her head to make sure she'd heard him correctly. "*You* are Silerith's Ruthless King?"

He gave a dark chuckle. "In name only, little villain."

"Stop calling me that."

He released her so suddenly that she fell back. "Run along, now," he said. "I'm tired."

Katrina got to her feet, brushing off her skirts and bending to retrieve the dagger and the vial. Trust her to fail at this, just like she failed at everything.

They won't think you're silly with me at your side.

No. No, she was *not* returning to that magepool with only Hawk's blood. It would not fully break the barrier; they would only send her back, their confidence in her shaken. Even with the element of surprise, she hadn't managed to win. She doubted she'd survive a second confrontation.

She drew herself up as tall as she could—which, unfortunately, was not very tall—and tipped her chin in the air to hide the way it was shaking. The way her whole body was shaking, and not only from the bone-deep chill of this place. "I'm not leaving without your blood."

There was a beat of silence. Then he twisted to face her, head tilted in what might have been a glimmer of interest. "Oh? And what are you prepared to pay for it?"

Kat stared at him. There was no way to keep the shock from her face. She couldn't tell if he was being serious. "What?"

He rested his chin on his fist, thumb pressing at the corner of his mouth. "You've been crashing through the Vales, taking what you want, always without asking. Did it never occur to you that someone might be willing to make a trade?"

"What kind of a trade?" She let the words snap out of her, hiding her hesitation behind a mask of annoyance as he looked up at her. Would he ever get up out of that damned chair?

He looked her over, eyes scanning the now filthy hem of her dress and up her torso, until he finally met her gaze. "I propose a trade. A drop of my blood for a drop of yours."

Suddenly, the vial she was holding became two. She nearly dropped them again in shock.

"What will you do with my blood?" she asked.

He raised an eyebrow. "What will *you* do with *mine?*"

He knew perfectly well what she planned to do with his blood. And he was going to let her do it. A drop of her blood, and he would allow her take his without a fight. Did he not care that she planned to bring the mages back to the Vales?

Perhaps he *wanted* her to.

She licked her lip, trying to think of how he might be tricking her. But in the end, it didn't matter. She needed his blood. This was how she would get it.

"All right," she said. "It's a deal."

He rose from the chair, finally, unfolding his body with graceful ease, and came to stand before her. Most people were tall in comparison to Katrina, but he seemed almost insultingly tall. Especially as he looked down at her, one corner of his mouth quirked in amusement, as if she were just so adorable for coming here and thinking she could best him. He had on black pants and a jacket, the shirt beneath unbuttoned and revealing more than a few inches of his chest.

He held out his arm. "Go on then."

"Can't you do the cut yourself?"

He shrugged. "I suppose."

But he didn't move. She snatched his hand, still expecting a trick, though something told her he would not flinch away.

This entire fucking castle was cold as the depths of winter, yet somehow Evren Avery's hand was warm in hers. It wasn't an entirely unpleasant feeling. In fact, she could almost imagine those fingers trailing farther up her arm, tangling in her hair.

He chuckled, as if he knew the reason for her delay, and she scrunched her nose in annoyance. And then she drew the dagger across an inch of his forearm, opening a short wound. She dragged the vial against it, collecting a few drops.

"And here I expected your blood to be black," she said sweetly.

"Oh? And what color is yours, little villain?"

She wiped the dagger on her skirts, then held it out to him. "Let's find out."

His cut was barely a pinprick, drawing the tiniest bead of blood from her skin. He met her gaze as he pressed the vial against it, allowing that single drop to collect in the vial.

She'd claimed a trickle of his blood, but he'd stuck with the letter of the agreement. One drop.

She half expected him to call her out on it, to demand some of those drops back. Or at least to make a snide comment. Instead, he merely held her gaze—and her hand—as he lowered the vial away from her arm.

"Why do you want it?" Her question came out as a whisper.

His lips parted, gaze sharpening, and for a second she thought he might actually answer.

But then he waved a hand, and the room began to fade. "Good luck building your empire, little villain," he said.

The last thing she felt before the magic whisked her away was the press of his fingers against hers.

CHAPTER 23

CALLUM

*T*hey spent most of the day ascending the mountain, Callum darting frequent glances back at Laena to make sure she was well. She did look pale, and she occasionally startled for no reason that he could see, her gaze lingering on some spot in the forest. Seeing the ghosts again, almost definitely. He wished he could understand what it meant, if they were hallucinations—a symptom of her illness—or something else entirely.

The air continued to cool as they climbed, the frosted tips of the foliage bowing under the weight of freshly fallen snow. The air was thick with it, their footsteps crunching on a thin layer— which would have been thicker, if Saria had not moved ahead of the group to clear a path with her magic. Not melting it, as Callum supposed Hawk would have done, but pushing it aside so that it piled up high on either side of the path.

When Laena asked about it, Maren said, "Air-speech."

As if that explained the matter.

It was late afternoon when Adrian announced they'd reached the peak. "All downhill from here," he said cheerfully, though Callum noted darkly that there could be two interpretations to that phrase.

He had to admit it did feel like a relief to head downhill after a day of climbing.

"This Petra," Callum said. "What is she like?"

Adrian shrugged. His favorite way to not answer a question. "You'll see shortly," he said. "Look."

The stubby foliage ended abruptly, dumping them onto a steep downward slope of granite. Which, based on the landscape so far, should have been covered in ice. Or at least patches of snow.

Instead, it was dry. The ledge they were standing on looked down on a valley. The trees there were in full bloom as if it were the middle of spring. Mottled shades of green mixed with pink and white blossoms, the grass lush where it was visible between the thick branches.

Not a flake of snow in sight. And it was *warm*. Not thirty seconds ago, Callum had been shivering in his cloak, lips and cheeks sore with the cold. Now, it felt warm enough to discard the extra layers altogether.

The roof of a small cottage was just barely visible through the blooms, a spiral of smoke curling out of the chimney.

"It must be confusing to live in Silerith," Callum said.

Adrian clapped him on the shoulder. "You get used to it."

The descent was tricky even without ice or snow. At first the slope was nothing more than a sheet of sheer rock that they scrambled down feet-first, searching carefully for footholds. A slide to the bottom might not kill them, but it certainly wouldn't be pleasant.

Callum fell to the back of the group once again so he could walk next to Laena, wishing he could hold her hand but knowing it would only make it more difficult for both of them to navigate the steep descent.

Still, he positioned himself so he might cushion her fall, in case she should slip. Which, of course, she did not. She was probably the most sure-footed of any of them.

When the slope eventually ended, it did so in a jumble of boulders that was only marginally easier to navigate. Even Adrian held his tongue as they worked their way down, his focus thankfully absorbed by the challenge of keeping his feet.

By the time they reached the valley floor, dusk was giving way to darkness, the stars beginning to shine through the aether. There were trees here, too, though they were arranged in the neat rows of a well-kept orchard.

Laena inhaled a deep breath. "Smells like spring."

It did. It smelled like damp earth, awakening flowers. A valley of spring, wedged in the middle of a range of wintery mountains.

Despite Adrian's claim, Callum didn't think he would ever get used to the strangeness of it.

Adrian strode confidently between the neat rows of trees, heading in the direction of the house. But Callum didn't miss the silent exchanges that passed between the rest of the group, lifted eyebrows and little head shakes that made him reach for his sword.

Which Laena immediately noticed. "Take it easy, Captain. I'm sure it's perfectly fine."

"Because everything else on this journey has been so safe."

She slipped her hand into his, forcing him to choose between her and the weapon, and added, "He brought his family."

His family. Was that who these people were? He supposed his knowledge of the matter was limited at best. Now that she said it, though, he realized it must be true. The way this little group of people cared for one another, the way they joked and shared a meal… they *were* a family. Albeit an odd one.

Adrian continued up to the little cottage, the existence of which was as strange—even stranger, perhaps—than the spring weather. Who had hauled the materials here to build it? And when? It looked old, the boards weathered and pocked in placed, but the paint on the shutters was fresh, the garden bursting with red and gold tulips.

Adrian knocked on the door, then stepped back and tucked his hands in his pockets in what Callum interpreted as a last-minute attempt at appearing innocent.

The door stayed shut fast. Adrian knocked again.

The window clattered open, and an old woman stuck her head out. Callum couldn't help thinking that her face resembled the inside of an aged potato. Her white skin was so wrinkled that her dark eyes looked like blemishes. She wore a red kerchief in her hair, but it was sliding off, revealing a strip of gray hair.

"What do you want?" she barked.

Adrian bent sideways, tilting his head to meet her gaze. As though a conversation through the window was exactly what he'd expected all along. "Hello, Petra," he said. "I thought we'd discussed installing a staircase over those fallen boulders."

The wrinkles in her nose deepened. "That would defeat the purpose, numbskull. Since we *also* discussed people not bothering me in my valley."

"We're both promise breakers, then. But I can make amends. I've brought you a gift."

Callum's fingers tightened around Laena's. She wasn't a *gift*. She was here to ask for help. Which this woman seemed very unlikely to provide.

Petra stuck her head farther out of the window, dismissing each member of the group until she got to Laena. She paused for a long moment, eyes narrowed.

"No, thank you," she said, slamming the window shut.

Adrian whirled around, hands still in his pockets. "That went well. Come. Let's make camp."

"That went *well*?" Callum asked. "She rejected us."

Adrian skipped down the steps, his gait relaxed. "She didn't expel us from the valley. So yes, I'd say it went well. Are you all hungry? I'm ravenous."

Callum watched him saunter through the trees. "I don't like him."

"We know," Laena said and patted his shoulder. "Let's go. I'm hungry, too."

———✳——

ADRIAN LED them to a clearing around the orchard and off to one side of the house, where Maren and the others immediately started foraging for firewood. They seemed to know this process well; Remy withdrew some carrots and potatoes from their bag to roast on the fire, while Felix disappeared and returned some time later with a pair of pheasants.

If they were worried about Petra's reception, they didn't show it.

Callum had no intention of dropping his guard in this place. So when the others filtered away to unroll their blankets, Laena following Maren and Remy toward a spot they claimed was the best in the orchard, Callum remained by the fire.

How long would it take before Petra agreed to help Laena— or expelled them from this valley altogether? And if she did expel them, what would their next step be? Adrian might not be concerned but Callum was. Laena was running out of time.

An errant spark spiraled out of the fire and landed on his knee. He let out a hiss, brushing at it until the small bite of pain dissipated. He frowned at the fire. What kind of wood had they piled on it to make it do that?

A tornado of sparks swirled out of the fire, billowing up to create a column of flame. Callum leapt to his feet, ready to call out, but the words died on his tongue when Hawk's form appeared before him, wreathed in fire. He rose to his full height

—taller even, as if he were standing on top of the fire. As if he were made of the flames.

Callum's stomach twisted with unease. There was no doubt in his mind, none whatsoever, about what the king was about to say.

"You're not so easy to get ahold of," Hawk said. It was his voice, and it wasn't. As if it needed the roaring crackle of the flames to amplify it. It sounded almost underwater—under *fire*—though his tone was clear enough.

"Been busy," Callum replied. He meant to add that he'd been busy trying to save Laena's life, but the words caught in his throat. He didn't want to speak of her to Hawk, unless it was to tell him the truth.

"I would have thought," Hawk said, "that you'd have contacted me after learning that your companions are *mages*."

Callum let out a breath. "Emilia and Gretchen," he said. "They made it to Vunmore? They're safe?"

Hawk stared at him. It was a stare he'd developed over time, one that seemed to cow the people around him into remembering he was king and doing exactly what he wanted them to do. But it had never worked on Callum. And it wouldn't work now, even though the flash of the firelight behind Hawk's eyes lent a new, darker element to the expression.

"We had an agreement," Hawk said. "I thought I was clear about my expectations for your trip."

Hawk had a unique ability to goad Callum, to condescend exactly when Callum most needed him to be a friend rather than a king. He was angry; that much was clear.

Callum drew in a deep breath, forcing himself to remain calm. Hawk was afraid, and that was reasonable. Callum and Laena had fled as soon as they'd learned about Adrian and the others. It was the last information Emilia and Gretchen had had, too: fear.

Callum needed to remain calm. Clearheaded. It would be the only way to convince the king to listen.

"You were clear about what I should do if I found Silerith's king using heart-tithes," Callum said. "This is—"

"Worse," Hawk interrupted. "It's *much* worse, Farrow."

It wasn't worse at all. It was merely different.

"Is Emilia all right?" Callum asked. He was stalling, his mind racing as he tried to think of a way—any way—to convince Hawk of the mages' sympathies. But he truly did want to know the answer, confirmation that Emilia was well.

"She's fine." The words were clipped. "She and her... companion explained everything."

Hawk disapproved. Well, that was hardly surprising. These days, Hawk disapproved of everyone and everything.

"Seemed like they're more than companions," Callum said. Though, it had taken him some time to realize it himself.

Hawk clenched a fist at his side. "That is between us."

"Seems like it should be between them."

Hawk held up a hand. "I will deal with Emilia. Your mission is unchanged."

He could not accept that. "These are good people," Callum said. "I think you should give them a chance. Meet with them. Allow them to explain."

It was difficult to make out Hawk's expression as the flames danced behind his face, obscuring his reaction. As if they were a part of him. "We also thought Katrina was an ally. And we were wrong."

"They're *helping* us," Callum protested. "They dropped everything to help... your betrothed."

The word tasted like ash on his tongue. He wished he could spit it out.

"You would not have questioned my father's commands," Hawk said, rage simmering behind his too-calm tone. "And you will not question mine."

Callum *should* have questioned King Magnus's commands. He should have questioned, avoided, and perhaps even betrayed those commands, from the very first day. He should have taken responsibility for the heart-tithers he'd locked up. He should never have crossed the border, or taken people out of Silerith.

He'd spent years defending his actions, convinced that heart-tithes were abhorrent by nature. Even though he'd spent those same years bending the law, knowing full well that Magnus would have denied any knowledge of his actions if Silerith had attempted to call them to account. It was luck that they had not.

Or it was fear that Aglye would discover their secret and destroy them.

Hawk wasn't finished. "I'm sending a stone through the flame. You can use it once, to travel a great distance. Grip the stone in your palm to activate it, and set your mind on your destination. I assume that if you don't yet know where the king lives, you have the means to discover it easily enough."

Bitterness coated Callum's throat. The magic sounded closer to Adrian's traveling powers than to the magic Hawk had been granted by the Vales. "How can flame powers create something like that?"

Hawk waved a hand, dismissing the question. "You can ask Thaddeus when you return. Which you will not do until the Ruthless King is dead."

"They call him the Mountain King," Callum said softly.

Hawk shifted forward, as if to step out of the flames and said, "He is a mage king, and his existence puts us all at risk."

No one's mere existence could put them at risk. "We don't actually know that he's a mage."

"I expect your loyalty, Farrow. Don't fail me as you did my father."

The flames died suddenly, Hawk's figure swirling out of sight, extinguishing the fire as if someone had dropped a blanket on it. In the middle of the smoking logs sat a coal-black stone set with flecks of orange sparks.

Callum could only stare at it. What would happen should he turn his back? If he refused to retrieve the stone at all? Would Hawk know?

He turned, intending to blink the fire away by looking up at the stars.

Instead, he saw Laena standing between the trees, eyes wide, lips parted. He could guess how much she'd heard from the look of shock on her face.

CHAPTER 24

CALLUM

*C*allum didn't know how to read the absolute stillness in Laena's posture, the coolness of her expression. She ought to be raging at him. She ought to be screaming at him, or at least stalking away into the forest. She ought to be turning her back and running away, and this time he would have earned it. He'd kept secrets from her, betrayed her, even as he'd made love to her. Even as he told himself he might win her over, convince her to choose him over the king.

But she didn't rage, and she didn't run. Instead, she just stood there watching him as the fire flared back up out of the cold ashes in a final burst of magic. As if her appearance had reawakened it.

He knew the feeling.

Callum turned away from her, bending to retrieve a long stick from the ground. He plunged it into the ashes, stirring a swarm of sparks into the air. A natural swarm this time rather than Hawk's magical one. He preferred it.

He knew it was an excuse to avoid her gaze, but he couldn't help himself. The fire felt safer than the accusation he would surely find in her eyes.

He knew he should wait for her to speak first, to start yelling at him. But maybe she wouldn't. Maybe she was waiting for him to tell her the damn truth. He certainly owed her that much.

"Hawk gave me another mission," he said.

"So I gathered."

If he was looking at her, he might have been able to interpret coolness in her tone. It was hard enough to hear the warmth of her affection fading from her voice. He was too much of a coward to witness it as well. The longer he delayed, the longer he could keep pretending she had no reason to hate him. So he kept his gaze averted, his eyes on the fire. Even as he felt her approach him, her presence sending prickles along his arms. Even as she reached down to tug the stick from his hand and toss it to the ground.

It wasn't until she pressed a hand to his cheek, until she drew his face toward hers, that he dared to look her in the eye.

Her expression wasn't one of anger, or even judgment. Her brow was smooth, her green eyes wide as she waited for him to continue.

"If we found evidence that Silerith's king had been heart-tithing," he said roughly, "I was tasked with the mission of killing him."

She studied him, scanned his face as if searching for some hidden hurt, some invisible injury. As if Hawk's flames had burned him. As if someone had been holding him in thrall like the mages of old, bending his mind until he obeyed without question, and she was trying to determine whether he was still held there. His actions not his own.

"That," she said, "might be the worst thing I've ever heard."

She was right. Of all his sins—and there were too many to count—this might be the worst one.

He couldn't stop himself from leaning into her hand. Her skin was cool to the touch, soft. So fucking soft. She was good enough to feel compassion for him instead of judgment, but surely she would never want to touch him again. In the pit of his stomach, it felt like a goodbye.

Now that he was looking at her, he never wanted to stop. "I let him endanger you. I'm sorry."

She didn't pull away. "I mean," she said softly, "Hawk—your *friend*—commanded you to assassinate a powerful king, one who is no doubt well guarded, should you discover him to be working dangerous magic. Which would make him even more of a threat."

Callum blinked at her. "And?"

She huffed out a breath of annoyance. "And? *And* he commanded you to do it alone. *And* a soldier is not an assassin. Are you an assassin, Callum?"

There had been times when he'd felt like one. He was meant to be a guardian, a protector of Aglye, but so much of his time had been spent hurting instead of helping. When he took in the indignation in her eyes, the offense—on *his* behalf—suddenly he could see it from her perspective. It made no sense at all for Hawk to assign him such a mission in the first place.

And he wondered, for the first time, whether Hawk—his friend, or so he'd once been—realized it would be a suicide mission to go alone into the depths of Silerith to kill their king.

"You ought to be objecting on moral grounds," Callum said. "Because it would be wrong. And also probably a political crime."

Her lips twisted. "Definitely a political crime."

He'd followed such commands from King Magnus for so long that he hadn't even considered that he ought to start questioning them.

He'd certainly never considered questioning them on his own behalf.

"You didn't answer my question," she said softly. "Are you an assassin, Captain Farrow?"

A lump rose in his throat, hard and painful. He covered her

hand with his, their fingers intertwining as she caressed his cheek. "No, my lady. I am not an assassin."

"And do you see how much he asks of you?" Her words came out as a whisper.

Callum swallowed. It was the least of his concerns. Or at least it ought to be. "I let his father die."

It didn't quite feel true, not anymore. But it was a difficult belief to shake. It had lived in the depths of his heart for a long time now, and Hawk's feelings only served as confirmation. He was not forgiven. He was not absolved.

Laena's eyes flashed, her anger quick to surface. "You brought his brother safely to Inasvale. To study *his* magic, and to help him control it. And because of that, you happened to be absent when assassins came for his father. You cannot keep punishing yourself for something you could not have predicted."

He wanted to say something flippant to deflect the pain of this conversation. He wasn't sure he'd ever be able to escape the guilt of King Magnus's death.

Even so, it was impossible to deny the truth: that when Hawk had needed saving, Thaddeus had uprooted his entire life to see it done. And Hawk had let Thaddeus do it, and had then blamed Callum for wanting to get the younger prince to his destination safely.

Thaddeus had given Hawk a chance to learn his magic. Now, he was withholding that same chance from Laena.

Yet still, Callum couldn't quite bring himself to condemn Hawk's actions. Callum might not agree with his approach, but there was no denying that Hawk was acting in Aglye's best interests.

"Hawk is afraid the Ruthless King is no better than Katrina," he said.

"Katrina's actions made her the enemy," Laena replied. "Not her magic. And you know it, too. If you didn't, you'd have contacted the king as soon as we learned about Adrian and the others."

Callum let his hand drop away from his face, pulling hers along with it and drawing her closer. Some part of him still expected her to flinch, to slap him for trying. Instead, she pressed her body against his, allowing him to settle her hand against his hip. "I will admit to having been somewhat distracted right at that moment. Something about a cave…"

She narrowed her eyes. "Don't try to flirt your way out of this conversation, Captain."

He wouldn't dare. He dipped his head closer to her, breathing in the earthy scent of her hair. "You should be angry with me, too. You should be *livid*. Hawk asked me to choose his dirty work over you."

"Do you intend to do it?" Her words warmed the shell of his ear, her breath making him shiver.

He didn't even have to hesitate. "I can't. I won't."

Much though he might have told himself otherwise, he'd never truly wrestled with it at all. His heart was hers, and so was his loyalty.

She tipped her head back, rising on her tiptoes. "Then I'm angry. But not at you."

This woman. She ought to be scorning him. He ought to be begging for her forgiveness on his knees. And here she was, looking at him like she wanted him on his knees for very different reasons.

He closed the last bit of distance between them and kissed her. She tasted of apples from the orchard, fresh and sweet. He moved to wrap an arm around her waist, to pull her closer.

She jerked away from him as something caught her attention over his shoulder. The color had drained from her face, her eyes wide and fearful. But when he turned, there was nothing there.

Another ghost. But why couldn't he see them?

Callum began to voice the question—a question she couldn't

answer, either—just as a wave of burning acid slammed into his nostrils, strong enough to knock him back a step. He grabbed for Laena, but her hands were stretched before her, brow knit in concentration as frost collected on her fingertips. He didn't miss the way she wavered on her feet.

"It's slipping away," she said. Her magic. Her magic was slipping away? "I can't hold it."

Callum drew his sword, his focus split between watching Laena and tracking the approaching wave of heart-tithe magic.

"You should go," he said. "Go to Petra. Convince her to talk to you."

"I won't leave you alone."

She said it without hesitation, through teeth that might have been gritted with concentration—or with indignation at the suggestion.

As if on cue, Felix and Saria came barreling out of the trees, swords drawn.

"How long have you two been watching?" Callum growled.

Saria wiggled her eyebrows. "Since the kiss, Captain. Nice moves."

At least they hadn't heard the part about him being here to assassinate their king. Though Callum had the impression that the revelation would not have surprised Felix in the least.

The smell of the heart-tithe thickened, and as Callum started toward it, Felix grabbed hold of his arm, hauling him back several steps. "The wards will hold," he said. "The heart-tithers cannot penetrate them. Our job is to make sure it stays that way."

How could they even see where the wards ended? Callum swallowed, nodding his thanks to the guard for keeping him within them. If for no other reason than that he needed Laena to go to Petra, and he needed her to do it now.

He turned to her, gesturing toward Felix and Saria. "I'm not alone anymore," he said.

She stared him down, like she didn't buy it. She was the one who trusted Adrian and his mages, at least enough to follow them all the way out here. She ought to trust them to watch his back.

"You heard him, my lady," he pushed. "The wards will hold. Go talk to Petra."

While you still can. Felix might be confident about the wards, but none of them could predict what might come crashing their way. He thought of Katrina's increased power in the cave, her determination. If she were to come here, who could say whether the wards would continue to hold?

Laena hesitated for another moment, then dropped her hands and ran to him, throwing her arms around his neck. "Don't you dare die," she said.

He smiled into her hair. "I wouldn't dream of it."

CHAPTER 25

LAENA

*L*aena tore through the trees. The sourness of the heart-tithe mixing with the fresh scent of the blossoms turned her stomach. She ducked beneath a low-hanging branch, flinching as an errant twig slashed a strip of pain across her cheek.

The wards would hold. Felix said it. Callum believed it. She needed to believe it, too.

The wards might hold, but Laena wasn't sure if she would. That one reach for her magic had set her head to spinning, even though she'd only managed to conjure a measly crust of frost.

She was nearly out of time. She could feel it.

She didn't stop until she'd burst out of the orchard and stumbled shoulder-first into Petra's door. She raised a first, intending to pound on it, expecting to have to beg for entrance.

Before she could, the door swung open with a loud creak, and the old woman peered up at her through the thickest pair of spectacles Laena had ever seen. "You going to punch me, girl?"

Laena lowered her fist.

Petra gave a *humph* that made her shoulders slump impossibly low. "Thought not. Come in, then. You like tea?"

"We're under attack," Laena said, breathless. "There's someone heart-tithing out beyond the orchard."

Petra *humph*ed again, then whirled around and thumped inside. "The wards will hold. Do you like black tea?" She looked over her shoulder, squinting. "Actually, no. You obviously can't handle a stimulant. Mint it is. Close the door. I hate it when the heart-tithe stink leaks between the cracks."

Laena inhaled deeply. She *had* seen the wards hold. She didn't quite share Petra's confidence that they'd shield this place indefinitely, but at least they had time. For now, they were safe.

Clearly, her best approach with Petra would be to act as if there was no rush whatsoever. Even as her magic churned in her gut like poison. Even as it showed her things that clearly weren't there at all.

It was breaking her mind. Slowly, yes, but there was a clear progression. She could hardly defend herself without causing more damage—if she could summon her power at all—and she kept hallucinating ghosts.

But Petra had let her in. It was a start.

The farmhouse exterior was clean, if aging, and relatively neat. Clean walls and windows, weeded gardens, and intact cobblestone walkways.

The inside was another matter entirely.

Hanging plants dripped from the ceiling and the walls, basking in rays of unnatural light that beamed down on their leaves. Laena recognized plenty of the flora from her time tending her own cottage: fat-leaved aloe and white blooming byflower, and several species of ivy with vines that snaked out of their pots, curling around neighboring fixtures and sneaking along the edges of shelves.

There were also plants she'd never seen before, with cone-shaped thistles and hanging peppers, and ferns with ink-black fronds.

But the plants, fascinating though they might be, were not

nearly as interesting as the vessels that contained them. Every single pot, vase, and basket was decorated with a face. Pudgy faces, wooden faces, red and orange and fuchsia faces, freckled faces, surprised faces, faces with thick eyebrows and lipstick and scars and masks. As Laena studied them, she could have sworn some of their eyes followed her gaze, and that a curtain of vines dropped just in time to shield a blushing face with seedlings sprouting from its ears.

The pots were far from the only objects in the room. The shelves upon which they sat were piled high with stones, with candle shavings, with bits of string. Every inch of the place was absolutely stuffed with… well, a less polite person might have called it junk.

Petra hobbled over to the table and set a steaming mug in front of her. "Stop gawking at my things. It's rude."

Laena risked a smile. "But you have such interesting things."

Petra narrowed her eyes, leaning on the edge of the table as she lowered herself into the wooden chair across from Laena. "You sure you're a princess?"

"Not at all." Laena sipped her tea, savoring the warmth as it slipped down her throat. Petra knew who she was. Interesting.

Also, she didn't seem so opposed to a conversation now that Adrian was out of sight.

She wished she could ease her way into this conversation, but there wasn't time to sip tea and slowly get to know each other. Not with heart-tithers stalking the border. Not with Kat out there brandishing wild powers. And not, she had to admit, with Hawk scheming to murder foreign monarchs.

She was going to need to address that situation. Just the thought of his betrayal, of what he'd asked Callum to do, made her want to scream with fury.

But Hawk would have to wait. She could only deal with one untenable situation at a time.

She had to get her magic under control first.

"Orchard's been out of control this season," Petra remarked, as if Laena had come to chat over nothings. "Too much rain."

"Don't you control the weather here?"

The old woman scoffed. "No one controls the weather. I *guide* it."

"Couldn't you have *guided* the rain elsewhere?"

Petra wriggled in her seat, indignant. "Didn't invite you for tea so you could criticize me, did I?"

"And I didn't come here to chat about the weather," Laena returned.

Petra was watching her, gaze sharp and hawkish, nose wrinkled. As if Laena's presence disgusted her and she didn't mind showing it. She seemed to know what Laena was about to say and wanted to avoid it at all costs. "Definitely not a princess," she muttered. "All right, girl, spit it out. What *are* you here for?"

The direct approach, then. "I need to ask you some questions."

Petra slurped her tea, not bothering to wipe the dribbles that escaped down the side of her mug. "Can't stop your tongue from wagging, can I?"

Laena suspected that Petra might well be able to stop her from saying another word, if she wanted to. But she decided to take the declaration as encouragement. "Are you a mage?"

Petra hissed, spilling hot tea all over her hands. She slammed down the mug so hard that Laena was surprised when the clay didn't crack right in half. "We don't use that term!"

Honestly, what kinds of questions had the woman expected? Advice on proper care of philodendrons?

"Adrian used it," Laena said.

"Adrian's a damned fool, and an arrogant one to boot. That's a bad combination, girl." Petra wiped the backs of her hands on her apron. "We *don't* use that term."

Laena set her mug on the table and leaned forward, meeting

Petra's dark eyes, and said, "I'm not a mage. My power was gifted to me by the Vales."

"That much is obvious," Petra grumbled.

Did the old woman know how much she'd given away with just that one sentence?

"But there's something wrong with it."

Petra sniffed. "Again. Obvious. I smelled the stink on you the moment you smoked up the mountain."

Laena suppressed the urge to hold her arm to her nose to see if she could smell it, too. Instead, she kept her attention locked on the old woman. She wasn't going to let Petra derail this conversation. "When I told Adrian about it, he brought us straight to you. Which makes me think you might be able to help."

"It's like I said. The boy's a damned fool."

Frustration lanced through Laena's chest. She forced herself to breathe. "You won't even *ask* what's wrong with my magic?"

Petra stared at the table, hands shaking. And all at once Laena understood that Petra knew exactly what was wrong. And that, whatever it was, it frightened her so much she didn't even want to acknowledge it.

"Please," Laena said. "It's going to kill me."

The old woman just shook her head, sending wisps of gray hair floating around like bits of her vines. "You're wasting your time here, girl. I can't help you."

CHAPTER 26

KATRINA

*T*he Ruthless King tossed Katrina back to the magepool. She could practically hear his smug voice in her head as she landed—tumbled, more precisely—boasting that while her magic had abandoned her halfway up a mountain, his was precise.

No matter. Soon her power would match his. Exceed it, even.

Katrina didn't bother to rise. She pulled herself up to sit, then reached into her pocket for the vial of Hawk's blood. She wedged the cork between her teeth, ripped it out, and emptied the entire bottle into the pool.

A single ring of orange flame pulsed out from the drop, then sank deep into the pool.

Power crackled through the clearing like thunder, raising the hair on her arms. There was no wind, no breeze, and yet the trees shook, their trunks bending in response to some unseen force.

Within her veins, the magic surged. But the mage king and his son did not appear.

Katrina rose, the power pulling her to her feet. Heat flushed her cheeks, crackling down through her neck, her spine, her fingertips, charging her body with unreleased magic. She was close now. So very close.

Her hands were steady as she withdrew the final vial from her belt.

Before she could uncork it, something crashed into her, throwing her to the ground. The precious vial skittered out of her hand and landed with a *clink* on the lip of the magepool.

Katrina shoved her attacker away with a surge of newfound power, and they grunted, falling back as she dove for the vial. Nothing else mattered.

A hand closed around her ankle, dragging her back over the stone as she struggled. She sent a wild stroke of power back over her shoulder, but the fingers stayed wrapped around her ankle like a vise.

She kicked, and her foot met flesh. Her attacker's grip loosened, just enough for her to whip around and face them, her dress tearing on the edge of the stone.

King Hawk's brother lay stretched before her, blood streaming from his nose. Thaddeus. The poisonkeeper. He lay sprawled before her, dusty brown hair tousled in every direction. His glasses were cracked. "I won't let you do this," he gasped.

Katrina ripped her ankle out of his grasp. Threads of lightning danced between her fingertips as she stood. "I don't see how you can stop me."

With a shout of rage, Thaddeus attacked.

CHAPTER 27

CALLUM

*C*allum watched until Laena was out of sight, every heartbeat urging him to follow her into the orchard. To protect her.

This, he reminded himself, was the best place to protect her. Out here, guarding the boundary of Petra's springtime valley. And giving her time to talk the old woman into helping them.

Felix hitched his chin toward the woods. "We'll go to the edge of the wards," he said. "See if we can find where the heart-tithers are clustering."

"How do I know you won't send me right through the wards?" Callum asked.

"Could've done that before," Felix grunted.

He wasn't wrong. He'd stopped Callum from barreling into danger.

Callum could only trust him.

As it turned out, the edge of the wards was more than obvi-ous. A dozen heart-tithers had gathered at the border, held back by the invisible shield of Petra's making. On some of them, blood flowed from cuts on their hands, their necks, their arms. Couples and siblings. Friends.

Some, of course, bore no visible wounds. Some had left their sacrifices behind.

It made his stomach turn. He wanted to scream at them, to demand why they would abandon humanity and sacrifice the pain of those they loved? Was it just for a taste of the mages' power, a cupful of their tainted magic? Nothing could ever be worth that.

Remy was already there when they arrived, their eyebrows raised, head cocked to the side as if listening for a far-distant sound. "No cracks in the shields yet," they said as Callum and the others arrived. "Adrian's circling the perimeter to see if they're testing any other spots."

Clearly, the wards protected against heart-tithes, but not against the smell of them. The air was thick with the stench of rotten burning, so strong he thought of pulling his collar up over his nose. How the heart-tithers themselves could stand the constant presence of it, he didn't know.

Lightning crackled across the cloudless sky like a warning.

"What in the name of the gods' cocks," Saria said, "is *that?*"

Callum followed her gaze back to the edge of the barrier.

At first, he thought she was referring to the columns of white smoke, or steam, that seemed to be appearing every-where. Like the sudden spray of geysers jutting out of the ground.

But as he watched, the smoke solidified into figures of men and women. Spirits. Their clothing was odd, and they all shared an expression of wonderstruck awe as they took in their surroundings.

Ghosts. Laena had been seeing them all along. So why were they only visible to everyone *now?*

He didn't know. He couldn't even guess. But it couldn't be good. It couldn't be good at all.

"I have to tell Laena," he said.

He ran.

CHAPTER 28

LAENA

*L*aena had been trained to negotiate with kings and queens, to face down powerful councils and generals alike. Yet somehow, she knew the old woman sitting before her was not going to yield.

She was so frightened that she would let Laena wither before she lifted a finger to help.

The door crashed open, and Petra leapt out of her chair faster than Laena would have thought possible. She reached for the old woman's elbow, to steady her as Callum stormed into the room, but Petra slapped her hand away.

"The ghosts." Callum was breathing hard, his eyes wild, his sword drawn. But not, Laena noted with relief, stained with blood. "Tell her about the ghosts."

Laena stared at him, not understanding. The ghosts were the least of her concerns at the moment. If she could get Petra to listen, she'd explain everything—including the ghosts.

"What ghosts?" Petra asked, her tone sharp.

"Laena has been seeing ghosts since Vunmore." Callum had to duck his head to fit inside Petra's house, the low ceiling brushing at his curls. He didn't even seem to notice, he was so focused on the old woman. "They interrupted the wedding with King Hawk. They were wandering the Grove. And now they're here, in the woods beyond your wards."

Laena shook her head, chest tight with embarrassment. "It's something the magic is doing to my mind. Twisting reality. They're just hallucinations, it isn't—"

"They're not," Callum interrupted. "Because I just saw one. And so did Felix and Saria."

Laena stared at him, shocked. He hadn't been able to see the one she'd glimpsed out by the fire. What had changed?

In a way, it didn't matter. Part of her wanted to weep with relief that she wasn't imagining these phantoms, but she feared what it meant that the others could see them now, too.

Petra whirled to face Laena, clamping her wrist between two fingers. "When did you start seeing them? *Where?*"

Laena flinched, trying to draw her hand away, but the old woman's grip was too strong. "At my wed…" She didn't want to recall it. Didn't want to remember the oath she'd sworn to marry a man who'd now very clearly betrayed her. "In Vunmore," she corrected. "And as Callum said. In the Grove, and on the way here as we scaled the mountain."

Petra released her arm, wheeling toward Callum. She had to tip her head all the way back to squint up at him. "And now *you* see them?"

Callum returned her gaze. "As I said."

"This is bad. This is *very* bad." Petra turned away, moving with such ferocity that Laena was surprised when she collapsed into a chair beside the fireplace, that motion abruptly stilled. She met Laena's eyes from across the room. "You were right. The wards will fail."

"When?" Callum asked, as Laena said, "How do you know?"

Petra waved them over, dropping her head to rest against the back of the chair. "Soon, in all likelihood. And I know it because of the ghosts. Which you should have mentioned from the beginning. Stubborn girl."

As if Petra had been begging to help, and Laena had been withholding the information. "You wouldn't let me tell you what was wrong," she said dryly.

Callum came to stand behind her chair, his presence immediately reassuring. "What are they? The ghosts?"

Petra dragged her fingertips across her forehead, hand trembling. "The poisonkeepers at Inasvale, they believe they guard the portal back from the Miragelands. And they do, in a way. Just not in the way they think."

Laena waited, breath stalled in her lungs.

"What they don't realize," Petra went on, "is that the pool is only a sort of beacon. Fiddle around with it, and it impacts any bits of the magepool that might be out there in the world."

The old woman hefted herself out of the chair, so suddenly that Laena feared she might tip all the way over in the other direction. Instead, Petra lurched toward one of the shelves, rummaging around, and finally withdrew what looked like a perfume bottle, molded into the shape of a feather.

"The Miragelands mages keep a few drops of the magepool with them at all times. They did it when they ruled the Vales, and they do it now. They *especially* do it now. They're always hoping someone will break the barrier and allow them passage back into the Vales."

Laena's head was spinning. How could Petra know what the banished Miragelands mages kept with them? That seemed like a less urgent question.

"But why do you have it?" she asked.

Petra waved a hand. "Wrong question, girl."

"What does it mean?" Callum asked softly.

Petra nodded. That was the right question, apparently. She replied, "It means that mages can enter the Vales from anywhere. Once they do, they're drawn to wells of power. Inasvale is one, but it's not the only one." She paused. "They'll be drawn here, too."

"And Vunmore," Callum said softly.

"The seat of their power," Petra agreed. "Yes."

Laena clutched the bottle. "Why is the portal opening *now*?"

Petra dragged her hands along her skirts as if to dry her sweaty palms. "It took human blood—royal blood—to seal the pool in the first place and send all the water-carrying mages back where they came from. A brilliant move, by the way, and one that humans orchestrated together with a few mages of the time."

"So someone's opening the magepool with royal blood now," Callum said.

"A drop from every king or queen in the Vales," Petra replied. "Each one thinning the barrier just a little more. They're ready to return. They've been ready for centuries."

Katrina. That was why she'd taken Laena's blood at the caves. It even explained, though perhaps not completely, why she'd spared Laena's life: as insurance, in case her dark spell failed and she needed to return for more blood.

Laena's chest twisted, the knot tight and painful, though she couldn't truly have expected otherwise. The little sister she'd known was gone; she knew that.

Petra plunged her hand into the soil of one of her ivy plants and withdrew a dagger. She made for the door, pausing to retrieve a stick from beside the coatrack. And then, to Laena's surprise, she flung the door open.

"If you're seeing ghosts, Captain," she said, "then it means they're almost here."

CHAPTER 29

KATRINA

*I*t should have been easy for Katrina to fight off a monk who spent his days hunkered over moldy old scrolls in libraries. But the poisonkeepers clearly studied more than just books, and when Thaddeus came at her, he came with surprising strength.

Thaddeus's hands closed around her upper arms as if he planned to restrain her, or perhaps wrench her away from the magepool. His grip was strong, fingers pressing into her flesh, and the hesitation was all too plain in his eyes.

He wasn't a vicious man. His desire to help overcame the necessity to hurt.

This fight would not be won without bloodshed. And it was not Katrina's physical strength that gave her power.

She no longer had to dig for it. Free of whatever hold the Ruthless King had put on it, the magic rippled back to the surface of her awareness. More fluid, more accessible with every second that passed. When she reached for the power, it rushed forward to greet her. The magic crackled through her skin.

Thaddeus staggered away from her, thrown back by a wave

of power she hadn't quite meant to release. He missed a step, losing his footing, and his fingers grazed the water as he fell.

At the last second, he angled his body toward the steps.

What would happen, she wondered, should he tumble into the water? Would he reach the Miragelands, or resurface here in the Vales? Would the magic of the pool pull him ever deeper until he drowned in its depths?

For a moment, she almost wanted to test it.

But she was here for one purpose, and one purpose only. She strode to the final vial, letting out a breath of relief to find it intact. She snatched it up.

"Don't." The skin on Thaddeus's hands was rough and raw, and he cradled them close to his body. Yet he didn't look away from her. "Don't do it."

It was far too late for that.

She told herself it was anticipation that lanced through her chest with every heartbeat as she uncorked the vial and held it out over the pool.

Excitement. Not fear.

"Please," Thaddeus whispered. "It's not too late for you, Katrina. You don't need them."

But it was, and she did. She most definitely did.

Katrina tipped the vial into the water, and the magepool erupted.

CHAPTER 30

LAENA

*T*hey arrived at the wards as it happened.

Laena held tight to Callum's hand as Petra bounded through the orchard, navigating the undergrowth like a young fawn until she scurried to a stop beside Adrian, Remy, and Felix.

They were staring out at a crowd of ghosts.

Laena had only ever seen three together at one time. Even as the sightings had become more frequent on the mountain, the ghosts had faded in and out of sight. As if, she realized now, they were trying to maintain a shaky hold on their connection to the Vales. And failing.

Now there were dozens, with more arriving each second. More and more of them, each glowing with that eerie inner light, until she thought she might need to shield her eyes against it.

And then, those lights began to dim.

At first it seemed like they were blinking out. Like some connection had been severed, sending them back to the Mirage-lands. Like Katrina had somehow reversed her actions, or that the poisonkeepers had found a way to defend against her.

But as her eyes adjusted to the deepening dark, the moonlight providing just enough illumination over the unfolding scene, her heart dropped into her stomach.

As the ghosts' inner glows faded, their figures *solidified*. The last bits of wispiness had vanished, their features sharpening, that unearthly white fading into full patchworks of color. As they arrived, physically and fully, out of the Miragelands and into the Vales.

Callum gripped her hand, and she squeezed back, dread sending a chill crawling up her spine.

"She got his blood," Adrian said. There was no question of who he meant, though Laena couldn't tell if he was even surprised. She would have expected Silerith's Mountain King to be the last holdout, the most difficult acquisition.

But Adrian just sounded resigned. As if he wasn't surprised.

"We're too late," Petra whispered. "They're going to take down the wards."

CHAPTER 31

KATRINA

*W*ater from the magepool surged over Katrina's head, the drops pattering around her like rain.

And then King Valdric stood before her, in real, solid flesh, his clothing impossibly dry, his son looming behind him. No more reflections. No more shadows. The fabric of his shirt flowed around his arms like water. Around his neck was a thick chain with a small vial dangling at the end. Identical to the ones he'd given to her, it contained a few shining drops of liquid. She squinted, trying for a closer look.

The king grabbed her arms, and Thaddeus scrambled onto his hands and knees as her power released him. Still he lurched forward, as if he could still hope to stop this.

It was too late. Even had the poisonkeeper prince possessed the ability to stop the king—unlikely—it was far too late.

Valdric's nails dug into Katrina's bare skin, power surging through him like a storm. When she caught Thaddeus's gaze, she wondered, distantly, if the look of horror on his face might be a mirror to her own.

But then the prince was gone, and she was falling. Smoke and darkness whipped around her in a thick cloud. It poured into her throat, burning her lungs, and her mouth worked silently as she tried to choke in a breath. She squeezed her eyes shut, but the magic washed over them anyway, leaking between her eyelids and forcing streams of tears down her cheeks. The magic coiled along her arms and snatched at her hair. It whipped at her ankles, her skirts.

Only the mage king's hands, still gripping her upper arms, tied her to the world.

With nausea churning in her gut and smoke burning her eyes, it was nearly impossible to pull together a coherent thought. Yet even here, in the midst of the chaos, the ghost of Declan's voice leapt to fill the silence.

All will be well, my queen. I'm here to clean up your messes.

For years he'd smoothed over her constant court faux pas and patiently worked to sand away all evidence of her wildness. For years he'd intervened on her behalf.

You will be fine, because you have me.

Only she didn't have him here. Because she'd killed him. She'd bathed in the power his death, his pain, had bestowed upon her.

She was alone and wreathed in smoke.

Regret opened a hole in her chest, though she wasn't sure whether it was Declan's murder she regretted, or the breaking of the barrier, or Laena—demons, everything she'd done to Laena. Maybe all of it. Maybe none of it. Her thoughts slithered away, impossible to grasp.

They landed in a forest.

The Vales had too many fucking forests.

But no. This wasn't a forest; it was an orchard, cultivated, the trees blossoming with the promise of fruit to come. As soon as the smoke dissipated, the king released her arm, withdrawing so suddenly that she stumbled. Her knees landed in a bed of pine needles and dying leaves. Whoever cared for the trees hadn't taken the same care with the paths.

Someone snickered, and she looked up to see Prince Koreth smirking down at her. She wanted to rip his face off. She blinked back her tears instead, all too aware which one of them would win in a direct fight. Choking in a breath of blissfully fresh air, she staggered to her feet.

Mages were materializing between the trees, the moonlight casting their silhouettes in silver. They were laughing and crying, embracing each other, every breath bringing more and more of them into being. As she watched, one of them threw his arms into the air and spun in a circle, his face turned upward to bask in the night sky.

They smelled of damp, of caves, of stagnant water. They smelled of sulfur, with a spiced edge that she knew, somehow, came from their magic. It made her nose itch.

Like their king, every single one of the newly returned mages wore vials around their necks or tied to their wrists, each one containing drops of shining liquid.

How did they know to come here when they materialized in the Vales? How did King Valdric?

"We're drawn by the power." She hadn't realized she'd spoken the question out loud until the king responded. He stood with his back to her, drinking in the joy of his people, though the prince had angled himself as if to keep one eye on her and one on the mages. He didn't trust her. And he didn't underestimate her, either, which was unfortunate.

"But they'll be reappearing across the Vales," the king added. "You forget, we've had centuries to plot our return."

Katrina hadn't forgotten. If anything, she'd been counting on it.

Valdric clearly didn't expect her to respond. He left her behind, meeting the first mage with a hand on the shoulder and a light embrace, and then the next, and the next, greeting them one by one. Looking them in the eye. And welcoming them home to the Vales. It was no wonder that the people beamed at him.

"You know," Koreth said, kicking at the ground and sending a knot of dirt and shriveled leaves scattering around their feet, "I rather liked the Miragelands. I expect your lands will be... a disappointment."

Valdric turned, noticing his son's absence, and beckoned him forward. The prince sighed, as if summoned to empty the refuse bin rather than to speak to his own people, but he went without argument.

Katrina could only watch as the mages greeted one another, uneasiness churning in her gut as the mage king raised his hands above his head and prepared to speak. Of course he would have a speech. Had probably prepared the thing years ago.

"We have triumphed over the weakness of the hollows," the king said, "as we always knew we would."

They had triumphed? *She* had triumphed. She was the one who'd collected the royal blood of the Vales. She was the one who'd masterminded it all. They wouldn't be here without her. One weak human. A hollow, as they called her.

Perhaps she no longer counted as human.

The king continued, "After generations of exile, we have finally broken the barrier and returned to the thriving lands of our ancestors. We'll paint the Vales with the hollows' blood. We will storm every corner of these lands, as our revered ancestors did so long ago."

Their ancestors. Sure. Katrina's heart hammered a wicked beat against her ribcage. She'd done this. She'd brought him here. She'd brought all of them here, with very little knowledge of what it was they intended to do once they arrived.

Not that she'd have cared. The power, she'd told herself, would be worth it. She tried to repeat that to herself now, but somehow the words felt distant. As if they had never been her own.

So many mistakes, my queen. But I will set them right.

Katrina set her jaw, forcing herself to unclench her fists. Fear had no place here. Declan had no place here. This was her move, had been her move from the very beginning. He'd had no say in it, and when he'd opposed her, she'd thrown him behind bars. And then used his betrayal to increase her own power.

Of *course* his voice would come to her just when her plans, and her own power, were finally coming to fruition, trying to sow doubt when she was so close to getting what she wanted. What she needed.

The power *would* be worth it. It had to be.

"There are wards just ahead," one of the newly arrived mages said. "We can't get through."

The king bared his teeth, eyes glittering. "Then we will tear them down. These lands belong to *us.*"

Did they even care what was on the other side of the wards? Or was it enough to know that there was a place in the Vales they couldn't reach?

Never mind that any ward—some kind of magical shield, she assumed—must have been set by the mages who lived here in Silerith. Not by humans. The mage king had conveniently forgotten to mention their existence in his little speech. Did his people even know Laena's little mage friends were here? That they'd remained in the Vales all these generations while they'd suffered in another world?

Their existence was a failure, surely. A remnants of the not-so-revered branch of their family tree, the descendants of mages who'd turned on their own people.

Valdric's mages pushed through the orchard, crowding together until they were practically standing shoulder to shoulder. Katrina couldn't see the border, the invisible line that barred their path forward. But Valdric strode ahead, his people parting to let him pass.

He lifted his hand and a deep note reverberated through the air, like the stroke of a gong. The shield had rejected whatever destructive magic he'd attempted to unleash. A pulse of power tossed him back several steps, but he managed to stay on his feet, regaining his posture immediately.

Shaking out his hand, he faced the crowd. "Together," he said.

In response, the air sang.

There was no other way to describe it. The breath vibrated in Katrina's lungs as, together, the mages unleashed their magic. The new power that boiled in her veins was nothing in comparison. Droplets within a flood. Sparks within an inferno. She watched, horror stinging down her spine, as the mage king singed the wards with a steady blast of blue fire.

Katrina took one step back, and then another. In all the history books she'd struggled through, none had described the exact nature of the mages' power beyond the horror of the poison-speakers—the mages who could enthrall humans and control their minds. The mages had been secretive, and they had left spare documentation behind. At least as far as she had been able to discover.

Every instinct told her to flee from this display of raw power. But she was the first human to witness such a display in centuries.

She would hold her ground. And she would watch.

Many of the mages spouted fire like the king's, in various shades of blue and green and purple. If the colors meant anything, she couldn't tell what it was. And she couldn't imagine that the wards would not melt in response to that overwhelming heat.

Some of the mages, though, produced no fire. She couldn't even see what they were doing, only the looks of concentration on their faces. And the way that they smiled as spiderweb-thin cracks began to splinter across the shield, stripping it of its invisibility.

Vines crept from the forest to attack. The very air twisted.

The wards quivered. But they were too damaged to hold.

When they shattered, the explosion tore through Katrina's body like a weapon, the sound reverberating through her ribs, her feet, her skull.

The world twisted, disappeared.

When it returned, she was on the ground. Blood leaked from a shallow cut on her neck, as if a branch had sliced through her skin. She staggered to her feet, ears ringing.

The mages were running toward the open shields. They were distracted.

Katrina turned and fled. Magic still ran through her veins, the magic they'd gifted her in return for helping them invade the Vales.

It would have to be enough.

She darted between the trees, aiming for a spot ahead where a tumble of boulders had crashed down the mountainside. She could make for the peak, for a place to obscure her retreat. She didn't want the mages to be drawn to the sudden release of magic she would need to whisk herself back to Etra. She didn't want them to notice her at all.

A wave of power lashed at her legs, and she tripped, tasting blood as her chin smashed into the ground. She dragged a breath into her lungs, but pain sparked across her scalp as she was lifted up by her hair.

Prince Koreth sneered at her with open disdain, his thin lip curled, nose wrinkled. She would have called it hatred if she thought she warranted such a strong emotion from him; it was more like she was a rat he'd caught rooting through the garbage. His necklace had slipped out of his shirt, a pendant hanging heavy around his neck. Like his fellow mages, he wore a vial of sloshing liquid around his neck.

"You've served your purpose."

She reached for her magic, managing to throw a pitiful trickle of power at his head, but he dodged it easily, as if she were no more than a nuisance. An insect to be crushed under his shoe. His power thrummed, the air around him vibrating like waves of heat from a fire, and she squeezed her eyes shut, flinching against the oncoming blow.

"Stop." Valdric. She'd thought he would be storming the land beyond the wards, killing and looting with his people. But he'd followed his son, and he stood here instead, looking down at her with disgust that equaled Koreth's. "Release her."

The prince tightened his grip on her hair, and she had to restrain a whimper at the pain. "She will betray us."

"We may yet have need of her," the king replied. "Let her scurry away to her hole. There will be ample time to deal with her later."

Koreth obeyed, releasing her so abruptly that her knees caved, dropping her back to the forest floor. Then he was gone, striding through the woods after his father as if she were not worth his notice. And yet...

We may yet have need of her.

Why? Why would they need her? Surely her role was complete.

It didn't matter. Katrina pushed herself to her feet, ignoring the pain in her right ankle, and called on her magic to take her away.

CHAPTER 32

LAENA

*T*he wards shattered.

Instinct pulled Laena to the ground as shards of magic exploded around her, glittering in the moonlight like glass. Callum dropped with her, covering her body with his own as if to protect from the sharp rain that seemed sure to follow.

But instead of falling like broken glass, the broken shield vanished into the aether.

Laena got to her feet as Adrian and the others fell in around her. Magic buzzed in the air, vibrating her inner ears and sending chills of awareness running along her spine. There was still the background reek of the heart-tithes, but it was distant now, covered by the thick, staticky brine of a very different kind of magic.

For a breath, no one moved. The returned mages stood immobile among the trees, radiating power.

A single man moved to the front of the crowd, long gray hair loose around his face. Moonlight glinted off the diadem he wore on his head.

"Hello, Valdric," Adrian said, like he was greeting an acquaintance rather than a conquering king. "Nice crown. A bit forward of you, isn't it?"

Valdric raised a hand as if to return the greeting.

A column of blue fire erupted from his fingertips, and his army repeated the motion, igniting a line of blue columns that stretched so far into the woods she couldn't guess where the last one was. How many mages were there?

If there were this many of them here, how many were Hawk and Emilia dealing with in Vunmore?

"The little queen thought me a king," Valdric replied, his face illuminated in the unearthly bluish light of his fire. "And with our own king so noticeably absent, I found myself rather taken by the idea."

The little queen. Katrina.

"Can't imagine that will go over well." If anything, the mages' appearance seemed to have strengthened Adrian's swagger.

"How is anyone to know, General? Except for yourself, I suppose."

Laena exchanged a glance with Callum. General? She had a hundred questions. A thousand. How could Valdric know Adrian, if he'd been locked in the Miragelands? How could they know him?

And who was their true king, if not the man standing before them now?

"Where is *your* king, then?" Valdric goaded, the emphasis on the word 'your' making it clear he did not claim the same sovereign. "Cowering in his mountain?"

The Ruthless King, Silerith's Mountain King, also ruled over the Miragelands.

But how? The Miragelands were sealed. There was no passage between the two realms.

Unless the magic made an exception for a man who wielded power from the Vales as well as from the mages. Unless the world bent itself in different ways to accommodate a king whose ancestry was rooted in both places. Human and mage. Vales and Miragelands.

Though it seemed he hadn't been doing much leading in either place. If Adrian served as his general, he'd been essentially ruling in his king's stead. How long had it been that way? And why?

Adrian shrugged, like Valdric's question meant nothing to him. "Off doing ruthless things, if the humans are to be believed."

"Ruthless indeed," Valdric agreed, "but to whom? From what I understand, he gave his blood willingly so the little queen could break the barrier."

Adrian's pause was brief, no more than a flicker of a hesitation. But Laena caught the way his breath hitched, just for a moment. The way his lips twitched as if he wanted to deny it. As if he was all too certain that it was a possibility.

And then Valdric saw it, too. He threw his head back and laughed. "Your playtime in the Vales is done." His column of fire widened to a flood. "Kill them."

Fire bloomed from the line of mages, columns of blue and green and purple flames. Impossibly beautiful, and impossibly terrifying. Adrian threw up his own hands. "Saria, contain them. Maren, vines. Remy, do what you can to shield us."

The forest came alive. Felix was already lunging into the battle, sword aimed at the closest fire-wielder, while vines snaked out of the undergrowth to pull weapons from hands and attackers off their feet. Remy dodged between trees, throwing up shields to defend Felix and Maren against the onslaught.

Laena could see no way to win this battle. The sheer number of mages… they'd be overrun in minutes.

"You gonna command me too, boy?" Petra asked.

Adrian blew her a kiss. "Petra, darling, I wouldn't dare."

Black smoke whirled around him, and then he was gone, reappearing in the center of the army with his sword drawn. Steel clashed as mages descended on him, and then he was gone again, disappearing and reappearing so quickly she could hardly keep track of where he landed.

Laena reached for her own magic and stumbled, nearly doubling over as it writhed away from her, cutting a hot line of pain through her body. She could barely feel the magic through that oily sheen, the familiar cold of it buried beneath waves of poison.

Callum put a hand on her arm. "What is it?"

"Nothing." Laena choked the word out from between gritted teeth, Petra's tea souring in her stomach. "I'm fine."

"So convincing."

If she hadn't been so focused on staying on her feet, she'd have smacked him.

And then he was charging into the battle, falling in beside Felix to lend his own sword to the fight.

Shoving her nausea aside, Laena plunged her awareness toward her magic, ignoring the wretched, rotting writhe of the poison as she gripped the magic, hard, and *pulled*.

It let go with a wrench, digging a searing thread of pain through her.

Shards of pitch-black icicles rained down onto the army like arrows, ice collecting in the air like it always had, allowing her some semblance of control as it knocked back a wave of their attackers. She threw them at Callum's opponent, and Felix's, already sweating with effort, begging her power to hold on for another minute. Another five.

Adrian reappeared beside her, hair drenched with sweat. "Any time now, Petra," he said.

"Thought you weren't going to command me," the old woman grumbled.

"Well, *I* thought you were going to help, yeah?"

With that, he vanished again.

"We can't defeat them on our own." Laena was wheezing, each breath digging a shard of pain through her ribs, her spine, and down through her gut. Even that one volley of magic had spotted her vision with little beads of darkness. She wouldn't be on her feet for long. "We have to retreat."

"So sure, are you?" Petra asked.

"There are hundreds of them, and eight of us," Laena replied. Callum had no magic, Felix had none he could make use of, and Laena's was very obviously failing. "So, yes."

Petra rolled her eyes.

Magic pulsed out of her like a storm, throwing waves upon waves of attacking mages to the ground. Their screams ripped through the forest, the coppery tang of blood joining with the thickening smells of smoke and fire.

"No hands," Adrian said, breathing hard. "Impressive."

"As I've told you over and over, there's no need for the dramatics." Petra turned, and another wave of mages went flying as the ground exploded beneath their feet, sending soil and rocks skyward with bits of tree roots. "My poor orchard."

"No one needs that many apples," Adrian said.

"Are you fighting, boy, or are you chattering?"

He winked. "Can I not do both?"

A column of fire shot toward them, and Laena wrenched the last dregs of her magic out of her body, meeting the fire with a sickly shield of charred ice that barely protected Petra from the hit. The fire melted the ice shield easily—if the term could be applied to the thick, tar-like substance that dripped from the ice shield. It coated the ground in a shining, writhing puddle of filth.

"That can't be good," Adrian said.

And then he was gone again, whirling away in a band of smoke, his sword flashing.

Petra turned on Laena, grabbing her wrist so hard it was painful. "Your magic. It's tainted."

Laena wanted to scream at her. Wasn't that the whole point of this journey? "I've been *trying* to tell you I needed your—"

Petra gave her arm a shake. "Did you battle a heart-tither?" she demanded.

"Yes." It was all Laena could do to hold on to the magic despite the pain in her ribs, her chest, her skull. She was distantly aware of Callum cutting down a pair of mages who tried to approach, of Petra's power pulsing out and pushing aside more of the army. "My sister."

Petra opened her mouth to speak.

A column of fire rocketed up over Callum's head, over Petra's magic, lighting the scene like fireworks shot high into the night. Like all of the mages had unified their powers, thread by thread, until they formed an arching whirlwind of flame. Laena reached for her power, but it slipped through her flingers, the world flipping to black for one second, three, more.

When she opened her eyes, the world was on fire.

And Petra lay beside her, blood coating the side of her face.

Laena ignored the stab of pain in her side, the ringing in her ears. She scanned Petra's body, searching for signs of injury. Blood pulsed out of a wound in her side, and Laena pressed the flat of her hand against it, trying uselessly to stem the flow.

Petra reached for Laena's cheek, hand shaking. "Your blood is cursed. Your blood is the cure. I'm sorry I didn't see it. Before."

Laena pressed her hand against Petra's to keep it from falling away, tears tracking down over both their fingers and blurring her vision. "Stay with me," she said. "You're all right."

But there was too much blood. So much blood staining the ground around her, soaking into the earth. Even with Petra's blood running over her hand, her fingers felt cold.

"What does that mean?" Callum whispered. "Your blood is cursed?"

She wasn't sure when he'd arrived, or how. And she didn't know the answer to his question. Petra's hand was heavy in hers, her eyes open and unseeing.

And then Adrian was lunging for them, wrapping them in a band of smoke and whisking them into the dark.

CHAPTER 33

CALLUM

*C*allum would rather trudge through the forest on foot for weeks, through rain and sleet, than travel through Adrian's smoke one more damn time. It was a choking, churning mess, and every second he spent inside of it without hurling up his guts was a fucking miracle.

Yet he couldn't regret it. Not with Laena's sobbing body crushed against his and the aftertaste of the mages' power on his tongue—so much power that even he could feel it in his bones, power unending, as if drawn from a bottomless source. The sight of Petra's motionless body was seared into his mind.

And the fear, still hammering against his ribcage, that Laena would be hit next. He cradled her against his chest, savoring each rise and fall of her breath.

For her, he'd endure ten such journeys. A thousand.

When the world returned, they were back in the fields outside of Vunmore. He couldn't see the city, but he knew these lands like no other: the knee-high grasses that stirred in the breeze, the distant rush of the twin rivers.

The city was nearly in sight. Just over the next rise, if he wasn't mistaken.

The others lay sprawled on the ground nearby, Maren and Remy still clasping hands as though Adrian had dragged them back here in a long chain. Felix's complexion had gone green. Even Saria looked unsteady, her usual composure replaced by shaking hands that she kept wiping across her mouth as if to dispel the taste of the smoke.

It was something of a comfort actually, to see that the mages found this method of travel as disorienting as Callum did.

"Not the smoothest exit," Saria complained. Blood stained the side of her shirt, but she was already getting to her feet, moving over to check the others, so Callum hoped that meant it wasn't hers.

"Why not bring us directly to the castle?" he asked. His voice sounded ragged, even to his own ears, and his throat felt raw, stripped bare by the smoke.

"I tried, Captain." Adrian staggered slightly, as if he'd been struck in the head. Or had a few too many drinks. "Something kicked us back."

As much as Callum appreciated a direct response, rather than a flippant one, the mage's seriousness was unnerving in a way he didn't quite want to describe. This man—this *general*, apparently—had just faced down an invading conqueror and his army with grins and pithy comments. If something had shaken him, Callum wasn't sure he wanted to know what it was.

Laena stirred, lifting her head from where she'd had it buried against his chest. He hated the tears that tracked silently down her cheeks, the raw grief in her eyes. He helped her to her feet, and she stayed close to his side as she looked around. Wavy heat lines rose from the land beyond the hill ahead of them, the only indication that anything strange was happening.

No shouting, no smell of smoke, no clash of steel. Just heat.

Still clutching his blood-streaked sword, Callum reluctantly unwrapped his arm from Laena's shoulder. "Stay here while I scout ahead." He directed the words to everyone yet meant them only for her.

The others could defend themselves. They could use their magic without killing themselves. Save for Felix, but the man fought like a beast. He'd be fine.

Callum hurried up the hill, legs burning as he climbed. He was afraid of what he would find and yet desperate to know. To see. As if every moment he delayed meant another second of torture for his city. As if seeing the truth could make it cease.

He crested the rise, not caring that it exposed him to whatever waited on the other side, and looked out toward Vunmore.

Flames engulfed the city, burning orange and red. So hot, so bright that there wasn't even any smoke. He had to shield his eyes against the burn of it. Even at this distance, he could practically feel the heat rolling across the hills.

"We're too late," he said, the words thick in his throat. "Vunmore is on fire."

Hawk was in the city, and Emilia. Gretchen. And all of Callum's soldiers, too—Edmun and Godfrey, and all the rest. They wouldn't give up without a fight. But what good would it truly do them? Even Hawk's power could not defeat so many. Not on its own.

Callum had failed his king, failed his city. Hawk was dead, or soon would be. And Callum had allowed it to happen. Just as he had with King Magnus. His chest was tight with pain, spots prickling the corners of his eyes as he struggled to draw breath.

"It isn't on fire." Laena wrapped her fingers around his arm. He hadn't even heard her approach. The crystal-clear note of her voice cut through the roaring in his ears, shaky yet confidence. Certain. "Look. It's a defense."

Callum blinked, forcing his vision to clear. The fire formed a clear arch around the city, wrapping around it in an unbroken wall. One so constant, in fact, that it even bridged the meeting point of the rivers—one of Vunmore's strengths, it was true, but also a potential weakness.

And indeed, an army of mages had gathered on the banks. Ready to invade the city but unable to penetrate the wall of fire by either magical or ordinary means.

"She's right." Adrian was breathing hard as he joined them. "That isn't magefire. Someone's shielding the city."

Hawk. He was maintaining this wall, by himself, and it was strong enough to prevent Adrian from traveling directly inside the city. Did he realize he was doing that, or was it a byproduct of the Vales magic?

"So how are we going to get to the king?" Maren asked.

Laena drew in a deep, shuddering breath, and Callum knew what she was going to say—wished he could snatch them out of the air before she could utter them. As if that would stop her from doing everything in her power to help.

"I can get us in."

—*—

SHE CREATED A ROAD.

It took several hours to circle around to the Sil side of the city. The fire had gouged a thick band of devastation through the old-growth trees where Callum and Laena had fled the city just a week ago. The fire had consumed every bit of foliage in its path but spread no further, leaving an eerie line of trees that stood mere inches from the still-raging flames. As if they were the army, ready to attack the moment the fire should falter.

It certainly looked as if it would burn forever.

The heat was intense, forcing them to stand back. Laena's eyes took on the distant sheen that meant she was calling upon her magic. Once, she had reached it so easily. He could see the way she struggled with it now, the sweat that beaded along her brow as she fought to pull it to the surface.

He would have stopped her, if he thought he could. If they'd had any other choice. Had he not discarded Hawk's magic communication powder.

But he couldn't stop her, so he stepped nearer, ready to catch her if she should fall.

A new sort of wall bloomed around them, under them. Frost crystalized into a tunnel made of ice, though it took a moment for him to realize it. The walls shone as black as obsidian. Only the wave of cold—and his knowledge of Laena's magic—told him the tunnel was not made of stone.

"Hurry," Laena whispered. "I can't hold it."

Adrian strode forward, followed by Remy and Maren. Saria ushered Laena and Callum ahead, with Felix ready to take up the guard spot at the rear.

The flames crackled to every side, making it impossible to hear anything above the roar, but within the narrow tunnel itself the air was cool. The only sign of the fire's onslaught was the trickle of water that ran down the wall, first a droplet here and there—like rain chasing itself down a window—and then forming a river as the fire wore down the protective barrier of magic from the outside.

He kept his hand in Laena's as she walked just ahead of him, her eyes narrowed in concentration. Her skin grew grayer with each step, as though the power was bleeding the life out of her.

By the time they exited the tunnel, purple bruises had appeared beneath her eyes, ominous in their suddenness.

As soon as Saria was clear of the walls, the tunnel melted away, an inky waterfall that sloshed to the forest floor in much the same way her ice shield had melted in Petra's orchard.

A beat later the flames returned, with a roar and a wave of heat that knocked Callum back several steps.

"*Now* I can bring us directly to the castle," Adrian said.

Callum opened his mouth to protest that it wasn't far, that

the building was right there, but smoke poured into his lungs before he could speak, smothering his curse.

—and then a sword was rushing at him, the world re-materializing in a flash of steel and stone.

Callum barely deflected the blow, knocking the attacker back far enough to make them stumble. Only then, with a second to draw in a breath, did the room come into focus. Adrian's smoke was dissipating over the stone floor of the throne room, where a small group of soldiers were collected by the door and ready to defend their king.

Hawk stood before him, his teeth bared, eyes flashing, and there was no doubt in Callum's mind that the king had been the one to come after him with the sword. Exhaustion had stamped bruises under his eyes, too, identical to Laena's. His blond hair was wet with sweat, his cheek smudged with dirt, and a beard of several days thickening on his face. Yet he held his blade like he meant to use it.

Though if he'd been paying attention, he'd have corrected his stance. The way Callum had taught him.

"Traitor." The king spat the word like a curse, and then he was flying at Callum again, brandishing his sword in an exhausted, clumsy sweep. Callum defended, meeting his attack without pushing one of his own. Hawk's blow reverberated through his body like the toll of a bell, but it was too easy to anticipate the king's next move. Callum deflected that as well, refusing to take the offensive.

"You brought them here," Hawk said, his words barely discernible through the heaviness of his breaths. "The mages."

"We're *different* mages," Adrian put in, though Callum didn't think Hawk could hear through his rage.

This fight had been coming for them for some time. It was a fight that Hawk had wanted, had itched for, ever since the death of his father. Magnus's murder had left him alone, or so he saw it. With secret magic to manage, a kingdom to run, and grief he appeared to confuse with weakness.

He'd needed someone to blame. Callum had been at hand.

But Callum should not have allowed it. He saw that now.

Hawk rushed for him again, and Callum met him blade-to-blade, disarming the king with a single stroke that left him stumbling back. No weapon. And, if one were to judge by the emptiness in his eyes, no hope either.

"Kill me, then," Hawk said. "As you did my father."

The guards hesitated by the door. They ought to be running in to shield Hawk, but they knew their captain. Knew he would not harm his king.

Callum bent and retrieved the king's sword. "I didn't kill your father," he said, offering the weapon hilt-first to the man who'd once been his friend.

Hawk's gaze didn't cool. And he didn't take the sword. Callum didn't know whether the king would attack with his bare hands—his nails, his teeth—or if he would give up and retreat.

Before he could do either, Laena stepped around Callum and went to stand beside Hawk. She placed a hand on his shoulder, and Callum couldn't repress the twist of jealousy that stabbed through his gut at the sight of her touching the king. Her fiancé still.

"King Hawk," she said, her voice soft. "These mages are on our side. You have my word."

Hawk blinked at her, as if her words had returned him to the world. He unclenched his fists, his breath softening as he took her in. "Princess Laena."

As if he were surprised to see her here, at Callum's side. What did the king think? That Callum would have abandoned her in Silerith? That he would return to Vunmore and leave her to fend for herself?

But then, that was exactly what Hawk would have expected

Callum to do, had she in any way interfered with his ability to reach Vunmore to help him. Wasn't it? Just as he would have bid Callum abandon Thaddeus.

Yes, he saw it now. Should have seen it from the first.

Adrian stepped forward, bowing deeply. "The shield you have erected around your city is impressive, King Hawk," he said.

Hawk wrenched his gaze away from Laena to meet Adrian's, suspicion driving deep lines into his forehead. "I cannot keep it up much longer." He spoke the words like an admission of guilt. "We will be overrun within the hour."

Adrian gestured to the other mages. "If you are willing, Remy can replace your shields. Provide some temporary relief."

It was, Callum thought, the most polite thing that Adrian had uttered since they'd first crossed paths. Not to mention the deferential tone.

Hawk narrowed his eyes, studying Adrian as if he were a cockroach who'd crawled into a cookpot. "Forgive me if I'm reluctant to trust you."

Adrian met his gaze, unmoved. "And forgive my rudeness when I say you look exhausted, King Hawk."

There was no denying that. Hawk looked like he could collapse at any moment. And when he did, the shields would go, too. Vunmore would be taken, its people enthralled. And the war would be lost.

"You can wait until your power gives out, which by your own admission will be soon," Adrian said. "Or you can trust us now and buy us time to make a plan."

"And what kind of plan will that be?" Hawk returned. "My soldiers carry no magic. My betrothed, powerful though she may be, looks as drained as I feel. I do not see how a few hours will help."

"I have a thought on that," Adrian replied. "But I will need time."

Hawk sighed, scrubbing a hand through his hair. "So be it. I see no difference, if you let them in now or in half an hour. We must face them either way."

Adrian nodded to Remy, who closed their eyes, concentrating. When they opened them, their gaze was clear. "You may drop the shields, Your Majesty."

Hawk released a breath, shoulders sagging as if a great weight had been lifted from them. "Thank you."

Thank you. That was... civil? Callum glanced at Laena, who still stood by Hawk's side, and she met his gaze with a small shrug. Maybe they could convince Hawk to get along with the Sil mages, after all.

Or maybe he was simply too exhausted to argue.

"Funny," Remy said, tilting their head to the side as if hearing some distant tune. "My magic is sticking to the remnants of yours. I think... I think it's getting stronger."

Callum could only hope that was true. They all needed as much rest as they could cobble together. Especially Laena. If Hawk looked exhausted, she looked a breath away from death.

He didn't want to think of it.

Hawk turned to Adrian, eyes sharpening in an expression that Callum recognized immediately. The one that came over him right before he started spewing orders at people. "Right. You have your time. Now what kind of plan—"

"I'll be back in a day," Adrian interrupted. "By sunset."

"What—"

But smoke billowed around the mage, swallowing him into the aether.

Hawk blinked. "And he's gone." He scrubbed a hand over his face. "What kind of trouble have you brought to our door, Farrow?"

CHAPTER 34

LAENA

*V*unmore's castle had, Laena knew, been designed as a fortress. The first coming of the mages had destroyed the original structure, though as Emilia had discovered, the bones still existed. The mages had then built up their own fortress to protect them against attack. From one another, from humans. From anyone who might threaten them.

It was the same fortress the humans defended now.

The outer walls were composed of thick stone, meant to slow any enemy who managed to breach the city. Beyond the band of courtyards and gardens, another layer of walls protected the interior chambers.

None of that had saved the mages, in the end. Nor would it save the humans who huddled within it now.

Hawk had turned the throne room into a central meeting place, a war room. Messengers ran in and out carrying orders, news, and announcements to Vunmore's population. The most urgent of which was to alert citizens to take shelter within the fortress, in anticipation of Remy's shields falling.

For now, though, they were intact.

For now, there was a lull. A breath, before the deluge.

It wouldn't be long enough.

Laena felt drained and shaky from the burst of magic she'd used to create the ice tunnel. Since then a constant pain radiated from her ribcage, a stitch that grew worse regardless of whether she sat or stood, rested or walked.

But who among them wasn't in pain right now? Maren lay curled in a corner of the throne room, her cloak tossed over her shoulder. Felix sat beside her as if standing guard. Even Saria had stopped moving for a few minutes, though Laena saw the way her gaze strayed to the windows every few minutes. As if searching for any sign of Adrian's return. They were all tired, to the depths of their bones.

Laena had tried to hide the pain as Callum went off to talk with Edmun, though she didn't think he quite believed her. Somehow she'd convinced him that she would be safe if he let her out of his sight for ten minutes, though he hadn't relented until after Emilia and Gretchen came tearing into the throne room to embrace her.

Well, Emilia had. Gretchen followed at a distance, watching the interaction as if she were concerned for Emilia's safety, and Emilia's safety alone.

Gretchen and Callum, Laena mused, had quite a lot in common.

She ate a bite of food and sipped a cup of water, and still the shakiness didn't resolve. As she'd known it would not. The black spots on the edge of her vision were a constant now, as if the poison could no longer be contained within her core well of magic.

There was nothing to do about it now. And yet she knew, as certainly as Remy knew their shields would eventually fall and Hawk knew he could not defeat the mages on his own, that using her magic again would mean her death.

Petra's last words echoed in her mind, a constant companion. Her blood was cursed.

And it would kill her. In time, she thought it would kill her no matter what.

Every time she used her power, she hastened the process.

Laena found Hawk standing over a table in the corner. The surface was piled with papers, bits of parchment curling out from under larger bits, scrolls scattered on the floor. On top of it all were several maps detailing the topography of the land around Vunmore. As she joined him, she could make out the precise twists and turns of the city streets, and the exact location of each village out on the plains.

Laena's heart twisted at the thought of the people they couldn't protect.

"So many years of studying these maps," he said as she approached. "I thought I knew them by heart, but somehow they look different in war. Every hill is a vantage point. Every patch of forest hides potential enemies."

"Every street houses souls that must be saved."

He looked up, offering her a tired smile. "The burden of leadership." He sighed. "And the honor as well, I suppose. I only hope I will not lead these people to their deaths."

It was as honest a thing as she'd ever heard him say. Perhaps he was too fatigued to wear that mask of his.

He didn't know that she was aware of the mission he'd assigned to Callum. She had plenty of reasons to be angry on her own behalf, it was true, but all she could think was how willing he'd been to send Callum to assassinate Silerith's king. Alone. Did he truly think so little of his friend, the captain of his King's Guard, that he was willing to send him to his death like it was nothing?

She was so lost in her thoughts that it took her a moment to realize Hawk had spoken. He was looking at her with his eyebrows raised, as if expecting a response.

"I'm sorry," she said, doing her best to smooth the anger from her expression. "My head is muddled. What did you say?"

"All too understandable," he said. "After everything you've been through. I said we ought to marry quickly. Tonight, before the shields fall."

Laena opened her mouth, then closed it. "But why?"

The words fell out of her mouth, completely beyond her control. If it was uncivil, well, she was exhausted. She hoped he'd forgive her for that.

He merely shook his head. "For morale. There's only so much planning we can do. With the citizens inside our gates, a wedding will distract everyone. Give them hope."

His words were kind, though he said them as if a wedding were just one more item on a long list of tasks. Because for him, it would be. Plan the battle, check. Shore up the defenses, check. Boost morale by marrying a near stranger? Check.

She hadn't thought to address this now. But if he was going to insist upon them marrying before the oncoming battle, then she could not delay the conversation any further.

Hawk was a king, used to getting his way, and Callum's history proved he could be unreasonable.

In this, she hoped he would not be.

"Your Majesty," she said slowly, "I think we must discuss—"

"I must go speak with Moore and some of the soldiers," he interrupted. "I'll find you when I return." Hawk gathered up several of the maps and rolled them up, tucking them beneath his arm.

"But—"

It was no use. The king was gone, hurrying across the room with two guards falling in behind him.

Doubt closed around her heart.

"He's always doing that," Emilia said, joining her at the table. She ran an idle handle over the remaining papers, shuffling them around. Her nails were ragged, her skin dry and cracked from days of traveling. She looked wistful, and Laena couldn't tell if it was out of fondness for her brother or frustration with him. A bit of both, perhaps.

"Always doing what?" Laena asked carefully.

"Oh, you know. Making plans no one wants but him. I was going to go out to the courtyard to check on our visitors. See how they're settling in. Will you come with me?"

Laena smiled. "Of course."

If the throne room was bustling with activity, the courtyard outside the castle was frenetic with it. Children chased each other through the gardens, clearly reveling in the chance to play in the castle grounds while their parents nestled sleeping pads together and set up cooking stations. It smelled of tea and linens. The shouts of the children provided a soundtrack that threatened to squeeze Laena's heart out of her chest.

These people were relying on them—on her and Hawk—to keep them safe. To protect their families.

The pain in her ribs only increased, as if her heart were beating a thick sludge of poison through her veins, like the one that had melted off the tunnel, and the shields.

Not long, she thought. *It won't be long now.*

Emilia went from family to family, cot to cot, checking on mothers and fathers and anyone who seemed to be alone. Laena followed as Emilia drifted from person to person, delivering blankets and even beckoning Laena to the kitchen so they could carry out an order from the housekeeper to retrieve an extra cook pot.

As they headed down the stairs to the kitchen, a little boy came tearing around the corner ahead of them, face flushed with excitement. He had a mop of unruly auburn hair and a splash of freckles on his round cheeks. And judging by the fire in his eyes, he was very clearly on a mission.

"Whoa there," Emilia said. "You're going to get trampled if you keep dashing around like that."

The boy skidded to a stop a few steps down from where they

stood, gazing up at them in wonder. "Princess Emilia," he breathed. "Queen Laena."

"I'm a princess, too," Laena said. "Technically."

He just stared at them, eyes wide as coins. He had a small pile of parchment tucked under his arm and a quill balanced between his fingers.

Emilia set her hands on her hips, tilting her head. "And your name, young squire?"

The boy giggled, his awe fading to delight. "I'm not a squire. I'm six."

"Squires can't be six?" Laena asked.

"No. They can't." He said it with the conviction of an expert in the field. "I'm Rowan. I'm writing a story. It's about a horse."

"Maybe you should add a princess," Emilia suggested.

Rowan wrinkled his nose. Then, realizing who stood before him, he smoothed it out again. "Maybe," he said.

Emilia waved her hands at him. "Off you go then, little bard. Before the cook sets you to peeling potatoes."

The boy was off like a shot, careening away through the hall as if she'd threatened him with banishment to the Miragelands.

"So," Emilia said as she and Laena returned with the pot, each holding one of the handles, "when are you going to tell my brother that you're in love with Callum?"

Laena coughed, nearly dropping her side of the pot as she stumbled over her feet. And here she thought she'd gotten used to the princess's cheerful directness. Love? Certainly, she cared for Callum. She cared for him deeply, and had from nearly their first meeting. But she hadn't thought...

Except that she had. Not in those words, perhaps. Every touch, every glance, every moment together had only made it more obvious. She was planning to call off the engagement, wasn't she? Not for political reasons, but because she could not go forward in good faith when she loved another man.

She busied herself with arranging the pot on the table, wishing she could hide the flush that had no doubt risen to her cheeks. "You read too many romances," she said, but her voice was too strained to pull it off as a joke.

"One," Emilia replied, forthright, "there's no such thing as too many romances. Two, I'm right. You love him, and he loves you, and everyone knows about it. Except for Hawk. And now that I'm looking at your face, maybe you."

A laugh bubbled out of Laena's throat, half strangled. "What does it mean," she whispered, "that I need someone else to tell me I'm in love?"

"I suspect it means you won't allow yourself to admit it, if you think it will mean hurting your people. But Laena, I've seen you together, and I think... who you are together, it can only help your people."

It was not so different from the words Callum had said to her. Not so different at all.

"All right," Laena said. "I'll tell Hawk about Callum when you tell him about Gretchen."

Emilia tipped her head to the side, lips pursed in a smug pout. "I already did. He yelled at me, insisting I'm supposed to marry some noble or royal. Of his choosing, naturally. I told him I won't do it."

Laena could picture the scene well enough. "Surely he's got bigger concerns at the moment."

"Yes." Emilia sighed. "Which is the only reason he hasn't packed me off to Inasvale to live with the monks." She paused, frowning. "That, and the army of mages standing between us."

"A small obstacle," Laena agreed.

Emilia brushed her hands on her skirts, then took Laena's hand, an earnest crinkle in her brow. "Callum is a brother to me. Just as much as Hawk and Thaddeus are. Sometimes, I think he's even more of a brother to me than they are." She squeezed Laena's hands, drawing her close and kissing her cheek. "As far as I'm concerned, I get you as my sister either way."

CHAPTER 35

LAENA

*W*hen Emilia shooed her away, apparently still full of boundless pre-battle energy, Laena tried to follow the others' example and close her eyes for a brief spell. But the pain in her ribs was intense, and she kept dozing off only to jerk back to consciousness, terrified that if she fell asleep she wouldn't wake again.

She didn't want to spend the last few hours this way, hovering halfway between sleeping and waking.

It would not help, anyway. At length, she threw off the blanket she'd wrapped around herself and stalked back out of the throne room. The halls were quiet as sunset approached, the others wise enough to take these hours to rest.

Almost all the others. Remy sat swaying in the arched door to the courtyard, clearly exhausted from the strain of holding the shield. Remy gave her a smile as she passed. Clearly not yet ready to give up.

Though Laena could not help but notice that they sat with a bell ready at their side so they could sound the alarm when the shields slipped out of their exhausted grasp.

Soon, though. It could not be long now.

She found Callum in the courtyard hauling crates to the walls. Steps for archers to reach the higher arrow slits. When she approached, he dropped the final crate and clapped Godfrey on the shoulder with a few quiet words. No doubt advising the young soldier to join the others and shut his eyes while he could. Then he turned to her and smiled.

He was clearly tired, his eyes rimmed in red, yet the smile was genuine in a way that made her heart hurt. And not because it was pumping sour magic through her veins, but because she didn't think she'd ever seen such a beautiful smile in her life. A king who'd betrayed him, an oncoming battle, and a mage who'd promised aid before disappearing. And still, he smiled at her as if her very presence could banish all those troubles away. At least for a time.

She held out her hand and he took it, allowing her to draw him away into the castle. Every space in the garden had been claimed; the courtyard and the interior halls were packed with Vunmore's citizens crowded in close, the children draped across bedrolls and laps and one another.

Not the ideal place to snatch a moment of privacy. But they needed to speak, so Laena led him into one of the stairwells and paused on the landing. Not exactly a low-traffic area, but at least it was quiet for the moment.

Callum didn't seem to care either way. He stood what should have been scandalously close to her, his chest nearly flush against hers, his breath warming the air between them. "Have you slept?" he asked.

She attempted a smile, though it felt forced. "Are you saying I look tired, Captain?"

He brushed a thumb across her cheek, and she leaned into his touch. "You're beautiful," he said. "But yes. You look tired."

So did he. So did everyone.

"The people are situated?" she asked, though she knew that they were. "The soldiers ready?"

"As much as they can be."

She wanted to keep talking to him of small things. To hear his voice. To feel his warmth and not his worry.

When she thought of telling him what she felt, what Emilia had coaxed—or ripped, perhaps—into her awareness, the words froze in her throat. He was looking at her with those eyes, that crinkle between his brow, his finger caressing her cheek so she could hardly breathe, let alone think. Or form actual words.

Somehow, those words felt more dangerous than the approaching battle.

So when she opened her mouth to speak, she found herself saying something very different. "Callum," she said. "I'm dying."

He shook his head. "No."

But these were the words she needed to say, and he was the one who needed to hear them. So she kept going. "If I use my powers again, I won't survive it."

"Then don't." There was a ragged, desperate edge to his voice, and the pleading look in his blue eyes matched it. "Don't use your power."

But he knew as well as she did that refraining would not be an option. He had to be thinking of all the people in their care, the children nestled in their parents' laps, the elderly folks and the craftspeople and young couples, all with their own dreams and plans, all relying on them.

He knew her, perhaps better than anyone ever had, and so he had to know that if using her power would save them—if it would buy them even a few minutes more—then she would do it. Without hesitation, she would do it.

"What did Petra mean," Callum whispered, his voice rough, "about the curse and the blood? The blood is the cure?"

Laena shook her head, the spots in her vision quivering as she moved, the world growing just a touch darker. "I've been puzzling over it. But I don't know."

Though, to be fair, there hadn't been much time for

puzzling. It was hard to think when her head felt as if it'd been stuffed with wool. And then set on fire.

"You can't die." He didn't say it as though he forbade it; he said it as though the very possibility was ludicrous. As if he could will the poison out of her veins, the sickness from her body.

He would, if he could. She knew him, too, and she knew he would scour every drop of poison from her body himself, if only he could.

"Hawk wants to marry," she said. "Tonight."

Though it would have to be this morning, at this point. She wondered if he'd been searching for her.

Callum dragged a hand through his hair. "Fuck, Laena. If I thought that would save you, I'd give you up. I'd mourn forever, but I'd do it." He took her hands, brushing his fingers over hers, running his hands up her arms to grip her elbows. "Will it?"

She shook her head, tears stinging her eyes. "I don't see how it could."

He pulled her closer, brushing his lips against hers. "Then," he said, "you're mine."

Neither of them said 'while you live.' They didn't need to.

Before she could kiss him again, Remy's bell began to clang, announcing the fall of the shields.

CHAPTER 36

CALLUM

*T*he bell vibrated deep into Callum's ears with such violence it felt like the toll was trying to crack his skull. A second bell joined Remy's from one of the watchtowers, and then a third, until the air was practically quivering the shrill alarms.

Their time was up. The shields were down, and the mage army they'd seen by the river would be advancing.

He'd been trained to leap into action when this particular bell rang out, but he'd never faced a true invasion. It had clanged upon King Magnus's death, he knew, but too late to do any good.

Laena stayed by his side as he made for the courtyard, his muscles remembering their training and carrying him toward the walls of the keep without so much as a moment of hesitation. Already, the reserve of soldiers was beginning to stream out of the barracks, weapons drawn. Some would join the shift at the city walls, while others shored up defenses here at the palace.

They were not trained to face mages. No one was.

He needed to join them, to make for the outer walls and the

257

city's first line of defense. Yet he couldn't bring himself to leave Laena. Not yet. She was looking up at him with those wide green eyes, her curls escaping the string she'd used to tie them back. Her lips were set in a determined line, as if she, too, planned to follow the stream of soldiers into the city streets.

He paused, turning to her shoulders. Trying to relish this moment, to breathe her in, even as panic threatened to force its way up his throat. "Try not to use your powers," he said. "Stay here, within the keep."

She was already shaking her head. "I have to help."

"If the city walls fall..." He trailed off, because in his mind it was a question of *when* they fell, not whether they would. But the shine in her eyes said she understood him, and he swallowed back the correction. Allowed his words to suggest the hope he didn't feel. "If the city walls fall, they will need you here."

She was already looking back over her shoulder, at the people who, even now, retreated from the courtyard. Children were covering their ears against the relentless clang of the bells, high and piercing, while the adults tried to usher everyone out of the courtyard. The interior corridors would be shoulder to shoulder with civilians. How many were in the city? Five thousand? Ten?

Maren's red hair appeared in the doorway, followed by Felix's hulking height, both of them weaving through the crowd in the opposite direction. Toward the outer walls.

Where the hell was Adrian and his promised help? They were out of time.

Laena hurried to join them, and Callum could only follow, hoping she would agree to stay behind. She was powerful, and she was strong. But her magic was killing her. And the people needed her here.

"Why don't the mages all just appear within the walls?"

Laena asked as she fell into step beside Maren. "Now that the shields are down?"

"Some of them will," Maren said. "But it's a pretty rare power. I doubt there are many in the army."

As if in response, a dozen columns of whirling smoke materialized in the courtyard, bypassing the outer and middle walls alike. They were like miniature versions of the tornadoes that sometimes plagued the plains in stormy weather, only these clouds solidified into something much more dangerous: mages, arriving in a storm of fire and lightning, that hair-raising sizzle of power he'd felt in Petra's forest.

"You just had to say it," Felix grumbled, drawing his sword.

Maren shrugged. "Can't help it if I'm an optimist."

And then they were off, Maren's power uncurling vines from the trees to whip the invaders off their feet and bring branches cascading onto their heads. Chaos filled the courtyard as the King's Guard joined them. They would defend their home. And Callum would join them.

He drew his sword. "Please try," he said to Laena. "For the people's sake, if not for mine."

"I'll try. For both of you." Laena pressed her lips to his cheek, lingering for barely a moment. He felt the weight of that kiss, even through the clamor and clang of the battle. If the worst should happen? It was a goodbye.

She withdrew, hurrying back through the palace doors as he shielded her retreat.

CHAPTER 37

LAENA

*L*aena allowed herself five seconds to fear for Callum as he ran into the fray, allowed the panic to seize her chest and demand that she go, that she run after him, that she spend everything she had to protect him.

Five seconds... before she pushed the panic aside, forcing herself to face the task at hand.

Protecting Vunmore's people.

She shut the door, barring it behind her—perhaps a useless gesture, but one she had to take nonetheless—and turned to the corridor. Shouts and clashes still rang out from the courtyard, the walls only muffling the chaos of the battle. Yet the back of her neck prickled with unease as she headed deeper into the castle.

How many people were taking shelter within these walls? There must be thousands. Thousands of them, and yet there was no noise. No whispering, no wailing, no crying. Not so much as the scuff of a shoe against the stone.

She entered the wide outer corridor, the artery of this side of the castle. And then she stopped, a gasp clogging her throat.

The people stood together in a silent, motionless crowd.

They breathed, and they blinked. Beyond that, there was no movement. The chatty shopkeepers and grumpy grandfathers she'd spent the day with were gone, replaced by these... shells.

There was no question in her mind: This was the horror of the mages' enthrallment, the mind control they'd inflicted on the people of the Vales. The power Felix didn't acknowledge, the second power that Adrian refused to use. Poison-speech, they called it.

Laena couldn't see the mage, or mages, who controlled them. But the result was obvious enough.

"What fun would it be to fight you," a voice said, snaking along the corridor like an insidious song, "when *you* can fight *them?*"

Laena's hands tightened into fists. "Coward," she returned. "Hiding in the shadows."

A laugh. "Perhaps. But I shall live, and you shall not. My king will no doubt grant *me* a boon to reward me for your death."

"Which king would that be?" she asked.

"The only one that matters. Goodbye, little hollow. Your royal blood will not protect you from a knife to the gut."

Laena frowned. Was her royal blood protecting her from enthrallment, then? Perhaps so. It was said that the original banishment had been done, partially, by a woman who'd been immune to their spells. Maybe it was all tied up in the Vales magic she could wield. Which had come first, she wondered? The magic or the royal status?

No time to consider that now, as a woman lunged from the front row of people, hands outstretched as if to wrap them around Laena's throat. Laena recognized her. She'd brought her a handful of ginger yesterday, for an uneasy stomach. As she ducked away, not wanting to hurt the woman, another pair of hands reached for her, and another. She ducked again, practically throwing herself to the floor as the people came for her, all at once. People she'd sat with, walked with, cooked with. People whose children she'd entertained.

There were so many of them, and she was hampered by the necessity of leaving them unharmed. But their movements were clumsy and slow moving. As if the single mage could not control so many minds at once. It was her one advantage.

She couldn't use her power against them, or even to protect herself. Who could say what it might do, if her control over it slipped?

She backed away, whirling to avoid hands that clawed at her skirts. A spark of silver slashed at her arm, and she cried out at the stinging pain but managed to knock the knife away. She felt naked without her power, her strength stripped away, especially in the face of this onslaught. This complete unwillingness to hurt innocent people.

Laena didn't want to turn her back on them, either. Didn't want to leave them in thrall, where this mage—multiple mages, perhaps—might grow bored and force them to turn on one another. The possibility turned her stomach.

But if Hawk were immune, as she was—and if she could find him—then he might be able to help.

Footsteps skittered behind her, and Rowan came streaking around the corner, nearly crashing into her. Tears streaked his cheeks, his hands stained with ink from writing his stories. "My mother," he said, his voice thick with tears. "I can't find my mother!"

Laena caught him around the waist and whirled him back behind her. She didn't know if she could shield him from the enthrallment, but she would try. As she ushered him around the corner, away from the throne room entrance, they found the passage filled with people, their stares vacant.

Laughter rang out through the halls, reverberating against the stones.

"Back to the courtyard," she said, but fear crawled through

her stomach at that idea, too. What if the mages took over the soldiers? What if they turned their swords on one another, or the people?

There was no choice. She was running now, practically dragging Rowan along with her, as she flung open a second door, pulling him around the side of the building and back to the courtyard.

If the raging battle were any indication, the soldiers were very much still under their own power. Hawk's fire burned, his red and orange flames meeting the eerie cool colors of the magefire.

Rowan whimpered, and Laena pulled him closer.

A bolt of magefire tore across the courtyard toward them, and she ducked, pulling the boy to the ground with her.

When she looked up, her eyes found Callum, locked in combat with two sword-wielding mages. Either they'd breached the walls or the travelers were smoking them in. They were everywhere.

And then one of them stepped in front of her, blocking her view. Magefire bloomed from his fingertips and coated his blood-drenched sword. He was grinning, mad with the heat of the battle as he raised his sword.

Rowan cowered under her arm, trembling.

And Laena had no choice but to reach for her power.

It answered, thick and slow, and she forced it to coalesce, forced the ice crystals to form. She met the mage's blow with a shield of icy poison that formed above her and Rowan in a wavy dome.

The ice burst apart, and the mage who'd struck at them fell back, screaming. The magefire on his sword withered into icy-black poison.

Callum was shouting her name, and she was vaguely aware of her head striking the ground, of vines collecting to break her fall, of Rowan's small form huddled against her side. And fire—so much fire.

She'd promised him she wouldn't use her magic.

She hoped he would forgive her.

The air smelled like fire and static. She blinked and Callum was before her, his fingers tangling with hers. She wasn't sure how she knew it, when her hands were numb. She wasn't sure how she knew that they were streaked with poisonous burns, so thick she could hardly see her own skin. She knew, like she knew that she would not be here much longer. Like she knew that Rowan was still trembling against her, and her hand had come down to rest on his back.

"Stay with me, Laena," Callum said—or maybe he was thinking it, and his words were echoing into her mind. It felt that way, as if her ears were bleeding. As if everything was bleeding.

I want to, she tried to say. But she felt him slipping away—she was so numb, so cold.

The mage who'd attacked her was there, behind him, sword raised. The blackened blade hadn't stopped him. She'd failed.

She had no way to warn Callum. She couldn't keep her eyes open. And her power—it was nothing but sludge.

Light exploded through the sky, blindingly bright, and the mage dissolved into a cloud of ash, his sword following. Through the light she could see the silhouette of a man standing upon the wall, hands open at his sides.

Adrian had kept his promise, then. Too late.

Not too late for Callum, she thought.

The world swam away.

CHAPTER 38

CALLUM

*C*allum was aware of Adrian's return, of the newcomer silhouetted against the searing yellow sky. He was aware that the battle had ceased, the clash of metal replaced by sudden silence. He was distantly aware that others had joined him. Maren. Hawk.

He didn't care, about any of it. All he could see was Laena, with the little boy tucked into her side. Maren knelt beside the child, coaxing him out of his protective ball. Tears ran down his cheeks, and his whole body was trembling, but he allowed her to lead him away.

The rise and fall of Laena's chest was barely discernible. A thick lacework of poisonous lines ran up her neck and traced down her arms. Even her fingertips were stained with it. A drop of blood trailed from her cheek, as black as it was red.

Your blood is cursed. Your blood is the cure.

Petra's words floated across his awareness, unbidden. Unbidden, and yet... yet, perhaps...

Callum looked at Laena's hand as he traced his thumb over her faint pulse. And he knew, suddenly and certainly, exactly what those words meant. And what he needed to do.

He'd spent much of his life chasing down heart-tithers. And now, he needed to become one.

He bent close to Laena's ear, wishing he could breathe his own life into hers. There were tears on his cheeks, and he could feel the others watching him. Watching *them*. He didn't care. "I need your blood, my lady."

Her pain. He needed her *pain*.

Her lips moved, almost imperceptibly. Her fingers twitched in his. He couldn't tell if she was aware of him. But he thought she was. She would trust him with this. Somehow, he knew that she would.

Callum unsheathed his dagger.

"What are you doing?" Hawk asked.

"Katrina's heart-tithe cursed her blood," Callum said. "Her own blood is the cure."

"*What?*"

Callum drew his blade across Laena's palm, wincing as the flesh parted. Blood bubbled to the surface, red tinged with black.

Callum touched his fingertip to the cut, then hesitated. "I don't..." He swallowed. "How does a heart-tithe work?"

"Heart-tithe," Hawk repeated. "That's forbidden. Farrow, you can't seriously—"

"Really?" Emilia's voice was thick with tears. "Forbidden? That's your concern right now? Not Laena's life?"

Of course it was. As it had been for Magnus before him. Their fear of magic, of heart-tithing, ran so deep that they would risk anything, sacrifice anyone, to see it eradicated. They were so focused on their fear that they could no longer clearly see the right path from the wrong one.

And Callum wouldn't allow them to force him along the dark path. Not anymore.

Hawk was still sputtering, confused. "But you have to care...

You have to love someone for their pain to grant a heart-tithe..."

"Dear gods, you are dense," Adrian drawled. Callum hadn't heard him arrive, but then that was hardly an abnormality. Unless it was because he'd managed to refrain from speaking until now.

"You have to reach." The voice that spoke over Adrian was unfamiliar. Callum glanced up to see a tall man standing beside Adrian, a stranger. Yet somehow he knew that this was the man who'd blasted the light into the sky, the one who'd incinerated the mages.

"Reach for her," he said.

Stranger or no, Callum did not hesitate. He *reached*.

And to his surprise, he could feel her. The fading thrum of her life force, the essence that was... well, *Laena*. Kindness and strength and humor—and cold. That fresh breath of winter, crisp and pure, sharp enough to cut him to the bone. To his very soul.

"Now you draw out the part that isn't her." The man's voice was by his ear now, and all he could do was obey. All he could do was hope that this person was indeed on their side.

At first, Callum wasn't sure what the man meant. This *was* Laena, as fully and purely as he'd ever felt her. But even as the words formed in his mind... even as he wanted to protest, he could feel it. The taint she'd described. The blackness of the poison.

So Callum reached further. And he *pulled*.

The poison fought him, like a snake coiling around a root to remain lodged in its den. But Callum reached, flinching as Laena's face pinched, as her lips parted with a whimper of pain. And he pulled, dragging the poison out of her magic, away from her. Separating the threads, like strands of yarn. Sweat beaded on his brow, but he ignored it, focusing on the magic. Separating cold from hot, darkness from light. Poison from life.

He'd never done magic before. He wasn't sure he liked it.

The strands snapped apart, and the poison lines leapt from Laena's skin, swimming in the air above her in writhing whorls of inky droplets.

Adrian's friend snapped his fingers.

The poison turned to ash and dissolved. Gone.

Callum let out a breath, the magic flowing out of him. He was left with a sudden feeling of fatigue. His lips were dry, his throat parched.

He didn't care about any of it. He leaned over Laena, brushing a strand of dark hair from her forehead. Willing her eyes to open. Her pulse had strengthened, quickened, and her breaths were coming more easily now. Without the ragged hitching.

In the corner of his eye, he saw Brin poke her head out of Laena's pocket. As concerned about her as the rest of them.

"Come on, Laena," Callum said. "Rejoin us."

"You love her." Hawk's voice sounded ragged, as if his fire had burned his throat. "The heart-tithe wouldn't work unless... You didn't tell me you *loved* her."

"So dense," Adrian muttered.

Hawk hadn't been someone Callum trusted. Not for a long time. But he could not have this conversation, not right now. Not when the person he *did* trust lay unconscious before him. Not when every second that passed increased the fear that pulsed through his body. The fear that she would not wake. That he'd been too late after all, that the poison had taken too much from her.

And that the world would now take her from him.

He could hear the boy, Rowan, crying behind him. Tears tracked down his own face.

"Far be it from me to command you," he whispered, "but you had better not leave me."

Laena opened her eyes.

CHAPTER 39

LAENA

*L*aena woke with her head cradled by a bed of vines, and a crowd of people staring down at her.

And ash floating in the air behind them, like seeds caught in the wind.

She blinked, and her vision focused. And then all she could see was Callum. Tears ran down his cheeks. His eyes were red, his hands shaking.

"Why are you crying?" she asked.

But she knew, didn't she? She'd nearly died. There was a stinging pain in her hand, and she lifted it to examine the cut. He'd asked her, hadn't he? He'd asked, and she'd trusted him. As she always had. As she always would.

"You heart-tithed for me," she said.

"Anything," he said. "Anything."

He cradled her hand in his, as if he were afraid to crush her against him. As if she were fragile and might break before him. But then, she *had* broken before him. She'd broken her promise, and in doing so had nearly broken herself.

She'd had to use her power. She'd had no choice. She looked around. "Rowan?"

The boy let out a sob, then he was breaking away from Maren. He threw himself into Laena's arms. Safe. He was safe.

When he pulled away, Laena sat up. The pain in her ribs was gone, the spots on the edges of her vision cleared away. The world was bright, and she felt strong again.

And when she stood, she found a crowd of people staring at her.

One of whom was King Hawk. He stepped forward, ducking his head almost tentatively. Not a posture she'd seen from him before. "Your magic, Princess Laena?"

"You're asking if she can still freeze things?" Emilia asked.

Hawk ignored her, but his eyes made it clear that that was indeed what he wanted to know.

What a question to start with. But she supposed someone had to ask it. It was, after all, the last test. Could she access her magic without falling ill? Or would the cycle merely begin again, forcing her to live in fear that another threat to the people she loved would force her to use it, force her to slowly poison herself over the years.

Laena looked at Callum. He didn't tell her not to reach for it, not to try. He merely nodded.

With a deep breath, she reached.

Snowflakes erupted out of the air above them. Pure, unblemished, joyful snowflakes. Rowan laughed, raising his hands to catch them, and she joined him. She couldn't help it. Her magic felt like it was singing, sighing breath after breath of relief. Even Brin scrambled out of her pocket to sit on her shoulder, her tongue snatching snowflakes from the air. Though whether because she wanted the snow, or because she'd mistaken them for flies, Laena couldn't guess.

And after a moment, she scrambled down Laena's arm and settled herself on Callum's shoulder. The little traitor.

"Your power is restored," Hawk said. He was hanging back, and it took her a moment to understand why.

He'd seen Callum do the heart-tithe. Which meant that he knew.

"We can still marry," he continued. "I don't... I made you a promise. I wouldn't mind, if Farrow..."

He cleared his throat, as if hesitating to voice what Callum's role would be. In her life. In her bed. As if there weren't a dozen people right here to witness the declaration. Or the almost-declaration, she supposed. It was close enough.

Laena looked at Callum. His expression had turned to one of caution, but she knew him. She knew the tick at the corner of his jaw meant he feared she would agree. She pressed a fingertip to it, looking into his eyes. "I can't marry you, Your Majesty," she said softly. "I need Callum. I love him."

Callum brushed a thumb across her cheek, and she leaned into him briefly before turning back to face Hawk. "And I need to take my place in Etra, instead of hiding here. With him by my side. If he'll have me."

Hawk looked back and forth between them as if he were still making calculations as to how this could have happened. Adrian stood to his left, shaking his head. Emilia's arms were crossed over her chest, while Gretchen stood close beside her and rolled her eyes.

Finally, Hawk bowed. "He'd be a fool not to. I wish you all the best."

He took her hand, pressing a kiss to her knuckles. Laena might well have been mistaken—she didn't know him all that well—but she thought she detected a hint of relief in the set of his shoulders.

Well, his people surely knew of his power now. They'd also seen him fight to protect them. Seen her do the same. He had no more need of a hasty marriage and a queen to help him weather the revelation. Or conceal it.

The king would have held to his promise, even with the

necessity of it now passed. But Laena would be willing to wager that he had no true desire to do so.

Laena had been too busy with her reunion, with checking on the people she cared about—noting Rowan's presence and then Maren's, Remy's, Saria's, and Felix's—to notice that a stranger also stood among them. He was tall, strikingly so, his raven-black hair tied in a knot at the back of his neck.

And now, he cleared his throat, as if reluctant to interrupt the reunion. "Unfortunately," he said, "this reprieve will be but a temporary one."

Hawk stepped back, the mask of the king sliding back onto his face as he turned to the newcomer. Adrian tensed, but Hawk made no move to draw any nearer. "Am I to understand that I'm addressing the King of Silerith?"

Laena blinked, surprised, though she supposed she shouldn't be. Adrian had gone to retrieve him, had he not? But the Ruthless King—the Mountain King—hardly seemed to live up to his reputation. He'd ended the battle, certainly, but now that he'd done so, he stood there with his hands in his pockets, shoulders rounded just slightly as if trying to minimize his threatening appearance.

Because his appearance was frightening, or otherwise might have been, had he not been so intent on appearing the opposite. His features seemed chiseled from stone, as if made to intimidate.

He inclined his head. "I am, technically, the king of that nation."

She could practically feel the power that buzzed in the air around him. A mage *and* a worker of Vales magic. The most powerful magic user of them all, or so she suspected. This man ruled both the mages of Silerith and those of the Miragelands.

What Vales magic had he been granted? The power of light?

"The three rightful leaders of the Vales, together in one place," Hawk said. "I never thought I'd see it."

And just like that, he accepted her ascension. Publicly, and without reservation. As if the abdication had never occurred. As if taking back her throne was a given, a simple mark on a list of tasks rather than another obstacle that stood before them.

The Sil king's mouth twisted. "Nor I, King Hawk."

Hawk gave a sharp nod. "Let us talk in my study, then." He turned to one of the King's Guard soldiers. "Have the physicians see to the wounded."

—*—

THERE WAS no question of Callum leaving her side or, as it quickly became apparent, of Adrian leaving the Sil king's. Though for different reasons, clearly; Laena saw how Adrian watched his king with narrowed eyes, as though he expected the man to vanish without notice.

But the Sil king followed Hawk through the halls without complaint.

Still, Hawk was the only monarch to enter the study without a second or a guard, though Laena hoped he knew he could count on Callum to defend him should the need arise. Not that it seemed likely. Silerith's king obviously had the power to defeat them all, should he wish it. So far, he'd done nothing but give them aid.

That didn't stop Callum from sticking close to her side. Not quite shielding her, as they entered Hawk's study, but ready to. What would happen, she wondered, if Silerith's king learned of Hawk's plan to have him assassinated?

She preferred to hope that particular detail would not come to light.

The study was nothing like she would have expected. Papers were strewn everywhere, most of them crumpled and battered. Piles of books and scrolls lay discarded in corners and on windowsills, some with pages half ripped out of the bindings.

Laena spotted more than one ink spill drying on the floor, and one seeping into the wooden desktop in the corner.

Adrian looked around. "Did the attackers target your study, King Hawk?"

Hawk shrugged, gesturing for them to sit in the chairs near the cold fireplace. "Not to my knowledge."

If he noticed Adrian's look of dismay at his answer, he didn't let on. Laena couldn't help but think of Adrian's meticulously kept treetop home back in the Grove as the mage swept a pile of crumpled parchment from a chair. He sat on its edge, as if the untidiness might contaminate his clothing. Which, she could have pointed out, was already crusted with dirt and blood from the battle. A fact that didn't seem to concern Hawk.

She glanced at Callum, who raised his eyebrows and gave his head a little shake. But she didn't miss the way the corner of his mouth was trying to hook up into an amused smile.

Hawk turned to the Sil king, who was quietly studying the room, his expression unreadable. "I'm afraid that while you know my name, I don't know yours," Hawk said. Polite. Unchallenging. The diplomatic king, direct but charming, his gaze cool and unthreatening.

Laena wondered if there was anything Hawk could do that would seem threatening to this strange, distant king.

"Evren Avery," he replied, as if it were an afterthought. He hadn't joined Hawk and Adrian by the cold hearth. He kept nearer to the door, his hands still stuffed into his pockets. "I am... royal by blood only, if you'll understand."

Adrian scoffed, but the king didn't look his way.

"I'm afraid that time is still against us," Evren continued. "We must reseal the magepool as soon as possible."

"How are we supposed to do that?" Laena asked. "What good will it do now, when the mages are already here?"

Adrian picked at his nails. "They still wear their vials, which means that what happens to the magepool will happen to them as well. *King* Evren has the right of it, I imagine." He said the word 'king' as if it were a joke, an insult. As if to mock his king's assertion that he was a royal in blood alone.

"Your sister used our blood to open the barrier." Evren directed these words to Laena, his tone cool and unaffected. "It stands to reason that our blood would seal it again."

It couldn't be that simple.

"As I understand it," Callum said, "you provided your blood of your own free will."

He certainly hadn't lost his directness.

Evren's gaze flicked to Callum. "And I gained a drop of hers. Which we will also need."

The Sil king didn't rise to the bait, nor did he explain himself. He merely stated the facts of what had happened.

"Causing problems just to solve them," Adrian muttered. "So shocking."

"That is enough." Evren spoke mildly, but Adrian shut his mouth, though the narrow-eyed glance he shot his king was nothing short of murderous.

Pieces of Silerith's strange puzzle were beginning to assemble into a picture, albeit a blurry one. Named general of Silerith's armies—which Laena had yet to see evidence of—Adrian had essentially been running the country.

While begging his king to take his place. His responsibilities.

That was where he'd been during the festival. Informing Evren of their arrival. And it was why it had taken him so long to return here. He'd had to convince the king to come. Why?

"Your power seemed... effective. Out there." Hawk spoke carefully, as if he, too, were unsure of how to properly navigate this conversation. "Why can't you simply incinerate the invading mages?"

Adrian clucked his tongue. "*That* doesn't sound evil at all. And you call *him* the Ruthless King?"

Evren's eyebrows ticked up, and he spared his general a glance. "Do they?"

"Yes, Your Majesty."

Evren made a humming noise, like it surprised him. "My power doesn't play well with itself."

There was a moment of quiet, and Laena expected the king to fill it with an explanation. When the silence stretched, it was Callum who finally said, "Are we supposed to understand what that means?"

"It means," Adrian said, "that King Evren wields mage powers *and* Vales powers. And when he uses them this much, bad things happen."

"Like the poison that was in Laena's magic?" Hawk asked.

Adrian opened his mouth, but Evren shot him a look that made him snap it shut again. "Too much of my power is danger-ous," Evren said. "That's all you need to know."

That was hardly true.

"Also, he gets cranky when he's around people for too long." Adrian smacked the arms of the chair, then stood. "You're all here, with your extra-special blood. We've got Katrina's blood, thanks to King Evren. So let's go to the magepool now and get it done, before our friend Valdric regroups."

Laena looked at Callum, who took her hand, looping her arm around his. "No offense, Your Majesties, but as I see it, there are far too many kings in the Vales. I think we should go kick one of them out."

"Valdric isn't a king," Adrian said. "He only wishes he was."

He'd done more than wish it. Laena didn't understand how Evren Avery could be king—*technically*, as he claimed—of both Silerith and the Miragelands. But this other mage, Valdric, appeared to object to the arrangement.

He'd promised her sister a wealth of power, guiding her through the steps of breaking the barrier so he and his people could return and conquer the Vales.

Laena found it difficult to believe that it would take but a few drops of blood to reverse what she'd done. "It can't be this easy," she said. "I just... have a feeling."

Callum nodded, squeezing her fingers. She wished they could step aside, have a few private moments—all right, a few private hours—now that they were free of her promise to Hawk.

"Whatever happens," he said, "we'll face it together."

Adrian's smoke magic whisked them away.

—*—

THE MAGEPOOL SMELLED of damp forest and blood.

Thaddeus was waiting for them when they arrived, with two other poisonkeepers at his sides. His eyes were bloodshot, and he had a wide bandage wrapped around his forearm, a deep gash across his forehead. He took a few limping steps toward them, as if he planned to attack, then stopped, eyes wide.

After a moment, he threw his arms around Hawk, who hugged him back, clearly surprised. "I tried to reach you," Thaddeus said when he stepped back. His robes were torn, his hair more disheveled than usual, and the frames of his glasses were bent. "You didn't answer. The mages. I saw them return. I tried to stop her, but she knew... she knows everything."

Katrina. Thaddeus had faced Katrina, fought her, but where was she now? She hadn't been present at either battle. Or at least, Laena hadn't seen her.

Perhaps the mages had killed her, now that they had no more need of her.

Despite everything, the thought made Laena's stomach ache.

Hawk put a hand on his brother's shoulder. "We know," he said. "Vunmore was attacked. But we had some last-minute help."

Thaddeus looked around, taking in the rest of the group as if for the first time. His eyes caught on Adrian and Evren and widened. "They're—"

"Mages," Hawk interrupted gently. "It's all right."

Thaddeus was frowning, as if it was very much not all right.

"We need to add our blood to the pool," Laena said. "Undo Katrina's spell."

Thaddeus's frown deepened, and he shook his head. "I don't think... I'm not sure that will work."

"We have Katrina's blood, too," Hawk said.

Thaddeus was still shaking his head, but Hawk turned away from him and took the steps up to the pool. He slashed a cut across his palm, allowing the blood to collect in his palm before tipping it to the side, releasing the small stream into the magepool. Evren did the same.

The cut on Laena's hand was still fresh, and she, too, held it over the pool, meeting Callum's gaze as she squeezed her hand into a fist, letting her own blood fall.

Finally, Evren withdrew a glass vial from his pocket. He looked at it for a long moment, brow furrowed, before finally tipping it into the pool, releasing a single drop of Katrina's blood onto the surface.

Nothing happened. Not so much as a ripple. The magepool simply accepted the offering as its due, absorbing their blood without so much as a flicker of acknowledgment.

They waited, hardly daring to breathe. But surely if it had worked there would be some indication. Some sign.

"How do we know if it worked?" Callum asked.

Thaddeus swallowed. "We caught one of them trying to sneak out through the monastery."

"Was he wearing the vial?" Laena asked.

Thaddeus nodded.

It was a matter of a few minutes to send one of the poison-keepers to confirm whether the mage had vanished back to the

Miragelands. They waited in tense silence, Thaddeus shifting his weight between his feet while Hawk locked his hands behind his back as if to hide his fidgeting.

Mostly, Laena looked at Callum. He had to be just as nervous, just as exhausted as the rest of them. But when she caught his eye, he winked at her, offering her a tired smile. Tired, but genuine.

Demons, but she hoped she was wrong. That the monk would come back and announce they were free of the mages, that the Vales had been saved.

It didn't take long for the poisonkeeper to return, with a grimace and a shake of his head. "The mage is still here," he said. "He claims to have felt nothing."

Adrian cursed, and Hawk let out a breath of disappointment.

Thaddeus turned to Laena. Like her, he had not expected the blood to work. And he was already thinking of what the next step ought to be. "Your sister knew of things I'd never heard of. She pieced things together in a way... It was truly impressive."

"That's one word for it," Hawk muttered.

Thaddeus attempted to adjust his bent spectacles, but he only succeeded in making them more crooked. "She might know how to reseal the pool. In fact, I think it very likely that she does."

"She didn't seem like she'd be all that willing to help us," Evren said.

Adrian glared at him, at the reminder that his king had spoken with her. Had helped her. Laena didn't know what to think of the man either, truth be told. She certainly didn't trust him. But that seemed like a problem, a complication, for another day. For now, it would have to be enough that he was on her side.

And he was looking at her. They all were.

If Katrina still lived, then that was surely where Laena would find her. Though whether or not she would be able to convince her to help... that was another matter entirely. "I'm overdue for a trip to Etra, anyway," Laena said. "It's time I had a visit with my sister."

CHAPTER 40

CALLUM

*C*allum could tell that Laena meant to go to Etra and face her sister this very minute. Her jaw was set, her hands curled into fists. As if she could will herself to stay on her feet.

Not even an hour had passed since she'd nearly died, and she would go tearing off into another battle without so much as a good meal and a night of rest. There was no telling what she would face in Etra. She needed her strength.

Perhaps he simply didn't want to risk losing her mere hours after he'd nearly lost her for good. If that made him selfish, then so be it.

But as Thaddeus led them away from the magepool and into the monastery, even Evren Avery was willing to see reason. "They will also need time to regroup," he said. "But make what haste you can."

Callum didn't much care for Silerith's Ruthless King, if he was being honest.

Thaddeus had to be beyond exhausted, yet he fell to assigning rooms and sending poisonkeepers to escort them through the monastery as though he had all the energy in the world. Someday, Callum would ask him to explain how he'd become so senior at Inasvale in such a short amount of time.

Soon the magepool's grove was empty, save for Callum and Hawk. Callum knew he ought to find his room, and yet he hesitated.

There was still a conversation that needed to be had.

The king sat at the edge of the magepool, much as Callum had seen him lounge on the dais of his own throne room, legs spread before him, arms propped behind. He looked more comfortable here, in a way, his shoulders relaxed even as he stared out at the trees. "It's a pretty spot," he remarked.

Days of battles, shields, and strategies, and still Hawk could appreciate the beauty of it. Honestly, all Callum could see was a few trees and a bunch of trouble shaped into the outline of a magical pond. But he supposed the king's magic made the place look a bit different.

For all of Hawk's apparent calm, Callum half expected the king to leap to his feet and start shouting accusations. For stealing his betrothed. For failing to execute Evren Avery—which, he had to admit, would absolutely have been a suicide mission—and for bringing the mages to Inasvale.

Callum waited, tense. But when Hawk looked up, he met Callum's gaze steadily. No flash of anger. Not even disappointment. Sadness maybe, the depth of grief that Callum had expected to see in his expression after Magnus's death—but that had always been overtaken by anger.

"My father taught me that ruling is a wretched business," Hawk said, his voice quiet enough that Callum felt the urge to lean forward, to catch every syllable. "That when given the choice between saving one or saving many, you always choose the many. And I can't say he was completely wrong about that."

Callum inclined his head. "I can see the wisdom in it."

In most cases, perhaps.

But Hawk wasn't finished. "To a point. Father also taught me that preventing war and slaughter was the most important thing a king could do for his people."

"Even if it meant crossing a line?"

Hawk leaned back, scanning the trees as if they might offer some wisdom. "My father was a good man. A good king, I think, but... an imperfect one, too. I've tried to emulate him. To make choices that would make him proud." He paused, as if these words had been simmering for some time. "But following his teaching without stopping to think, and letting my anger at his death guide my choices... I can't lay those mistakes at his feet. Most of the choices I've made have not considered the many, not in the long term. And they certainly haven't considered the few."

Callum swallowed, allowing himself to absorb the king's words. Hawk spoke so plainly, it was almost like looking into the past. To a version of the man, the brother, he'd once known. To the man who'd gone directly to his father and admitted his part in the disaster the first time he'd passed into Silerith. To the man he respected as a leader and a friend.

The king stood, brushing his hands on his pants. And then he held his hand out to Callum. "I'm sorry, Farrow," he said. "I never should have sent you into Silerith with such a hateful mission. And I should have stopped the hunting of heart-tithers across their borders as well. I hope you can forgive me."

Callum blinked. This entire conversation surprised him. He'd begun to think that Hawk would talk around the apology, offering his reasoning without quite taking the responsibility. And yet here he was, saying the words outright.

"Are you sure you want my forgiveness?" Callum asked. "I did steal your betrothed."

Hawk laughed. "I rather think I stole her first. Yes?"

Callum snorted. He wasn't wrong. "I think she'd smack our heads together if she heard us speaking like she has no mind of her own."

"And we'd deserve it, too."

Callum accepted the king's hand. "You're a brother to me. That hasn't changed. Of course I forgive you."

Hawk grasped his hand, and then pulled him into an embrace. "Brothers," he said. "Thank you, Farrow. I won't forget it."

Callum clapped the king on the shoulder. "I do think you ought to speak with Thaddeus, too. When all this is over, if not sooner."

The king frowned. "Thaddeus? Why?"

Well, one couldn't expect too many miracles overnight. Hawk would need to talk to his brother himself. "Give it some thought," Callum said. "And get some rest, Your Majesty. I think you're going to need it."

—※—

CALLUM ACCEPTED the room he was given—no longer banished to the outer guest rooms, he noted—and made use of the minimal bathing chamber to scrub the grit and blood from his skin. But the bath did nothing to calm his anxiety at being separated from Laena so soon after she'd almost died. And he emerged with the sudden, awful worry that she might have left for Etra without him.

He opened the door, intending to go and find her. Only to find her standing there, hand raised as if ready to knock.

When she saw him, she smiled. Just a smile, and it was the most beautiful damn thing he'd ever seen in his life. "We had the same idea," she said.

"I thought you would be preparing to go," Callum said as she entered, bringing with her an intoxicating wave of honeysuckle soap.

And snow. Always that fresh, sharp tang of winter snow.

Laena ran a fingertip along the windowsill. "There's not

much to prepare, really." She gave him a rueful smile. "Except myself. And Kat's gone so far down this path, I'm not sure there's much hope of convincing her to help."

"There's always hope," he said.

She nodded, eyes shining. Her curls were damp and heavy around her shoulders, and she wore a simple dress, something one of the monastery's maids might have lent her. His cock stiffened just looking at her, just breathing the same air as her. He swallowed hard, trying to tamp down his desire. She needed to rest; she didn't need him pawing at her all night.

His dick had other ideas, especially as she stepped closer to him, pressing light fingertips to his cheek. He closed his eyes as she trailed her fingers down his neck, pausing at the open collar of his shirt. "I thought death would take me." She spoke so softly he could barely hear her words. "I thought I would never see you again."

He swallowed. "And now we have forever."

"No one has forever." She loosened the first button on his shirt, and then the next. "But we do have now."

And for once, they could take their time.

She pressed her hand to his chest, running it up over his shoulder and stripping the shirt from his body. The last two buttons tore free as it dropped to the floor. Every touch was like fire against his skin. Fire, and ice.

She kissed him, undoing the buttons on the back of her dress and tugging it down over her collarbone, laughing as the garment caught on her elbows.

He could have listened to her laugh all day.

"A bit tight around the shoulders," she said.

"Not to be borne." He eased the gown down her arms, tugging the fabric until her breasts were bare before him. He dipped his head to kiss one nipple, then the other, sucking it between his teeth and reveling in her gasps as he eased the dress down over her hips.

He raised his head to kiss her again, and she pushed him toward the bed, lips skimming against his as his knees hit the mattress. He fell back, her hand still pressed against his chest as she fell with him, her legs tangling with his.

"So aggressive," he murmured against her lips. Her breasts were pressed to his chest, every curve fitting against his body so perfectly.

"We haven't been together in a bed," she said.

He ran his hand down her body, pausing to cup her ass, to drag her body against his. He reached a finger between her thighs, running it along the inside of her slit. She gasped, grinding against his cock, which was now straining against his trousers.

"A clear oversight," he said, "and a testament to how strange this courtship has been."

"And in a poisonkeeper's bed, no less." She broke their kiss, trailing her lips down his neck to his chest, her lips hot and needy. She reached the waist of his trousers and pulled, stripping the clothing from his body.

When she returned, she did so on her knees.

"Laena," he gasped, intending to pull her back to him, to protest. She silenced him by swiping her tongue up his cock in a single, languorous sweep. He let his head drop back to the mattress, the world contracting into one finite space. Her lips closed around his cock, her tongue swirling the head. Teasing until he growled her name again. This time, it was a plea.

She took him into her mouth and sucked, all wet heat and glorious pressure, and he couldn't keep himself from bucking his hips to drive deeper into her throat. Until finally he pulled her up, not wanting to spend himself in her mouth.

"I need you, Laena," he said, and his voice was ragged.

She positioned herself above him, fitting him against her entrance and rocking, dragging his head along her slit, gasping as his cock teased her clit.

And then she sank onto him, and he was lost. The pleasure was everything as she leaned down to kiss him. He ran his hand over her breast, pinching her nipple, and she cried out, riding him harder, deeper with each thrust.

She rolled, and he flipped her onto her back, keeping his cock inside her. He wanted to be deeper, to be everywhere, and he slid his hand between them to press a thumb to her clit as he thrust deeper, worshipping her breasts with his mouth as her breaths became ragged. As his breathing matched hers, desperate and seeking, he drove harder and harder into her.

She screamed his name as she came, her orgasm arching her back, her hair spread around her on the bed. When he spilled his own pleasure, the intensity of it washed the world in white light, the edges of the room sparkling.

He came back to the world with one hand gripping her breast, the other tangled in her hair. He stayed there for a long moment, looking into her eyes. He kissed her gently, and she touched his cheek, meeting his gaze with those lovely green eyes.

"I love you, Callum," she said, her voice low and husky against his lips.

They were the sweetest words he'd ever heard. She loved him. She belonged to him, of her own free will. And he would never be foolish enough to let her go again.

CHAPTER 41

KATRINA

*K*atrina wanted to grab the captain of Etra's army by his regulation-short beard and throw him across the council chambers. Followed by every member of the hastily assembled council that she'd brought together. To make an action plan. To prevent the mages from storming Etra and enthralling all their people.

As soon as they defeated Aglye, they would be here.

It would not take long. Her sister's magic would not be enough. King Hawk's magic, and the power they could cobble together with their little band of mage friends, would not be enough.

Her own magic, gifted by the very mages she now feared, would not be enough, either.

Even if she could access it.

Ever since the fight in the Sil mountains, her magic had abandoned her. She'd used it to wrench herself away from the battle, to appear on her own shores. And then, it had disappeared.

It was still there; she could feel the hot well of its power in the back of her mind. But she couldn't access it, no matter how hard she tried.

King Valdric must have done something to her to lock it away, to sever her access to it. Or the prince, she supposed, though she'd have expected Koreth to boast while he did it. Either way, it seemed that they couldn't fully retract their gift once it was given. Whether they'd even been the ones to give it, or whether it had somehow come from the magepool—or the Miragelands themselves—she couldn't say.

Honestly, she didn't much care. Her magic wouldn't help, anyway. But her military could.

And now Captain Jarvid, who was supposedly under her command, stood directly opposite her at the end of the oval-shaped table. She had just finished telling the story and admitting the full truth of her quest to reawaken the mages. She could feel the council members' stares on her, like they were not sure how to react.

But Jarvid? He was smiling at her, softly, with a sparkle of amusement in his eyes. Like he was comforting a silly daughter who believed in fairy-tale monsters.

Hence her desire for beard-grabbing and hurling.

"The queen," he said, addressing the other councilors, "is falling victim to her own hysterics. Forgive me, Your Majesty. But the mages are long gone. There is no way to return them to the Vales. And even if there were…"

He trailed off, even his traitorous mouth clearly unwilling to articulate the rest of that sentence.

Even if there were a way to return the mages to the Vales, Katrina would not be the one to do it. She had neither the wits nor the fortitude.

He was a fool.

"Our queen has been missing for weeks, while we've held both Riles and Etra's coast." The captain's tone was placating.

Patronizing. "Councilor Riennad's security plans are well in hand."

"That security will be useless against the mages," Katrina replied.

If she could access her magic, they would see. But perhaps that was the cruelest wound of them all: not that the mages had hobbled her power to prevent her from defeating them, but that they'd left her without a way to prove her story.

"Regent Riennad—" Captain Jarvid began.

"Declan is dead," Katrina interrupted, her own voice betraying her by trembling at the worst possible time. "I am the queen."

Leave it all to me, my dear. There is no need to worry.

Captain Jarvid smiled that smile again. She imagined taking a dagger and peeling it off his face. "Perhaps a bit of rest would do you some good, Your Majesty."

Katrina sat at the table as the council dismissed themselves, leaving the chamber without so much as a parting glance in her direction.

It didn't matter, anyway. Captain Jarvid and his soldiers could believe her every word, could give their very best effort, and it wouldn't matter. The mages would still come.

They'd finish their assault on Vunmore and eventually— soon—they would come for Etra.

And it was all her doing.

CHAPTER 42

LAENA

*A*t dawn, Adrian came to retrieve Laena.

She'd been awake for some time, watching the gentle rise and fall of Callum's chest. Savoring the moment of calm, brief as it was. Motes of dust drifted in the early-morning light, and the room smelled pleasantly of cedar and light incense. As though it had been burned here long ago, and the room had absorbed its essence.

Then Adrian rapped on the door—she supposed she shouldn't be surprised that he knew to find her here—and she extracted herself from Callum's arms, meaning to let him rest.

She certainly hadn't allowed him to do much of that last night.

But he stirred immediately, rolling onto his side and pulling her down into a long kiss. The kind of kiss that had stirred up plenty of trouble last night. More than once. The kind of kiss that made her want to melt into him and stay there.

On the other side of the door, Adrian cleared his throat. Loudly.

"I dislike him," Callum said.

In this moment, Laena disliked him a little bit, too.

Reluctantly, she pulled away. This time Callum allowed it, joining her as she dressed and walking her to the door as if he were escorting her home after a stroll in the park. Instead of sending her off on yet another dangerous mission. After a night of... well, a different kind of courtship, she supposed.

And now they had to say goodbye. But only, she told herself, for a short time. A very short time.

"Are you sure I can't accompany you?" he asked.

She wanted him to. Demons, but she wanted him to. Mostly because she didn't want to let him out of her sight again. But she'd been ignoring her instincts for too long, and this one said she shouldn't approach Katrina with Callum by her side.

She had to believe her sister could still be reasoned with. She had to.

"You're needed here," she replied. And it was true. For strategy, for defense. Even for Hawk. Callum had told her how they'd come to a tentative understanding. It would be good if he had a chance to further solidify the peace between them. "And I think... I need to speak with Katrina alone. She won't like it if she sees this as an attack."

He was clearly hesitant, frowning as if he wanted to come up with a reason to come with her. But all she could do was to kiss him again, long enough to prompt another flurry of annoyed knocks. "Besides," she murmured, "Adrian will be with me."

"Not," Adrian's voice came from the other side of the door, "if you don't hurry up."

Callum kissed her lips, and then her nose. "Be careful."

She opened the door to find Adrian leaning against the frame, his arms crossed over his chest. "I was about to travel directly into the room to take you away," he said.

Laena adjusted her satchel, then shut the door behind her. "Good thing you didn't. Callum would have killed you."

"A risk I was prepared to take." He straightened and started down the hall, his strides long and sure. "Might as well travel from outside, lest the monks think we've started a fire in the halls."

Laena supposed it made sense. The halls were silent, the monks either resting or, perhaps more likely, attending to their early-morning prayers.

"If your king has so much power," she said, "why can't he bring me to Etra? Or is that part of the danger he mentioned?"

Adrian huffed out a breath. "As a matter of fact, he most definitely could bring you to Etra himself. Some might even call it his duty. And yet, here I am. Preparing to travel. At the ass crack of dawn."

Laena wondered if this traveling power had an official name, like poison-speaking for enthralling humans and green-speaking for growing plants. Travel-speaking didn't exactly have the same ring to it.

If they got through this, there would be plenty of time to map out the types of power the mages could wield, along with all their names. Or someone would. Thaddeus, perhaps. Assuming he actually wished to continue studying magic.

For now, Laena was more interested in the individuals who wielded that magic. "You're his general," she said.

He gave her a sideways glance. "Was that a question? Yes, I am his general. A familial obligation from which I cannot escape."

Laena raised her eyebrows, surprised. The king didn't bear much resemblance to his general. "Brothers?"

"Cousins. Unfortunately."

Laena wasn't sure whether to laugh. "I'm sensing you're not a morning person, General."

"For the love of everything sacred, don't you start calling me that. And on this particular morning, no, I'm not. Not all of us spent the night crying our lover's name to the rhythm of multiple orgasms, darling."

"Seems like a failing on your part, not an embarrassment on mine."

Adrian threw the door open, letting them out into the court-yard. "Touché. Now if you will please take my hand, I'll whisk you away on yet another ill-reasoned mission."

She let his fingers close around hers. His hand was warm and dry.

A twist of magic, a mouthful of smoke, and then they were there.

She knew it before she even opened her eyes. The flirty welcome of the breeze that rifled through her hair like a greet-ing, bringing with it the briny smell of the sea, the rush of the waves.

They were in Riles. She was home.

When she opened her eyes, she was looking at the interior doors to the palace. Adrian had bypassed the outer gates, drop-ping them directly into the entry hall. The breeze she'd felt was skipping in from an open window, batting at the familiar tassels on the tapestries. And urging her deeper into the palace. As though it wanted her to know she had an ally here.

Suddenly, her knees felt like they might not support her weight for much longer. She forced herself to breathe deep as she stared at those doors, with their wave motifs, their spots of shining silver paint wearing thin in places, but still enough sparkle to bring tears of nostalgia to her eyes. As a child, Katrina had convinced herself that there had to be real silver in the paint. Incensed, she'd come to Laena with a plan to separate the silver out and refine it. And distribute it to the people.

Laena had dismissed the idea. Until, a week later, when the palace painters had appeared at her study, begging her to convince her sister that the sparkle in the paint was just mica. She'd had to find the purchase receipts before Kat could be convinced of it.

How old had Katrina been then? Nine? That would have made Laena fourteen.

It felt like so long ago.

Adrian hovered by her shoulder, all traces of impatience vanished as he watched her. She didn't want to meet his eyes, so she kept hers trained on the doors. Wondering if she'd ever be able to reach for that handle.

"Did you and King Hawk have a moment yesterday?" she asked, stalling.

"Indeed, my tastes run to kings with sloppily kept offices and loose interpretations of peace treaties."

Laena licked her lips, attempting to dispel the sudden dryness. "I feel like you had a moment."

She didn't have to see Adrian to know he was giving her the same flatly unimpressed look he'd spent yesterday leveling at his king. "You're merely delaying the inevitable, darling. Shall I go in with you?"

Laena shook her head, her throat dry. "Best not."

Before she could talk herself out of it, she reached for the handle and tugged open the doors.

Inside, the halls were quiet. As quiet as the monastery, yet here it felt... off somehow. It wasn't that the place had fallen into disrepair, not exactly. But every hearth she passed was cold, and cobwebs had collected in many of the corners. As if the staff had fled.

Certainly, Laena couldn't blame them for that. Her sister had not been in residence here for some time. And when she had been, she'd been deep in her heart-tithing. Still, it was difficult to fathom how the place could have changed so much in such a short period of time.

Thaddeus was sure that Katrina had gained her knowledge of the magepool and the Miragelands by digging through ancient manuscripts. Going on that logic, Laena headed for the second floor, and the library.

Where the mess rivaled that of Hawk's study. Books and scrolls were strewn across the floor, along with piles and piles of papers. The papers were everywhere, each page covered in frustrated scrawlings and rips, and spots of spilled ink.

Katrina had been here. Had spent time here, certainly.

But Katrina hadn't been *comfortable* here, among the dusty pages and the smell of ink. She never had been. Now that the lessons she'd needed had been learned, she'd have abandoned this place as quickly as she could. Laena ought to have known that.

She found her sister on the roof.

Kat sat perched on the flat part of the ridge, just before the point where the shingles began to slope downward. All these years, all this roof to explore—and no one to command her to come down—and still, she'd chosen the stretch of rooftop between their childhood bedrooms. As Laena had known she would.

Katrina had drawn her knees up to her chin, and she was looking out at the sunrise, her hands resting on her shins. A protective pose, as if to shield herself from whatever was to come. She wore a pair of soft trousers and a loose white blouse, her now-unruly golden curls tied back with a string. Though Laena did nothing to conceal her approach. She'd slid the stubborn window of her old room open with a loud thump and let her footsteps fall loudly. And yet Katrina gave no indication that she was aware of her sister's presence. She just sat there, watching the sunrise.

And what a sunrise it was, with both sky and sea drenched in brilliant shades of purple, pink, and red.

"I think Etra keeps the Queen's Journey tradition just so we'll appreciate that we have the best sunrises," Laena said.

When Katrina didn't stir, Laena took a step in her direction, testing her balance. Somehow, this rooftop hadn't seemed so high the last time she'd done it. "This was easier when we were children," she said. "Bit of vertigo now, if I'm being honest."

Katrina didn't look her way. "Did you come to kill me?"

Laena's heart lurched. "No."

"If you don't, they will." Kat's tone was forthright, in a way Laena hadn't heard for so long. Forthright, and... bare somehow. Dull. Like she'd stripped every bit of hope from it along with all the fake cheer and confidence, and the costumes she'd been wearing. "They'll make a spectacle of it, too. At least you'll make it quick."

Laena tipped her head to the side. "Is that an apology?"

"No." Katrina snapped the word like a curse. "I'm not sorry."

But she was still avoiding Laena's gaze. Still focused on the sunrise. And Laena decided that she didn't believe it.

The last time Laena had been up here, she'd just finished packing her things to leave the palace with Ben. He'd been waiting, in fact, the horses already prepped and ready to go. Telling herself she was up here for a last glimpse of the view, she'd inched that same window open and shimmied out onto the roof.

Where she'd found Katrina sitting here, in very much the same posture. Not apologizing for running to the regent with her story of Laena's tryst with the farmer. Not apologizing for seizing hold of Laena's birthright.

Which had been a good thing, at the time. Laena hadn't wanted her to apologize, or take it back. That had been the whole point.

"Don't worry," Katrina had said then. "Declan will see to things."

Now, Laena thought that perhaps she should have been the one to apologize. For ensuring her sister would happen upon her with Ben. For dumping the burden of leadership on her. Kat had wanted it, true, but she'd been so young. Too young to make that choice. And Laena had left her without one.

301

Laena had left her sister alone with Declan. Because she'd feared what her magic might do, and who it might harm.

She'd been young, too. But still. She hadn't truly considered the consequences. And no, she didn't believe she could have predicted... whatever had happened between Katrina and the regent. Yet she'd owed her sister more than a manipulation. For it had, most definitely, been a manipulation.

Throwing her arms out for balance, Laena crossed carefully to where Katrina sat and lowered herself down. There was no delicate way to ask what Katrina might have endured in the intervening years, no easy way to approach the subject. But she could not leave it unsaid. "Declan," she said. "Was he—"

"I can't." Katrina wiped a tear from her cheek with a shaky hand. "I can't."

Laena nodded, her throat tight. "All right."

She let the moment stretch, watching the way Katrina's hands trembled against her legs, the tears tracking down her cheeks. There was no reason for her to trust Laena enough to talk about it. And with his death so recent, she might not know what to say.

Laena found herself wishing she could kill the regent all over again.

But that would do nothing to remedy their situation. And the hourglass, if King Evren were to be believed, was slowly draining its sand. The mages would regroup soon. They'd slay the poisonkeepers or enthrall them. They'd enthrall and enslave every human in the Vales, then take control of the magepool, cutting off any possibility of returning them to the Miragelands.

The Vales would belong to them.

So Laena took a deep breath. And she said the only thing she could think to say: "We need you."

Katrina let out a hysterical burst of laughter, tears still tracking down her cheeks. "*My* help? I'm nothing. I *caused* this."

"If anyone else said that about my sister," Laena replied, "I'd kick their ass. You are *not* nothing."

Katrina gave her a look that said she knew how ridiculous that was, coming from a sister she'd betrayed, schemed against, and left for dead. Multiple times. "Except that I am. I can't even access the magic they gave me, so there's nothing I can do to help. This world will fall to the mages. Again. You might as well accept it."

Fear pulled at Laena's gut, and for the first time since stepping out here—for the first time ever, in all the times she'd been out here with Katrina—she feared her sister's reason for being up here.

To fall from this height... it would not end in a mere injury.

"Your magic is gone?" Laena asked carefully.

"I *said* I can't access it. It's there, but it's also... not. I can't help you."

Not 'I won't,' but 'I can't.'

Laena studied her sister's face, trying to understand how she'd come to a place where Kat thought her only value to the world was in the magic she could wield. "I don't care about the magic," she said. "I care about the fact that you're the only person who knows how to reseal the magepool. We tried to do it with our blood—mine, Hawk's, and Evren's—but it didn't work."

Katrina scoffed. "Of course it didn't."

Thaddeus had been right. "So you *do* know," Laena said.

Katrina rubbed her fingernail against her thumb, digging deep enough to redden the skin. "Maybe."

"It would have taken months of study to figure it out." Laena chose her words with care. A direct compliment would be thrown back in her face. But to point out how much work it would have taken, generally... "Years of concentration."

"I'm a terrible student," Katrina returned.

"And yet."

303

Katrina didn't fire back a retort, or scream at her, or try to throw her off the roof. She didn't whip up a band of dark magic. She merely sat there, looking out, and so Laena waited, breathing in the salty air and hoping. Hoping to everything that they could turn this around. That this wouldn't be the end.

Katrina wiped another tear from her cheek, resting her chin on her knee. "You should kill me, you know. You're too trusting."

"Perhaps." Laena risked reaching out, risked a brief touch to her sister's shoulder. "Will you help us?"

Katrina stood, the sunrise painting her face in a symphony of red and orange. Laena wondered what her sister was thinking, if she was remembering Declan or cursing him, or if she would allow herself to make this one decision without his ghost looking over her shoulder.

"All right," Katrina said. "I'll help."

CHAPTER 43

LAENA

*L*aena feared that Katrina might turn and run at the sight of Adrian waiting in the palace halls below, despite her attempt at forewarning her sister of his presence. But when he greeted them with a bow and said, "Shall we?" Katrina merely accepted his hand silently and allowed him to smoke them back to Inasvale.

Laena wasn't quite sure whether she ought to be relieved or concerned by her sister's docility.

Adrian landed them in the middle of a private dining room. Everyone was in the midst of loading their plates with food, Hawk at one end of the table, with Callum seated to his right. Emilia sat at the other end, with Gretchen on *her* right. Judging by the delight on her face at their arrival, they'd interrupted a tense conversation.

The rest of the table was taken up with Thaddeus, Felix, Saria, and Maren. All of whom were gaping at them in unrestrained horror. Like they'd just dragged a wraith into their midst, or the bleeding head of some mythical monster.

Really. What had they thought would happen, if Katrina agreed to help?

Laena put a hand on Kat's arm, but her sister shook her off. Still, the movement was enough to break the icy silence.

"You couldn't have traveled to the *outside* of the monastery?" Saria complained.

"It's breakfast time." Adrian strode to the table, reaching around Saria to pluck a grape from her plate. "No wine?"

"*Breakfast,*" Saria said.

Adrian popped the grape into his mouth. "Shame. Where is our illustrious king?" When Hawk lifted an eyebrow, Adrian waved a dismissive hand at him. "Not you. The annoying one. No, wait, you're both annoying. I meant King Evren."

"Too many kings," Emilia lamented.

Saria reached into her pocket and handed a vial to Adrian. "He left his blood."

"Do we have to do that at the table?" Gretchen asked.

Adrian snatched the vial out of Saria's hand, shoving it grumpily into his pocket. "He took off." It wasn't a question, and no one denied it. "I don't know why I'm surprised."

"He's not here?" Katrina asked sharply. "King Evren?"

Laena looked at her, trying to decide whether Katrina was relieved or disappointed. But her sister's face merely held a stubborn expression, her lips set in a firm line, brow furrowed.

"Scuttled on back to his hidey-hole, it would seem," Adrian muttered. "Leaving the hard work to his general, as usual."

"Calm down and eat some bacon," Maren said, "before you give yourself a complex."

Adrian dropped into the empty chair beside her as Callum rose, crossing the room to kiss Laena on the cheek. Katrina rolled her eyes.

But when Callum spoke, he directed his words to her, rather than to Laena. "You must be hungry," he said. "Please, join us for breakfast."

And he said he was no good at diplomacy.

"How would *you* know if I'm hungry?" Katrina grumbled.

But she followed them to the table, ignoring the fruit and sausage Laena immediately started heaping onto her plate in favor of staring at her hands.

Everyone at the table stared at her. Hawk did so openly, his utensils resting by his plate. Emilia kept darting glances at her, while Gretchen looked back and forth between Emilia and Katrina as if attempting to calculate whether she'd need to leap in front of her princess for protection. The others were similarly furtive, stealing looks between bites and loaded glances.

Well, she *had* tried to end the world as they knew it. And it wasn't yet a certainty that she hadn't succeeded. Laena supposed it would take a bit of doing to get them to trust her.

"Katrina knows how to seal the magepool," Laena said.

"I have a theory," Katrina corrected. "That's all."

"All your theories have proved true thus far," Hawk said, his tone like acid. "May I ask why you're choosing to help us now?"

"What if she says 'no, you may not'?" Adrian whispered.

Hawk spared a brief, irritated glare for the mage before turning his attention back to Katrina. Waiting for her response.

"I regret bringing the mages back to the Vales," Katrina said, her voice surprisingly steady. "You want to send them back to the Miragelands. So our interests are aligned."

Not exactly a passionate oration. But Laena couldn't deny that it was a diplomatic one. Kat had entered this conversation like it was a negotiation. And perhaps, in a way, it was.

Hawk sat back in his chair, regarding her with open suspicion.

Laena caught Callum's eye, begging for his help. He grimaced, like he wasn't sure Hawk was in the wrong. But still, he cleared his throat. "I think we should hear her out, Your Majesty."

"If nothing else," Adrian said, "we're out of other options."

Hawk sighed. "Well, I cannot argue with that. Tell us what you've learned."

Hands folded in her lap, Katrina met his gaze. "And my end of the bargain is what?"

Hawk leaned forward. "Your end of the bargain is, as you said, that we rid the Vales of the invading mages that *you* have inflicted on our lands. Further, it is that we do not execute you in front of the entire population you put at risk in doing so. *That* is your end of the bargain."

"A cell, then."

"Perhaps."

Katrina regarded him for a long moment. Laena wondered if she would try to negotiate for more, for leniency or even immunity. Or stand up and flounce out of the room, as she'd been inclined to do, or even force them to beg for her assistance.

Perhaps she'd reveal that she still had plenty of access to the magic she'd claimed had drained away—and hurl it in their faces before they could defend themselves.

It wasn't easy to trust her. Especially when her expression was so guarded, so impossible to read. Had Laena ever been able to read it? Or had she only thought she could?

"Someone has to seal it from the other side," Kat said finally. "From inside the Miragelands."

Silence.

"I'm sorry," Hawk said slowly. "I'm going to need you to say that again."

"We all heard it, Your Majesty," Adrian said.

Hawk placed his hands flat on the table, like he wanted to push himself off of it and launch himself at Katrina. "She's implying that one of us has to sacrifice ourselves to free the Vales from the mages."

More than implying, Laena thought. Katrina was saying it outright. Though, judging by the looks everyone was exchanging, and the weight of the silence, Laena could tell they didn't fully believe it.

What did Kat hope to gain from such a lie? Laena wondered.

Thaddeus chewed his lip, his expression pained. "I think she may be right," he said.

"How kind of you," Kat said dryly. "I don't know why you even need me at all, when you have Prince Thaddeus here to explain the obvious."

It was almost a relief to hear her bite back at them like that. Almost.

Thaddeus gripped his hair so hard it looked like it must be hurting him. "I would not have come up with the idea myself. But it makes sense."

"It's how they should have done it before," Katrina said. "Or that's the theory. It's what makes heart-tithes possible. It's why these mages"—she flicked her hand toward Adrian—"get to keep their powers without regular visits to the Miragelands."

Adrian pressed a thumb to his lip and sat back in his chair, unable to conceal his surprise.

"Yes," Kat continued, as though he'd asked a question. "I know about how your ancestors used to return to the Miragelands to recharge their powers. And that you've wondered why you've maintained your own powers for all these centuries when they ought to have drained away."

"You know a great deal, it seems," Adrian murmured.

"Yes. I do. The theory that makes sense to me is that the humans who sealed the mages away in the Miragelands—"

"And the mages who helped them," Saria said.

"Sure. And the mages who helped them." Kat blinked, somehow making it look like an eyeroll. "They didn't complete the process. So the door was left ajar. Someone has to close it from the other side."

She punctuated her sentence by pushing her chair away from the table, as if her part in this was finished and it was their turn to fight it out. She didn't rise, merely went back to staring at her hands.

"I should be the one to do it." Thaddeus adjusted his spectacles. "I've spent the last year preparing to do whatever I need to protect the Vales from the mages."

"But not," Hawk said, "of your own volition."

Laena lifted her eyebrows, looking at Callum. He didn't look quite as surprised as she felt. She knew that he and Hawk had talked, had come to an agreement between themselves. But it was somehow still shocking that Hawk so fully understood this —and that he was willing to admit, in front of a group, that his brother had only come to Inasvale in the first place to help him learn about his own magic.

It raised her estimation of Aglye's king.

Thaddeus held his brother's gaze, eyes wide. It was as if he, too, could not quite understand what Hawk was suggesting.

"You've sacrificed enough," Hawk said.

Thaddeus was quiet for a long moment, his surprise clearly mirroring Laena's own. Exceeding it, even. "I appreciate that," he said finally, his voice soft. "But there is no one else."

Hawk opened his mouth to interrupt, but Thaddeus held up a hand, and Hawk sat back, willing to let his brother silence him.

"I will not ask any of the mages to go to this place they dread," Thaddeus said. "Not after the way they've been treated in the Vales, forced to remain in hiding. And the rest of you are needed here."

"*You* are needed here," Hawk insisted.

"I am." Thaddeus was firm. "I'm needed for this. To go into the pool. To seal it from the other side and see to it that the Vales live on. I gave an oath to do this."

"So did the other poisonkeepers." Grief crumpled Hawk's expression. "One of them could—"

A horn called out, long and loud, interrupting the king's protests. Thaddeus jumped to his feet. "We need to get to the magepool," he said. "They're here."

CHAPTER 44

CALLUM

*C*allum held tight to Laena's hand as Adrian smoked them away to the magepool, the room falling away as Saria and the other mages ran for the door to help defend the city, Gretchen taking her place beside Emilia as if she could personally shield the princess from all harm. Well, who was to say she couldn't? Callum had seen the woman's skill with a bow.

Hawk held on to Adrian's shoulder, while Katrina grabbed Callum's arm at the last minute so she wouldn't be left behind. As far as they knew, they still needed her blood, and she seemed willing enough to bestow it.

Laena might trust her not to stab them in the back, but Callum certainly didn't.

Rain drenched the magepool forest, falling heavily enough to make it through the dense foliage and splatter onto the cobblestone path, the steps, and the pool. The drops that hit the pool skittered across its surface in unnatural patterns, water-falling down the steps as though the pool had rejected them.

Hawk wasted no time in opening the cut on his palm, squeezing a few drops of blood into the pool and prompting those petals of fire. Adrian went next, tipping the vial of Evren Avery's blood, which hit the water in a flash of blinding light.

Katrina stepped up to the rim of the pool. "I don't know why you all mess with your hands," she muttered. She slashed a cut on the back of her wrist, allowing several drops to fall onto the surface. They fell without fanfare, without smoke or fire, merely melting into the pool like another drop of water.

Laena met Callum's eyes as she opened her own wound once again, the same one he'd cut into her flesh. The one he'd cut again, in a second, if it meant saving her life. She allowed several drops to fall, watching as blooms of frost crystalized, holding for a moment before sinking down into the depths.

How, he wondered, had the magepool come to be here at all? This well of magic, this passageway of sorts that connected their two worlds? Had the mages placed it, or had they discovered it? Judging by the works Katrina had found, the ways of magic, the mages, and the Miragelands had all been studied in much more depth than he'd ever assumed. Someone else must have been asking these questions, too.

For now, though, he set them aside. Hawk could assign a scholar, or fifty, to study the pool's origins once they'd banished the mages back to their own world.

Thaddeus stepped up onto the rim of the pool. Hawk was quiet now, watching his brother with unconcealed grief, and Callum wondered whether they ought to watch him, in case he should try to take Thaddeus's place.

Black smoke churned into the clearing, and a trio of mages materialized among the trees. They were moving before Callum had fully registered their presence—demons, but he hated all this smoking from place to place—fanning out to begin their attack. Callum recognized Valdric, the man who'd claimed to be king, magefire pouring out of his hands and wreathing his chest in strange, colorful flames. Beside him was the man Adrian had said was his son. Koreth.

Koreth lunged toward the pool with unnatural speed, features blurring as he tore past Callum to the edge of the pool. Callum released Laena's hand, but he was still unsheathing his sword as Koreth knocked Thaddeus down the steps.

The prince fell, smashing his head against the stone path. He didn't move.

Koreth turned toward him, but Callum moved to defend Thaddeus, dashing to intercept the mage even as fire bloomed from Hawk's fingertips. Ready to come to his brother's aid.

But Valdric intercepted him, raging toward Hawk with a whirl of power, and the two met in a clash of fire and sparks. Leaving Callum to defend Thaddeus on his own, as Adrian and Laena engaged the third mage.

"Would be so nice to have a bit of light magic right about now," Adrian grunted, but his words were nearly lost behind the roar of fire, the crackle of ice.

Koreth, who'd paused briefly to watch his father's attack on Hawk, renewed his own attack on Thaddeus, who still lay motionless on the cobblestones.

Koreth threw a pulse of magic at Callum, as if to bat him away with a mere flick of his wrist. But Callum didn't have a chance to see what kind of power he'd tossed out—not that he was complaining—as the magic slammed into a wall of ice. Laena, sending her own desperate surge of magic to protect him.

But the mage merely smiled and raised his hand, and Callum was momentarily distracted by the shift as his fingers transformed into long, crystalline claws.

"How many powers do you even have?" Callum said.

Koreth's smile stretched. "At least one more."

"That was a rhetorical question," Callum said, lunging to take advantage of the opening the mage had left and aiming his sword directly at Koreth's gut.

But that was where he stopped. Against his will.

His raised sword was mere inches from gutting the mage down the middle, yet his muscles no longer obeyed his commands. His legs burned with the effort of staying in this position, yet he could do nothing to alter it.

"Callum!" Laena cried, but there was nothing he could do, no way to fight the enthrallment. She had royal blood, Vales magic that could protect her from it. He had none. He was susceptible.

Koreth strode toward him, claws extended. "I do love hollows," he said. "You're so… maneuverable."

Callum's muscles strained, but his sword might as well have been locked in stone for all that he could move it. The prince pushed past him like he was nothing, aiming his own blade directly at Thaddeus's heart.

A fresh blast of ice shattered against the mage's shoulder, knocking him sideways. He yelped in surprise as several of the ice chunks sank into his arm and shoulder, blood blooming out of the wounds.

Koreth lost his footing, dropping the enthrallment as he staggered, and Callum stumbled, barely managing to keep a hold of his sword.

They had mere moments to act. To finish this.

He could run to protect Thaddeus. He could run to fight beside Laena.

But Thaddeus wasn't the only person who could leave the Vales without destroying everything they'd built. He wasn't the only one who could seal the magepool from the other side.

Callum dashed for the pool.

CHAPTER 45

KATRINA

*F*rozen with shock—but not, thankfully, with enthrallment—Katrina watched as her sister's lover staggered toward the pool. The fight had taken him almost all the way across the clearing, but his intention was clear enough.

He would dive in. He would seal it from the other side.

He would leave her sister here, alone.

Katrina was aware, distantly, that Hawk was kneeling at his brother's side. That Koreth, wounded as he was, would soon regain his balance. And that he would not stop until he'd skewered the Aglyean prince.

More likely than not, none of them would leave this place alive.

Valdric stepped up beside her, as if they were attending a party together rather than a battle. "I told you I would come for you," he said. "Though I did not suspect it would be so soon. You do still have a few surprises in you, little hollow."

Laena was screaming her lover's name. It was wrong, Katrina thought, that he should go to the Miragelands. That they should be separated.

Life isn't fair, Declan's voice said. *But you can turn events to suit your own pleasure.*

And she saw, in a burst of understanding—a vision, a truth, the kind of thing she would have sneered at, had someone else claimed it—she saw exactly what needed to be done.

Her own dagger was in her hand, though she didn't remember drawing it. Didn't even remember bringing it here.

"I'm not hollow," she said.

Then she plunged the knife into the false mage king's chest.

CHAPTER 46

CALLUM

*C*allum had seconds to take advantage of the chaos.
No time for regrets. No time for goodbyes.

Prince Koreth screamed in rage as his father's knees buckled, Katrina's blade lodged in his breastbone. She'd bought Callum precious seconds, just enough for him to do what needed to be done.

She stood with unnatural stillness, watching dispassionately as Valdric fell. Almost as if she were seeing someone else.

"Thank you," Callum said.

Katrina looked at him, and time seemed to slow as she put her hands on his arms. For a moment, Callum thought she meant to pull him into a hug.

Instead, she shoved him, with enough strength to send him stumbling back down the steps and into the clearing. "Take care of my sister," she said.

He blinked, trying to understand her meaning.

Laena, of course, already did. "No." She spoke from behind him, her voice breaking with emotion. "They'll kill you."

Katrina gave her a small smile. "They can try."

The prince lunged for her, his face a mask of grief and fury. But he was too far to close the distance in time.

Katrina turned and dove neatly into the pool.

Laena let out a quiet sob as her sister's form disappeared beneath the surface.

The water went still, as still as it had ever been, and Callum found himself reaching for Laena's hand as Koreth shouted in rage. Caught halfway between the pool and his father's fallen body, he chose the pool, stumbling toward it as though he could hope to yank Katrina back from its depths.

The water shivered, the darkness fading to a brilliant shade of violet. The vial of water around Koreth's neck glowed in response, matching the color as a sharp tone cut through the air, as if the two portions of the pool disliked their close proximity.

Koreth's vial flashed, the light so intense that Callum had to shut his eyes against its brightness.

When he opened them, Koreth had disappeared.

CHAPTER 47

LAENA

*T*he forest was achingly quiet.

Laena clung to Callum like he was her last tether to this world, as if his hands, closed around hers, could keep her from falling into the depths of the earth. The blaze of light still swept across her vision, and she blinked to dispel the last of it.

The mages were gone. Or, at least, the Miragelands mages were; Adrian still stood a few paces away where, only seconds ago, he'd been fighting one of the invading mages alongside her. Her fingertips were still coated in frost, her magic still primed to throw another blast of ice.

But their opponent had vanished along with Koreth. Even Valdric's body had disappeared. As if it had never been.

She scanned the clearing, trying to take in everything at once. Thaddeus was stirring, hand scraping the ground in search of his spectacles. Hawk knelt by his side, concern etched across his face.

"Are you all right?" Callum's voice was close to her ear, and she looked up to meet his gaze. The crystal blue of them nearly made her lose her balance, the intensity of it boring into her like he meant to measure and obliterate any injuries, large or small.

So intense. And so very, very infuriating. "What the fuck did you almost do?" she whispered.

He blinked. "I'm sorry?"

As if he'd forgotten everything about the last few minutes. She let go of his hand so she could smack him on the shoulder, hard. And then she threw her arms around him, burying her face in his neck. "You were going to sacrifice yourself," she said. "You were going to take Thaddeus's place."

His lips were on her hair, her neck, her cheeks. "I was the only other person who could be spared."

She kissed him, hard enough to make him stumble. She didn't care that they weren't alone. She didn't care if the others watched or turned away. She scraped her teeth against his bottom lip, clashing against him like a storm. Messy and harsh, and desperate.

When she broke the kiss, she smacked his shoulder again. "You can*not* be spared."

He wrapped his arms around her, holding her tight. "I'm sorry." He whispered the words like a prayer. "I'm here. I'm not going anywhere."

"Thanks to the traitor, I suppose," Adrian muttered. "King Evren and his reasons. I swear."

Katrina. Laena broke away from Callum and ran for the edge of the pool. He kept pace with her, steadying her when she nearly tripped on the steps.

When she reached the rim, she gasped.

The water had drained away, leaving behind only a funnel-shaped shell of obsidian stone. Smooth as a rock tossed about in the sea, and polished to such a shine that she could see the silhouetted treetops reflected within its walls. The funnel ran deep, though she could not make out where it ended. Assuming it ended at all. No doubt Thaddeus and the poisonkeepers would be swarming the clearing in short order and working to discover whether the rock swirled all the way shut at the bottom.

If there was even a pinprick's-width of a tunnel remaining, they would find it.

Laena peered over the edge, Callum still holding tightly to her hand as if he feared she would fall—or leap in after her sister. Her mind tried to wrap itself around the impossibility of Katrina disappearing through such a gap. But this was a thing of magic; it would not be explained by the physical realities of this world.

Adrian joined them at the ledge and gazed into the shining abyss. "That's unexpected," he said. As if it were a mild curiosity rather than the complete upending of everything they knew. The disappearance of the passage that would lead to his ancestral lands. And, if Laena understood Kat's explanation, the eventual leeching away of his own powers. If she was correct, the closing of the barrier meant that the mages would eventually lose their powers.

The last few minutes seemed impossible. Fighting the mage with Adrian, she'd been helpless to assist as Thaddeus had fallen, helpless to stop Callum from taking his place—and helpless to intervene as her sister leapt in front of him. Sacrificing herself to save a man she claimed to hate.

Sacrificing herself for Laena's sake.

"What did you mean," she said, "about King Evren and his reasons? You think he knew what would happen before it did?"

Adrian hesitated, shifting his weight. "I don't completely understand his powers," he admitted. "It's just a feeling."

What, that he'd given Katrina his blood so that she could sacrifice herself to the Miragelands? That didn't exactly warm her to the man. If the Sil king had the power of foresight, if he could have prevented this from happening, then his disappearance was unforgivable.

The weight of her sister's sacrifice squeezed her chest.

Katrina had made many mistakes, but this fate... Laena would never have wished it upon her. She would never have wished it upon anyone.

"They'll never let her live," she choked. "Not when she murdered Valdric. Not when she closed the barrier."

If Katrina could even survive in those famously inhospitable lands, the mages would hunt her down and surely execute her for what she'd done. Valdric might be dead, but the agony on his son's face was burned into Laena's memory. Koreth would not let his father's murderer live. Nor would he be likely to let her die without suffering.

Callum squeezed her fingers, drawing her close against him. "I wouldn't count her out."

And maybe he was right. If anyone could best the mages, even in their own realm, it was her little sister.

Kat had taken Callum's place so that he and Laena could be together. Laena would be a fool to throw away that sacrifice.

Footsteps approached from the path, and she tore her gaze away from him as Emilia and Gretchen appeared, hands clasped, with Saria and Remy a few steps behind.

"The mages," Emilia said, breathless. "They've disappeared. It was chaos up there, and then suddenly poof! Everyone vanished."

"Best battle ever," Gretchen said.

Saria frowned. "Your last arrow went through a dissolving mage and almost hit Felix."

"Yes," Gretchen said. "*Almost.*"

Emilia laughed, then threw her arms around Gretchen's neck, pulling her into a kiss. When Laena looked at Hawk, he just shook his head. Accepting his sister's choice.

Laena looked to Adrian. "Will you lose your magic? Now that the magepool is sealed?"

Or gone completely. Or both.

Adrian shrugged. "Won't know for a while yet, I imagine.

But if so, then it's a rather small price to pay for permanent freedom." He jumped from the rim of the magepool and strode down the path toward the monastery. "Battles make me hungry. Let's find something to eat."

Hawk watched him pass, blinking rapidly. "I'm not sure I understand him."

Laena wasn't sure that anyone could.

Callum brushed a strand of hair behind her ear. "Where to next, my lady?"

There were messes awaiting them all over the country. In Vunmore, in Inasvale, and likely across many of the other towns and cities across the Vales.

Laena couldn't fix them all. But she could start with one: the one that was counting on her.

"I think it's time to go home."

EPILOGUE

LAENA

*L*aena's shoes were blissfully soft.

She stood before the mirror in her dressing room in Riles, wearing a gown of rose gold. Etran colors. The dress had been tailored to her specifications, with silky material that flowed softly around her legs, making her want to swish her skirts constantly. And, of course, a pocket for Brin. The shimmerling poked her head out now, her bright pink scales a pretty contrast to the golden glow of the dress.

She'd had no other requests for the dress, honestly. Only for the shoes. She'd asked for comfortable shoes.

The council had accepted her travels in lieu of the traditional Queen's Journey, a concession they'd made so eagerly—along with enthusiastically accepting her marriage to Callum as a tie to cement Etra's alliance with Aglye—that she suspected they'd have accepted any arrangements she proposed, as long as it meant she would return to claim her crown.

She'd made a point of walking the streets daily since her return, of holding long sessions that were open to the citizens, often staying with them late into the night. She had work to do to regain their trust after revealing the truth of her abdication, and of her magic. In time, she hoped they'd come to rely on her again.

She and Callum had remained in regular communication with Hawk, and with Adrian, though no word had come through from King Evren, who seemed to have slunk back to his hermitage in the Sil mountains.

It was too soon to say whether Adrian and the other mages of the Vales would retain their powers, or if the magepool was well and truly sealed, cutting them off from the source of their magic. They likely wouldn't know, Thaddeus and Adrian agreed, for several years.

There had been no word from Katrina, either. Nor would there be; Laena knew this. Yet it was hard to be back in Etra without thinking of her sister. Of all she'd sacrificed. Living in the Miragelands, she would not know a day's peace. The mages would hunt her, punish her for her part in their downfall. Not to mention whatever challenges she would face when it came to the land itself. A barren place, full of monsters. From the little she knew.

But Laena didn't intend to waste Katrina's sacrifice.

Now, Callum stepped up behind her, adjusting her hair so he could bend and press a kiss to her neck, then her shoulder. She breathed him in, the comforting presence of woodsmoke and fresh air.

"What do you think?" she asked.

"I think I want to peel that dress away and see what's underneath."

She rolled her eyes, laughing. "You've seen what's underneath, Captain. Multiple times."

His lips trailed down toward her collarbone. "But not as queen."

"I'm not queen yet."

"You don't need some stodgy politician to place a crown on

your head to make you the queen," he murmured, his breath warm against her skin.

She laughed, pulling away and smacking him lightly on the arm, though her cheeks were flushed with heat. She didn't understand how he could do this to her, make her head spin with just a touch. "Later," she said.

He grinned. "That's a promise. Are you ready?"

Was she? The road had certainly been long enough. Still, she hesitated. "Do you think they'll come to trust me? Despite the magic?"

He pressed a kiss to her temple, a secret smile on his lips. "I suppose," he said, "that we'll have to wait and see."

She narrowed her eyes. "What is that supposed to mean?"

He raised an eyebrow, offering her an arm.

He was, she thought, terrible at secrets. Well, let him keep them. She'd find out what he was grinning about soon enough.

The palace halls were busy with staff preparing for days of coronation celebrations. Her guards fell into step behind them as they left the palace, and though most were not the familiar faces she'd come to know in Aglye's King's Guard, there was one of Hawk's soldiers who'd accompanied them to Etra: Godfrey, who'd come to beg Naomi's hand in marriage.

And she'd accepted it. Yet another reason for celebration, among so many.

Laena had wanted her coronation to be out in the city. Not in a throne room or a council chamber, but in the streets, out in the open. Before the people she was about to swear she would protect. Another arrangement to which the council had readily agreed.

She wondered what they would think when she proposed her idea to add a second council, one made up of Etrans from across the country.

She'd save that for another day. When the crown sat firmly on her brow.

When the guards opened the outer gates, Callum leaned in close and whispered, "This is where we met."

Laena smiled. "So it is."

"I believe, my lady, you'll find that they recognize you now."

Laena stepped onto the street, then stopped.

Riles had been transformed into a winter wonderland. Paper snowflakes hung in every window and dangled from every balcony. A web-like network of strings crisscrossed the street before them, the snowflakes so thick it looked like a true winter storm. They'd even covered the streets with white cloth.

And the people. Rather than Etran gold, they wore shades of blue and purple, silver and white. Children circled their parents' legs, weaving through the crowd flying wintery blue streamers from sticks.

A show of acceptance. For her. For her magic. She'd left them, and still they were willing to take her back. Still, they trusted her to lead them. It was the most beautiful thing she'd ever seen.

They were waving to her, cheering, but she could barely hear their shouts above the beat of her own heart.

"Did you do this?" she whispered, unable to hold back her tears.

"It was all them, my lady," Callum replied.

With Callum's hand in hers, Laena stepped into her city, ready to take her place as queen.

THE END

—*—

Learn more about the time of the mages in a stand-alone prequel novel, *Hollow & Venom*! It's FREE when you join my email list, Amelia's Letters.

Sign up now at AmeliaMacLeod.com/newsletter!

Fake courtesan. Real feelings. Impossible odds. Some lies are worth dying for.

Neve has spent her life hiding a deadly secret: she's immune to the magical thrall that controls every other human in the Vales. When her defiance catches the attention of Prince Sylvan Everstone—the notorious Soulslayer—she expects torture or death.

Instead, he claims her as his courtesan to save her life.

Claim your FREE copy of Hollow & Venom at AmeliaMacLeod.com/newsletter

———*———

Laena and Callum's story is complete—but there's more to come within the world of the *Poisoned Kingdoms*.

Get ready to journey into the Miragelands:
Shadow's Price (Poisoned Kingdoms #3) will be out on February 11, 2026!

Pre-order your copy now!

(Or join Amelia's Letters at AmeliaMacLeod.com/newsletter so you'll be sure to know when the book hits Kindle Unlimited!)

ACKNOWLEDGMENTS

Laena is like me in so many ways.

You'd think that would have made this an easy couple of books to write. I knew her from the moment she stepped into my mind, after all.

Instead, it felt vulnerable to let her live out here, in real, tangible words. With real, tangible fears and flaws and messes.

Thank you to everyone who picked up this book, and who found even a small piece of themselves within it. This is one of the many ways that stories connect us, after all.

Of course, who Laena *is* and what *happens* to her are two different things. I want to give a shoutout to my sisters, Shana and Susan. And of course, I'm not only thankful the fact that you're not even a little bit murdery. Your support while I walked out on this limb has been everything—ordering paperbacks and giving me pep talks and telling your friends about the books… I could not be more thankful that I got you as sisters. How lucky am I?

Thank you also to my writing besties: Sara, Jessie, Wade, Chelscey, Mark, and Heather. You're always a text or a Slack away, and I appreciate it so much.

This book wouldn't exist, because I wouldn't be writing anymore at all, without the help of Roni Loren, who coached me out of burnout. Your patient and practical advice was everything I needed; you helped me to find the joy again. And shoutout to Becca Syme and Claire Taylor as well, whose work has just been so important to my journey. Thank you all for what you do.

Thank you for my mom, who doesn't know this pen name exists and probably shouldn't. But she's a great lady, and I'd be remiss not to mention that here.

Thank you to my kiddos, who are always excited to see my covers; one day, you can be embarrassed to read these books. (Or you can just pretend they don't exist. That's what I would do.)

Thank you to my husband, Moshe: the most supportive partner in the world, who believes in me more than I believe in myself. Our banter will always be the best banter. I love laughing with you.

And finally, thanks to everyone who's picked up these first two books in my romantasy journey. It is no small thing to trust your time to a new author. Every message of encouragement you've sent, every reel you've posted, every review—you make want to continue doing this, and to keep improving with every book.

I tell these stories for *you*. Thank you.

Sincerely,

Amelia

GLOSSARY - WP

Spoiler warning: this glossary contains some new characters who appear in Winter's Power, and whose existence might be considered a spoiler depending on your preferences. Proceed with caution!

PEOPLE, PLACES, AND THINGS

Adrian (Ay-dree-ann): A Sil mage with traveling powers.

Aglye (AG-lie): One of two mainland kingdoms; led by King Hawk.

Brin: Laena's shimmerling companion. (See also: *shimmerlings.*)

Callum Farrow: Famed magic hunter from Aglye. Formerly the Captain of the King's Guard.

Declan Riennad (Deck-lan Ree-EH-nad): Regent of Etra; assisted in running the country until the queen comes of age.

Etra (EH-trah): A small island nation that takes pride in its long line of queens

Felix (fee-licks): A Sil mage and guard to Adrian.

Hawk: King of Aglye.

Heart-tithe: A brand of magic requiring the pain of a loved one to access remnants of the mages' power.

Inasvale: A city in Aglye where the poisonkeepers' monastery is located. (See also: *poisonkeepers*)

Katrina Montrose-Aboret: Sister to Laena and heir to the throne of Etra following Laena's abdication.

Laena Felicia Montrose-Aboret: Former heir to the throne, she abdicated five years ago, supposedly because she loved a commoner. In truth, she left out of fear of her forbidden magical abilities.

Landon Moore: Newly promoted to Aglyean general.

Mages: Banished to the Miragelands after years of controlling humans in the Vales.

Magepoool: The barrier/gateway between the Miragelands and the Vales.

Magnus: the late King of Aglye; Hawk's father.

Maren: A Sil mage with plant-speaking powers.

Miragelands: The home world of the mages. After ruling over the people of the Vales for hundreds of years, the corrupt mages were banished back to their native world, known as the Miragelands.

Poisonkeepers: An order of monks charged with guarding the passage between the Vales and the Miragelands.

Remy (REH-mee): A Sil mage with shield/warding powers.

Riles (rih-LESS): The capital city of Etra.

Saria (sah-REE-ah): A Sil mage with air-speaking powers.

Shimmerlings: Rare, newt-like creatures with magical properties. Legends say their bones were used to were used to control humans during the time of the mages — and that they helped liberate the realms.

Silerith (sih-LER-ehth): The secretive country that shares the mainland with Aglye. Known to be lenient toward magic users, they are ruled by an elusive king; most refer to him as the Ruthless King.

Sunflower Cottage: Laena's home after abdicating the throne.

Thaddeus: King Hawk's younger brother and a prince of Aglye, he took orders as a poisonkeeper and lives at the monastery in Inasvale. (See also: poisonkeeper, Inasvale.)

Vaelthorne (VAY-ehl-thorn): Dormant volcano overlooking the city of Vunmore.

The Vales: Common terminology for the combined realms of Aglye, Etra, and Silerith.

Vunmore: The capital city of Aglye.

—✳—